Two
Roads

JOSEPH BRUCHAC

PUFFIN BOOKS

To my grandfathers
with gratitude for
everything they taught me

PUFFIN BOOKS
An imprint of Penguin Random House LLC, New York

First published in the United States of America by Dial Books for Young Readers
Published by Puffin Books, an imprint of Penguin Random House LLC, 2019

THE LIBRARY OF CONGRESS HAS CATALOGED THE DIAL BOOKS FOR YOUNG READERS EDITION AS FOLLOWS:
Names: Bruchac, Joseph, 1942- author.
Title: Two roads / Joseph Bruchac.
Description: New York, NY : Dial Books for Young Readers, [2018] |
Summary: In 1932, twelve-year-old Cal must stop being a hobo with his father and go to a Bureau of Indian
Affairs boarding school, where he begins learning about his history and heritage as a Creek Indian.
Identifiers: LCCN 2018001784 | ISBN 9780735228863 (hardback)
Subjects: LCSH: Depressions—1929—Juvenile fiction. | CYAC: Depressions—1929—Fiction. | Tramps—Fiction. |
Fathers and sons—Fiction. | Veterans—Fiction. | Identity—Fiction. | Creek Indians—Fiction. |
Indians of North America—Oklahoma—Fiction. | Oklahoma—History—20th century—Fiction. |
Washington (D.C.)—History—20th century—Fiction. | BISAC: JUVENILE FICTION / People & Places /
United States / Native American. | JUVENILE FICTION / Social Issues / Prejudice & Racism. |
JUVENILE FICTION / Historical / United States / 20th Century.
Classification: LCC PZ7.B82816 Tw 2018 | DDC [Fic]—dc23
LC record available at https://lccn.loc.gov/2018001784

Puffin Books ISBN 9780735228870

Printed in the United States of America

CHARACTERS

ON THE ROAD

Cal Black (Blackbird)—narrator
Pop (Will Black)—his war vet father
Red Campbell—war vet
Miz Edith Euler—war widow
Jack—tramp who steals from Miz Euler
Boney—rude hobo
The Professor—educated hobo
Corporal Esom Dart—Negro hobo war vet
Cap—mayor of the hobo jungle
Shorty—hobo
Sheriff Boyle—prejudiced lawman
Eljay and **Arjay**—cowboys
Mr. E. Wimslow—Stable owner

AT CHALLAGI

Charlie Cornsilk—boy who dreamed of a witch and died
Ironhand Bayner—School disciplinarian
Superintendent Morrell
Possum (Charles Aird)—Creek student
Mrs. Wilton—School nurse
Bear Meat—Head of Creek Gang

Creek Gang members:

Little Coon

Grasshopper

Deacon

Skinny

Dirt Seller

C.B.—dorm adviser, former student

Ray Chapman—student sergeant (Cheyenne Arapaho)

Mr. Mallett—geography teacher

Mr. Handler—shoe repair and harness shop teacher

Mrs. Tygue—English teacher

Tommy Wilson—white Creek

Mr. Pond—math teacher

PART 1

ON THE ROAD
MARCH 1932

CHAPTER ONE

KEEPING UP

The red road stretches out before us, a long ribbon of light.

"Keep up, Cal."

I am the right size for my age, which is twelve—this being 1932 in the year of Our Lord. I can run as fast as the Dickens. But when it comes to marching I always fall behind. Despite Pop's limp, he always gets a few steps ahead of me.

I cannot help but sigh.

Pop doesn't hear that. Though he can still catch the songs of the birds in the trees above us—like the redbird he pointed out a mile back—real low noises escape his ears. It has been that way since the sixth of June in '18 when he was partially deafened by the booming of the big guns.

We keep marching along. I'm doing a better job now of keeping up. I don't mind walking like this, mile after mile, just as long as it doesn't start my father remembering.

Pop looks up at the sun. "It was hot like this that day. It was about this time," he says. "Exactly three forty-five p.m." There's a faraway look on his face now. He's telling the story to himself, almost unaware of me listening.

"'Over the top and take that wood,' General Hartford orders

us. And then the whistle blares. So over the top we go. Every one of us as green as grass."

It's the place where Pop always pauses. Sometimes we'll walk as much as a mile before he says more.

"And then the Devil's Paintbrushes opened up and down we went, like a wheat field being mowed."

Another silence as another mile passes.

"No," he says. "Not like wheat nor rye. Mown grass does not bleed or make the ground so slippery you can't hardly stand."

He pauses, shakes his head, as if trying to wake up from a bad dream. Then he starts walking again. That faraway look is gone from his face. I'm not sure he even knew that look was there. He's finished that story for now, leaving it behind.

Which is what I would like to do. But almost as soon as he started the story, as it sometimes happens, something took over. This happens to me now and then. I'm drawn backward. I find myself in the middle of someone else's life. Not remembering it or seeing it. But living it moment by moment.

I'm no longer walking down a Southern road in the here and now of 1932. It's years ago—over there. I'm someone else in full uniform. Crouched next to my father in the muddy trench. I'm holding a gold pocket watch in my left hand, looking at the letters inscribed on the back.

S.K.E.

My heart's pounding like a drum as we wait for the signal. Sweat is beading my forehead. That loud shrill whistle sounds. We scramble up over the top, stumble forward through the broken strands of barbed wire, the half-buried bodies of men who took part in the last wave. We leap over craters left by shells. The only sounds are heavy breathing, the thudding of feet on the frozen ground, the rattle of our canteens against the metal buckles of our belts.

Then the Huns open up with their MG 08 machine guns— the Devil's Paintbrushes. Bullets hiss around us, moving faster than the speed of sound, followed by the cracking of the air. Men start bowing their heads and dropping to their knees as the earth beneath us is painted with blood. Their blood. Our blood. My father falls, but I pick him up, throw him over my shoulder to carry him . . .

"Cal? Cal?"

I'm so lost in that vision of a France I've never really seen that I've been in a daze, not even seeing my feet crunching the red roadside gravel.

I run my hands back through my long hair, waking myself back up to the real world.

"Yes, sir!" I say. "Present and accounted for, sir."

That makes Pop chuckle. It's not hard for me to amuse Pop, unless he is in one of his black moods. Then nothing will bring the light of a smile to his sun-browned face, even though I have to try.

I take care of you, you take care of me.

That's the deal, as Pop puts it. All we have is each other.

I pick up my pace to match his. I'm counting my steps, keeping my face calm so as not to let on where my mind has been. Pop would feel bad if he knew where his speaking about the war

9

sometimes leads my overactive brain. I know he always has my best interests at heart. He just wants to take good care of me.

For example, to help me know what to do when there's trouble, he tells scary stories. Like the one about a giant all made of stone that likes to eat people. Or the story of monster birds that would fly down and carry away children. I do not know where he got them from, but those tales about bloodthirsty monsters are really something. He doesn't tell me them just to scare me, though. Take courage from the story, he says. In every one of those stories, those monsters end up getting defeated—usually by a boy or girl who's listened to the advice of elders and learned the monster's weakness. It's also been there in the books I used to read in the little library in the school—stories of boys managing to win against all kinds of odds. *Treasure Island. Tom Sawyer.* Being able to get stories like those is the thing I miss most about school.

I feel the weight of the few books I do own in my pack. Mrs. Hall, who was my sixth-grade teacher, gave them to me when the school closed. She made sure every one of the few boys and girls still left when it shut down got one or two books. Me, being the one who read the most, I got three.

"Here, Cal," she said. "I know you'll treasure these."

And she was right about that.

I'd buy more books if I had the money and a place to keep them other than my pack. One day, probably years down the road, when Pop and I have a place of our own again—as Pop promises we will—I am going to have a whole shelf of books in my room. Maybe two.

But even without school, I have kept on learning. Pop knows a lot. Though he doesn't often share what he writes, he keeps a sort of journal—an old half-used ledger book that he was able to buy for a nickel from a storekeeper we did some odd jobs for. Now and then he will pull out this half pencil he keeps in his shirt pocket to write down his thoughts as he takes note of things. Maybe the weather or where we found a good place to camp, or the name of some farmer who treated us friendly-like.

Some of the other things he writes down, as he remembers such things his own parents taught him, are about plants. He has read to me from that journal the names of all sorts of things and how they might be used—like how chewing green willow bark cures a headache or how tea made from pine needles is good for a cough.

I'm studying the trees and plants by the road as we trudge along. It being March and us being in the southland, there's the chance of finding things ready to gather. Yesterday there was a fine cattail marsh I pointed out. No houses around. No one likely to drive us off. We took off our shoes and waded in. Red-winged blackbirds—Pop's favorite birds—were calling all around us and bobbing on the tallest stems. The young stalks pulled out easy. The bottoms of their stems were white and crunchy to taste. Better than celery.

No marshes today, though. No nut trees ready to harvest yet, it being months too early. But the brush bodes well for the presence of rabbits.

11

"See that, Pop?" I say. "Rabbit run."

"All right, Cal," he replies. "Good eyes, son. After we make camp, we'll set up some snares."

Sometimes, in addition to finding myself in the past in someone else's body, I can also sort of look ahead to what's coming. Where we camp for the night will be high enough on a hill that no rain will flood us out. A nice dry oak grove.

I can hear Pop talking to the rabbits as he puts out the snares.

"Hey, you, we need you.

"Come on, rabbits, we need you.

"Hey, you, we thank you.

"Come on, rabbits, give us food."

"Where-all you boys think you're a-headin'?"

That rough, unfriendly voice jolts me out of that future to an unpleasant present. A big man on an equally big white horse is blocking the road in front of us. There's a double-barrel shotgun cradled loose over his left arm, half-pointed our way.

The man's square face is as red as his hair. His mouth is set hard.

"Morning, Captain," Pop says, snapping a salute. His voice is friendly and polite. I'm glad of that. When my father's voice is otherwise, things may not turn out so well. Pop's stance is relaxed and easy, not like a coiled spring.

Pop drops his hand to untie his kerchief and unbutton the top of his shirt. Then he wipes his neck with that kerchief. His doing so makes that man up on his horse relax some. I know why.

He's caught sight—as Pop intended—of the slightly paler

12

skin of my father's neck and chest. Both Pop and I are dark. And we tan fast. We become brown as berries from living out as we have done since losing the house and farm when the bank failed. That man on his high horse might have been taking us for Negroes.

We are in the South. Here in the South, though I have never understood why, those whose great-grandparents came from the Dark Continent are not treated fair.

"Y'all serve?" the rider asks.

"You could say that. Corporal. Second Division."

"Belleau Wood?" the man says.

Pop nods. "Soissons, too. PFC. Under Marine Brigade Commander John Lejeune, Captain."

"Ah'm jes a corporal, too, brother," the red-haired man says. There's a hint of a smile on his lips as he shakes his head. "Only got that rank on account of all them officers getting kilt off. Jes' a peckerwood doughboy who didn't know no better than to join up to kill him some Huns. Never expected they would do such a job of killin' us."

Neither of them says anything for a while.

I try hard not to think too much about what I just heard. I don't want to find myself there again in my imagination. I concentrate hard on listening to what's close by. The soft huffing of that big horse. The sound of the red-haired man's heavy breathing. That bit of a wheeze in his throat is like what I've heard from others who served in the poisoned air of Belgium and France.

I am not going to let myself get taken over. I'm here in the South.

13

There's a redbird calling *wheet-wheet-wheet-wheet wheeyou wheeyou wheeyou* from somewhere farther down the red earth road.

That's the best thing for me to listen to—that birdsong being repeated again and again.

Wheet-wheet-wheet-wheet wheeyou wheeyou wheeyou

Wheet-wheet-wheet-wheet wheeyou wheeyou wheeyou

"We are," Pop finally says, "knights of the road. My son, Cal, and me. Heading to Rustburg, assuming we are on the right road."

The big man pulls lightly on his reins to move his horse out of our path. He lifts his shotgun—uncocked now—up over his shoulder and points with his other hand.

"Some twenty miles," he says, coughing to clear his throat. "Red House crossroad up ahead. You all want to go straight. Right turn'd take you to Appomattox."

"Thank you," Pop says.

"I would ride a ways with you," the man says, turning his head to the side and spitting a gob of pink phlegm, "but I'm-a due over Pamplin City. Tell you what, though."

He gestures down the road with three outstretched fingers. "Third house on your left. Half mile up. My place. Wife's there. Rose. Tell her Red sent you." He claps his palm on his chest making a hollow thump, loud as a drum. "Red Campbell. She'll give you dinner. Boy of your'n looks hungry."

"Thank you," Pop says, drawing himself up a bit. "But we, my boy and me, we would like to work for what's offered. Might you need some wood split or a fence mended?"

14

Red Campbell nods as he clears his throat again. "That is how you folks be, right? Different from them beggars or bums looking for handouts."

"We're hoboes, sir," I say, speaking up for the first time. It surprises me almost as much as it does Pop, who looks at me with one eyebrow raised. "We have an ethical code."

Pop raises that eyebrow a little higher. Staying silent most of the time is my nature. But when I do start talking, especially about our way of life, I sometimes do go on a bit. Right now Pop is wondering if I am about to begin spouting that ethical code which he used to read me from his journal but which I now know by heart. Starting off with *Decide Your Own Life, Do Not Let Another Person Run or Rule You*.

I could spout that out now—but I've said all I intend to say.

Red laughs, loud and deep as thunder. He leans down to slap me on my back in a friendly fashion that nearly dislocates my shoulder. The grin on his face is wide as Jack's Old Lantern.

"Wood splitting it is," he says. "And tell Rose to give this eth-ee-cal son of your'n the slab of corn bread she was savin' for me."

He slides his shotgun into the sheath hung from his saddle, kicks his heels into the big horse's sides, and they gallop off, dry red dust rising from the road behind them.

CHAPTER TWO

NOT ALL THAT MUCH

There's not all that much wood to split and stack. No more than a cord. But Red's wife, Rose, as big-boned as her husband, makes like we got enough done to heat their cabin and stoke the cookstove for a year.

"Come on in now, boys," she says.

I finish washing at the pump. Then I take out my comb and run it through my hair a dozen times. Just to make sure my hair's not tangled, but slicked neatly back.

"Ready?" Pop says.

I nod and we follow the sweet aroma of home-cooking inside.

I'm served a big slab of corn bread. I eat it slow, sopping up the gravy from the squirrel stew she spooned into tin plates for each of us.

"Thank you kindly, ma'am."

Those are the only words out of my mouth the whole meal. But they are sufficient to earn me a second piece of corn bread.

Try to Be a Gentleman at All Times.

That is part of the second rule of the ethical code. I do my best to live by it.

The sun is a few fingers past the top of the sky when we finish eating.

There is no time for us to boil up. But rinsing and wringing out our shirts at the pump renders us presentable enough for polite company. The sun is warm enough to dry our shirts as we walk.

"Off we go, Cal," Pop says, shouldering his bindle.

I nod and we start off.

Pop is just tireless when we walk together. Miles fall away under our marching feet. It is still two hands from sunset when we come in sight of Pop's destination. It's a small farmstead. It's not within Rustburg proper, but at the outskirts of the little town where there's mostly fields and farms.

Pop stops at the rail fence a hundred yards from the house. Between the house and fence is a field of cotton. White plumed stalks wave at us like little hands as a wind comes up.

Pop is shaking his head. He's studying three hobo signs scratched into the corner post. They are no more than a foot from the ground. Not where a member of John Q. Public would look.

The first sign, older by the way it's weathered, is a square missing its top line. It's the sort of sign a hobo loves to see. It means this is a safe place to stop for the night.

But the second two signs, more recent, are ominous.

The first of those newer symbols is a square with a slanted roof and an X drawn through it. The second is a triangle with two raised hands.

"Dang and blast," Pop says. It's as near to cussing as he ever gets.

17

I nod and look back down the road. Time for us to start padding the hoof.

Pop shakes his head.

"Nope, Cal," he says. "Let's see if we can set this right. You stay back of me."

We walk up the driveway that leads to the small farmhouse. It has a single story. No more than four rooms by my estimate. I do as Pop says. I stay back, but not too far. If someone suddenly comes out that door with a gun, my plan is to push Pop aside and try to duck the shot. With that bad leg of his he can't always move that fast.

I take care of you, you take care of me.

As we walk, I am thinking about those signs we saw. I am feeling perturbed about whoever the tramp was who did the homeowner wrong. This is a person who was friendly to 'boes before, but now is no longer open to honest men of the road such as us. That second sign, the one of a house with an *X* through it—meant that hoboes were no longer welcome. The third one, that triangle with the two hands on it, that was even worse. It meant a homeowner with a gun!

Had the one who turned this place unfriendly been a thief? It was surely no real 'bo. Us honest to Pete hoboes follow the code and work for what we get. More likely it was a tramp, someone too lazy to work and apt to steal your boots while you was sleeping.

We're now within sight of the front door. So far there's been no barking from a dog and no shout of "Clear out, Bums!" from

18

anyone inside. That's good—unless they're waiting for us to come close enough to get a better shot at us.

The screen door opens just a crack. But that crack is plenty big enough for what appears to be the barrel of a rifle shoved through it.

"Mauser," Pop says, his voice soft. "Saw too many of them pointing at me in France." He reaches a hand back to stop me from doing anything. "Stay back, Cal."

I should do something. But what?

"Go away, you two! You got no business here. Go on now before I shoot you!"

The only good thing about what was just shouted at us, in a woman's high voice, is that what we heard was words and not the crack of a German rifle.

"Edith," Pop calls out. "That you in there?"

The barrel on the gun drops. I catch a glimpse of a face peering out above it.

"Who are you to know my name?" the woman says. Her voice is more quizzical than challenging now.

"It's Railroad Will," Pop says, his voice turns singsong, "Child of the Open Road, Heir to the Throne of the Wind, the same Son of the Soil who served by the side of your husband, Sam, in the War to End All Wars."

"Will Black!"

The door swings wide open and a woman comes running out. She throws her arms around Pop, almost braining me with that rifle still in her right hand.

19

Pop carefully extricates the rifle from her grasp without removing her arms from around his neck. He hands the gun to me. I hold it carefully, parade rest.

"Edith," he says, her feet not touching the ground as she hangs about his neck like some sort of scarf, "you are looking well."

The Edith-woman leaves go of her hold, plops down onto her own feet, and reaches up her left hand to push a thick lock of brown hair back over her forehead.

"Why thank you, Will Black," she says.

"I just speak the truth," Pop replies.

They stand there a moment. It makes me feel awkward. It's as if there's something between them that goes back a ways, something they don't seem to need to talk about because both of them know it so well.

"And who is this?" the Edith lady says, suddenly turning her eyes on me.

Pop swings his chin my way, the gesture he does instead of pointing a finger the way most do.

"Meet my boy, Cal," he says. "The finest companion any traveling man could hope to have by his side."

It makes me proud to hear Pop say that, his voice so sincere. I stand a little straighter, swing the rifle from parade rest up to shoulder arms, and snap a salute with my right hand.

"Yes, sir," I say.

That brings a grin to Pop's face and an outright laugh from Edith. It's a pleased laugh, not her laughing at me.

"Well," she says, "and who taught him that?"

"Give Mrs. Euler back her gun," Pop says in reply.

I try to hand her the gun, but she shakes her head.

"No," she says, smiling at me. "You bring it on in with you. It is not loaded, anyway."

"I know, ma'am," I say, opening it to show the lack of any shells in its breech.

That broadens the smile which seems to be a natural expression on her face.

"Come on in." She gestures at the door. "There's a chicken stew on the stove and a mince pie in the oven, as well. More than a widow woman can eat by herself."

As we sit at her kitchen table she small talks about her little farm. How the hired man who comes by three days a week is a good enough worker. How the chickens, Sam's Plymouth Rocks, have been laying their eggs good and regular. How that big field of cotton is leased out to a man she calls the Colonel, who pays her a fair enough price for the use of the sixty acres.

Pop listens, nodding his head now. He is paying careful attention to her words, as if his life depended on them. Whenever she seems about to falter or lifts a nervous hand to push back that thick brown lock of her hair, he speaks a word or two of encouragement.

Yes. Go on. I see.

That is one of the things I admire about Pop. He has a way of paying attention that makes people feel good about themselves. I am not sure where he learned that, but it is something I intend to emulate whenever I have the opportunity. There is nothing fake about it. He's not just pretending to be interested, even in things that might seem boring. He just finds people interesting.

Finally, Miz Euler reaches a point where her words finally run out, like a pot from which the last drop has been poured. Like the actual empty coffeepot from which she has poured no fewer than four cups for Pop over the last hour.

She takes a breath, looks around the kitchen, sighs.

"Time I set the table. You two go wash up," she says.

As I reach for the pump handle, Pop holds out a hand to stop me.

"Sam Euler," he says. He's looking over his shoulder toward the house.

I wait, knowing there's more about to be said. But instead of speaking, he just points with his chin over by the woods behind the house. I see right away what is there.

We walk over to it together. It's a rough-cut rock, not the smoothed granite you seen on rich folks' resting places.

"Local sandstone," Pop says, squatting down as best he can with that stiff leg. "Cut it himself, carved in his name and the dates when he knew he was about out of time."

SAMSON K. EULER

1898–1928

S.K.E., I think. A shiver goes down my back. Those were the initials on the watch I saw in my vision. Pop has a gold watch like that one.

"It was the gas," Pop says. "Sam had only half a lung left when he got back. It was a near miracle he survived as long as he did. Long enough to set this place up, pay off the mortgage. Then he could let go."

I reach out my hand to help Pop up. He could do it alone, but then again as he often says, there are plenty of things a man can do alone, but do a sight better with just a little help.

"Never met a man stronger than Sam. That Biblical name surely suited him. It was him who carried me over one shoulder back to the trench, running, leaping over the shell holes and the bodies of fallen men, right through the barbed wire, paying no heed to bullets and shells. I would have been pushing up poppies in Flanders were it not for Sam."

We walk back to the pump. Cool, sweet water comes gushing out as I lift the creaking handle up and down, up and down. But Pop just stands there.

He has that faraway look on his face again. He doesn't like to talk about the Great War. It's too painful for him. Maybe feeling that pain of his is what makes me imagine I was there with him. Though that vision of the gold watch is still bothering me. I imagine it could just be coincidence. But what about the part of my vision when I see Sam picking Pop up and carrying him to safety?

There's no explaining that. No question I could ask about it. But I know I should say something now to bring him back.

"Pop?"

"Yes, Cal?"

"You saved him, too, didn't you?"

"You could say that," he replies.

Pop sticks his whole head under the gushing spout. He's

done talking. He wipes his face with both hands and slicks back his thick black hair. Then he shakes the water from his hands, making dark spots on the dry red earth to the side of the trough, as if he's offering the ground some of that water.

"Your turn," he says, taking the pump handle.

I bend and wash my face and hands as he did, sluicing away not only the dirt, but also as much as I can of a memory of pain and loss—a memory I've somehow shared.

We're back at the table again. The two of us are scrubbed to the point where our faces are nearly as red as apples, our fingernails as clean of the usual dirt as the points of our jackknives can make them. Pop is not talking. He's looking, just as I am, at the big bowl of chicken stew that Miz Euler just placed in the center of the table. The steam rising up from it carries an aroma that makes my mouth water.

But I have to wait. My father and I are civilized travelers of the highways and byways and not lowlife scroungers. Grace comes first.

Miz Euler and Pop are each waiting for the other to say the words. But neither seems ready to pipe up with a blessing or pass the burden of saying grace to the other.

"Go ahead," Miz Euler finally smiles.

"Creator," Pop says, his voice deep and resonant, "we three who have gathered here give thanks for this food, this gift. We thank the bird that gave its life, the plants that also allowed themselves to be sacrificed to feed us."

Pop pauses, takes a breath.

"We are thankful for the good company around this table and for the everlasting love that still echoes through this home, the love of a good man and a good woman. We are thankful for the brief time we will shelter here in this blessed place before we set our feet again to that long path you've placed before us to travel."

Again he pauses. Though I do not look up, my eyes glued to my bowl as he speaks, I can hear a soft drawing in of breath from Miz Euler and I am pretty sure there's a tear or two in her eye.

"Amen," Pop says.

"Amen," we say.

I am halfway through my second bowl when I feel something wrapping itself around my leg. I don't jump, except in my mind.

The last time I felt something like this was at a jungle camp near the railhead at the outskirts of Tucson, Arizona. Two months ago, it was, Pop and me having ridden the rails south to escape the harshness of a northern winter by seeking that balmier clime.

A feeling like a long hand pressing on my ankle, moving around, up, tightening. And then a soft hiss.

"Don't move, son," Pop's voice whispered. "I heard it."

I opened my eyes to look down, lifting my head only a hair. All I saw at first was Pop's shadowed figure crouching, outlined by the low glow of the campfire behind him. Then he struck a match.

And chuckled at what the light disclosed.

It was a snake all right. A big one. But even in the small amount of light cast by the lucifer we could see its smooth tail and the shape of its head. It was not a rattler.

"Bull snake," Pop said, his hands gently uncoiling it from around my calf. "Come to warm itself up some."

It wrapped around his arm, its head raised to look at him as he lifted it. It was a good six feet long, thick bodied and black as jet. Its eyes caught a gleam from the fire that made it seem as if they were filled with stars.

I reached out a hand and stroked the big bull snake's back. It hissed again, a sound I took as approval.

For some reason, Pop and me always have gotten along with snakes. Most fear them, to the point of hysteria. But, as Pop says, snakes just want to go their own way. Though, to be honest, I would far prefer that their way not lead into my bedroll.

Pop placed the bull snake on a blanket off to the side, a spot where the fire's warmth would be felt.

"You keep watch," he said to it. "We give you heat, you keep us safe."

Then the two of us settled back down and slept the night. One thing about bull snakes is that they tend to discourage rattlesnakes from coming around. Not that Pop nor I feared rattlers all that much. Rattlers are an honorable sort of snake, generally warning you before they strike. But a bite from a poisonous serpent that responds after being stepped on—or rolled over onto by accident—is just as bad.

This time, though, what's wrapping itself around my leg feels different, especially when I hear a sound that tells me the one paying attention to me is no snake.

"Mrrroooww."

"Rudy!" Miz Euler says. "You stop that!"

She reaches down under the table and pulls a fat, purring tabby up onto her lap.

"No manners," she says. "But I spoil him. Typical widow woman with her cats."

Rudy glances at Pop and then me, a self-satisfied look on its broad face.

"Twenty-three pounds," Miz Euler says. "About breaks my back to lug him about. Doesn't it, you rascal?"

Dinner is now finished, including a sweet-tasting mince pie. Pop leans forward to look toward Miz Euler's back. There's a quizzical look on his face.

"Will Black," she says, "what are you staring at?"

Pop shakes his head. "That pie was so heavenly," he says, "I thought for sure it had to be prepared by an angel. I was just looking for your wings."

Miz Euler laughs out loud and Pop and I join in the laughing. That sort of gentle joshing is typical of my father. It is one of the reasons why those who know him are always glad to see him appear.

Miz Euler rubs her face with her apron. "It feels good to laugh again," she says. "I am right glad that you and your boy stopped by, Will. You know Sam never stopped talking about you."

Pop looks down at his hands.

"I wish I could have seen him more often, but . . ." he pauses a moment before speaking the words I've heard him say a hundred times or more ". . . we never know where life is going to take us."

"True enough," Miz Euler agrees.

"You been having some trouble with tramps?" Pop asks, saying that last word as if it brings a bad taste in his mouth.

"Indeed I have," she says. "But how'd you know that, Will?"

Pop does not mention our hobo signs. No need for anyone outside of our society of knights of the road to know.

"Well," he says, "getting welcomed by the barrel of a rifle was a bit of a giveaway. Steal from you?"

Miz Euler nods, pressing out her lower lip as she does so.

"Three chickens thus far, my best butcher knife that I had left on the back porch, and an iron kettle I could ill afford to lose."

"How long ago?" The tone of Pop's voice has changed now from idle questioning to focused intent.

"Two weeks ago was the first chicken. I would have thought it a fox or a weasel if I had not seen the footprints around the coop. The knife was next to vanish a day or so later. That was when I started keeping watch, and keeping Sam's gun at the ready. I used to not mind someone coming through offering to work for a meal. But after that knife vanished I started doing what I did with you—warning anyone away before they got close to the house. They might have been honest hoboes, but I felt I could not take the chance."

"Shame you had to do that," Pop says. I can hear anger below the calm surface of his voice. "And when did that kettle turn up missing?"

"Two days ago."

"Ah," Pop says.

I know what that means. We are, for certain, going to do something.

CHAPTER THREE

TRACKING

"We'll be back in a bit," Pop says, pushing away from the table. "Just going to take a little walk."

Out back a few small maples have grown up along a rail fence. Pop uses his jackknife—just like the one I own—to cut a thin six-foot-long stick from one of those trees. Then he peels the bark off that stick, which he will use for measuring. It's shiny yellow, and its scent, which I love, is bitter and sweet at the same time.

We start off at Miz Euler's chicken coop, a well-built little house with a screen door at the front and two dozen nest boxes across the back wall. It is spotlessly clean, probably swept out twice daily. Painted white, with little flowers drawn on the outside walls, it's bigger than most shelters Pop and I have rigged up whenever we're stayed a day or two in a jungle. Truth be told, it is better made than any of the shanties in the Hoovervilles, growing up like weeds all over the land these days.

Pop sees me studying the henhouse. He pats the side of it with his hand.

"Sam made this," he says. "A man who always took pride in his work."

I peer inside. All the nests but two are filled with hens that lift their head to look up at us. Seeing no threat, they settle back, making the chuckling little clucks you hear from contented chickens. Another dozen hens, none of them layers, and a strutting rooster occupy the fenced-in yard behind the coop.

Pop walks around behind the house, slow and careful, his eyes on the ground. I stay two paces behind.

"Here," he says.

I look down at what he is pointing at with the tip of his measuring stick

There, in the soft earth, is the print of a man's right boot.

Pop puts his own right foot next to it, presses down to make an impression of his own, then steps back.

"What do you see, Cal?" he asks me.

I kneel down by the two prints. I notice right off that the unknown man's boot is two sizes larger than Pop's. From the depth of the impression, he's considerably heavier than Pop's hundred and fifty pounds. I don't mention either of those deductions, though. Pop takes it for granted—with all he's taught me about tracking—that I'll see such.

Picking up a twig, I point to a line at the back of the heel print.

"Yup," Pop says. "Good eyes, son. Something made a cut across his boot heel. That makes his print like no other. Now there's the left print and another right one."

He takes his stripped stick and measures the distance between strides as well as the direction that trail leads toward the woods.

Then we commence to follow.

Where the ground is hard, Pop uses his measuring stick, laying it end over end until he locates another track. He also takes notes of such thing as broken-off dead branches where the chicken thief forced his way through some small pines. Pop is an ace tracker. Learned from his own father, a grandpop I never met—him having passed on before I drew a breath.

Beyond my parents, I have never met any other of my kin.

There are good reasons for that. After going off to school, Pop explained, he lost touch with his own relations, most of whom passed on while he was away—as did his mother and father.

"There's no other Blacks to be found," he sometimes says.

As far as my late mother's side goes, there's no way I can ever make any connection there. That was so even before her sickness took her two years ago. Mom had come West as one of the children on an orphan train.

"Look here," Pop says, bringing me back out of my cogitating.

We have gone about a mile and found ourselves on the other side of the woods with an open field before us. There are no tracks, cut heel or otherwise, to be seen ahead of us.

"Thinks he's clever, don't he?" Pop says.

I nod.

"So what did he do?"

I point with my chin toward the pine tree behind us where a low branch has been broken off so recently that the sap is still oozing. A branch meant to serve as a sort of broom by a man walking backward and sweeping away his tracks behind him.

"So what do we follow?"

31

I look ahead of us. A six-foot-wide swath of smoothed earth stretches across the red soil of the field.

"The trail of no trail," I say.

Pop smiles and slaps me on the back.

"Lead on," he says.

The footprints begin again a few feet past the edge of the field where that pine-branch broom, its needles just beginning to turn brown, has been cast aside.

I keep following the trail, Pop a few feet behind me, till the land drops off into a small valley. I reckon it is not far from the train tracks, which I remember being on the other side of the next hill. Sure enough, as we stand there we hear the distant whistle of a locomotive still miles away.

Pop pulls out that pocket watch, which he regards as his one and only useful valuable—aside from his service certificate. That paper, to be honest, he describes as "almost valuable" seeing as how he still has to wait thirteen years before he can cash it in.

"That'll be the three-o-five," he says. "If we were planning to ride it, we'd have plenty of time to reach the uphill grade where it slows on the back side of that ridge."

Pop snaps his watch shut and slips it back into his vest pocket.

"Now, though," he says, "duty calls."

We go quiet down the slope, using the toe-to-heel walk Pop started teaching me as soon as I reared up on two legs. Neither of us makes more noise than wind through tall grass.

On the level ground at the base of the hill I note a single deep footprint, a cut across the heel. Not that I need to see it. The chicken thief's camp is in plain sight.

It's a ramshackle affair. A tent constructed of a piece of canvas stretched over the low limb of an oak tree. It's tacked to the branch on top with bent nails and held in place at the bottom by rocks at the base. Five feet in front of the shelter, a black pot is balanced on the stones of a cold fire pit. The mess of feathers, hacked-off chicken legs, wings, and heads off to the left of the pit leaves no doubt that this is our man.

Two boots are sticking out from under the lean-to. As we get closer, still quiet walking, I see the right shoe has that telltale cut across the heel. Though the rest of him is concealed by the low-hanging canvas, his feet are in those clodhoppers. The sound of snoring leaves little doubt we've come up unnoticed, helped, no doubt, by the drained whiskey bottle next to the fire pit.

I shake my head. Not only is this man making it bad for other 'boes by being a thief, he is ignoring the sixth rule of our ethical code:

Do not allow yourself to become a stupid drunk and set a bad example.

There's a stack of newspapers on a stump. One thing in the fellow's favor, I suppose. That he can read, I mean. On the other hand, there's little chance he spent a penny to buy a paper. Likely stole that pile from people's porches. Maybe he is just using those papers to start his fires.

Pop picks up the topmost paper, which seems to have caught his eye. He reads a bit of it, folds it, sticks it in his back pocket.

Then Pop looks at me and nods. He walks over and kicks the sole of the man's left boot.

"Rise up," Pop commands, in a voice like that of Jesus lifting Lazarus from the dead.

The result is more dramatic than I expected.

Rise up is indeed what our cut-boot chicken thief does—propelling himself from horizontal to vertical so that he brings that makeshift tent right up with him, making him look like some sort of a ghost in a canvas shroud. It's a funny sight to see.

Or it would be funny were it not for the fact that the man is clutching a butcher knife—no doubt the one he purloined from Miz Euler—in his right hand.

He's big—both in height and girth. As he swings that blade wildly every which way he is growling like a gorilla and bellowing out a series of homicidal remarks.

"I'LL CUT OUR YER LIVER! DANG YEH! I'LL KILL EVER ONE OF YEH! YER DEAD MEN EVER ONE OF YEH!"

His blind soliloquy is cut short by Pop stepping to the side and taking the man's legs out from under him with a quick kick to the big tramp's ankles. As the heavy-bellied man thuds down—hard enough to shake the nearby earth—Pop reaches in, quick as a hawk diving onto a rabbit, relieves the man's hand of the blade, and steps back to stand beside me.

There was no anger in what Pop just did—luckily for the stunned hulk of a man gasping for breath. But what my father just accomplished was done with such easy efficiency that it's taken my breath away.

I hope I can just grow up to be half the man Pop is, I think to myself.

Pop nods at the black pot. I pick it up. He hands me the butcher knife.

Then he grabs the canvas and yanks it off the chicken thief so we can see his face for the first time. It's a small face for so big a man, reddened and veined by too much drink. His nose is bulbous, his eyes set close together under a mop of straw-colored, dirty hair. I would wager a dollar that no comb has touched that unruly mess for months.

The man pushes himself up on his hands to a sitting position, looks at us with bleary eyes.

"Yeh can't do this to me," he says, his voice stupid from drinking. "I got friends."

"I doubt that," Pop says. He squats down, his stiff leg off to the side. "You got a name, tramp?"

"Jack," the man says after a moment of hesitation. "Just Jack."

"Got any money, Just Jack?"

"You gonna rob me?" asks the man who's called himself Jack—and is likely named something entirely different.

"Show us what you got," Pop says. The tone of his voice is such that even as fogged by alcohol as our Jack might be he knows there is no way to refuse.

Jack digs out a dirty change purse from a back pocket.

"Dump it," Pop says, tapping the ground with an index finger.

It takes a moment for the half-drunk man to untie the strings of his purse. His hands are pale white, his palms and fingers

35

free of any of the calluses like the ones Pop and I have earned by doing honest work. This man is no hobo; he is a light-fingered and lazy tramp for sure.

He pulls free one last knot and shakes the purse open. Four quarters and a dime plop out onto the red earth.

"All of it," Pop says, having noted as I did that Jack is pinching the purse at its middle, holding back most of the contents.

Whining like a pig being prodded, Jack loosens his grip. The rest of his stash falls out. Another seven quarters, four fifty-cent pieces, and two shiny new silver dollars join the other coins. Jack starts to reach for them.

"No," Pop says, his voice quiet but firm. Jack pulls his hand back.

"You got anything else?" Pop asks.

"I am a veteran," Jack replies. "I served in France. You can't treat me this way."

"Where's your Tombstone Bonus?" Pop asks.

The man looks confused. It's plain to me that he is no vet at all, just one of those pretending to have served to get pity while begging on the street. But Pop gives him another chance.

"Your Compensation Certificate," Pop says, speaking the words slow and clear. "The twenty-one-year endowment life insurance policy every man jack of us was issued in ought-twenty-four." He stares Jack straight in the eyes and waits.

Jack looks even more confused than before. He drops his gaze to his feet.

"You hurt my ankle," he complains, rubbing it.

Without looking in my direction, Pop holds his right hand out toward me. I put the handle of the butcher knife in his palm.

Jack shrinks back, pushing himself against the tree and holding his hands out in front of him.

"No," he whimpers. "No."

Pop pays him no heed. He reaches out with the knife and divides the coins into two piles. The two and four bit pieces to the left, the silver dollars to the right.

"Now we got back this knife and the pot you stole," he says. "So no compensation needed there. But those hens you took?"

Pop picks up the two silver dollars. "This will pay for them."

Pop flips one coin and then the next back toward me. Both land in the black pot, where Pop was aiming.

Pop stands up, slips the knife under his belt.

"Now Just Jack," he says, "we will be coming back here tomorrow. By then, you will be long gone. Savvy? Or you will be even longer sorry."

Pop walks away and I follow him. Neither of us look back.

A part of me, though, is thinking how sad it is. When a man gets like Jack with only himself to think about, there's really nowhere he can go. Not like Pop and me, us always having each other to take care of the other.

CHAPTER FOUR

NEWS

Miz Euler is right pleased. Not only has she gotten her knife and kettle back, but the two shiny silver coins Pop is placing in her palm are fair payment for her purloined pullets.

"You take half, Will," she tells Pop.

"I cannot," he says, his voice soft and gracious. "What Cal and I did was not for money."

Miz Euler puts the coins into a front pocket in her apron as she turns away quickly.

"Thank you and bless you," she says, her voice choking a little on those words. Then she turns back to us, a smile again on her face.

"Well," she says, "there was no way I was going to allow you to refuse a sit-down dinner and night's lodging."

"A dollar means a lot to a widow woman," Pop says to me as we walk down Miz Euler's lane.

It's the following morning. We've not just had a huge dinner last night, but a breakfast this morning big enough to satisfy the appetite of a grizzly bear.

I look back over my shoulder. Miz Euler is still standing on her porch. I reach my hand into my right pocket and feel the quarter she slid into my palm as I was helping clear the breakfast dishes.

"You must take this," she said fiercely.

So I'd accepted it, knowing it would be bad grace to refuse.

I have no doubt she wished us to stay far longer. She must be lonely. Her cooking was surely good. And that barn was warm and comfortable. But we are men of the road, Pop and me. Clutching her apron in her left hand, she is still waving good-bye with her right, her arm held high like a brakeman with a lantern. Maybe she will stay there waving like that long after we've gone. But I do not turn back again.

Rather than heading for the place just past the rail yard to hop the Southern, we swing first by Jack's mess of a camp. As I expected—since few men ever choose to go up against Pop when he has laid down the law—Jack is gone. So, too, is the piece of canvas that served as a shelter.

But his campsite's not empty. There's not one, but two whiskey bottles—plus something else left right in the open for us to see. Rather than use a pit latrine, Jack has left it there.

Pop shakes his head, but there's a little smile on his face as he does it. He knows such a gesture of defiance is the mark of a coward, one who hightailed it as soon as he did it. Probably catching the very train Pop told him to take yesterday.

We go down to tidy things up before we leave. That is what the ethical code teaches a knight of the road to do.

Always respect nature and do not leave garbage where you are jungling.

Pop takes out the fold-up trenching shovel he always carries. He'd no more be without that than I would be without a book or two in my own pack. *Bullfinch's Mythology* and *Call of the Wild* being my current companions, along with my dictionary.

We bury Jack's mess, then roll the stones away from the fire pit and shovel enough dirt onto the still warm coals to make sure no stray sparks get into the surrounding dry brush. Few things make folks resent us 'boes more than when a careless left fire pit sets the surrounding woods and fields ablaze.

When we are done there's no sign anyone was ever there.

"Time to ride, son," Pop says.

There's already half a dozen men crouched down in the weeds and brush a half mile past the switching yard. We approach through a gully, bent low so that we do not attract the attention of the railroad bull, whose job it is to police the yard, walking back and forth by the train. He's checking all the boxcars hooked on behind the passenger cars, looking into them, atop them, under them, a heavy club in his right hand.

I suspect he must know there's a passel of us knights of the road waiting outside his yard, but he is either lazy enough or cautious enough to not stray far from the open tracks.

"ALL ABOOOOOAAARRD," is carried to us on the morning wind.

We're ready. I can feel the tension in the men around us. They're all on this side of the tracks because of the hillside rising on the other side. The grade here keeps the rate of the train at just the right speed for a man to lope along next to it, then

40

grab a handrail. My breath is deeper, my heart pounding heavy and strong. About to latch on to the power and speed of a train. About to be part of it. I love this feeling. Wild and free!

I don't know if there's a better feeling than this. I can see why Pop chose this life before he met my mom and decided to settle down. I can understand why he has come back to it. Unlike a good many of those millions of folks who became homeless when all the banks failed, Pop had already experienced the hobo life and didn't have to struggle to adjust to it. I've seen men wearing rags that once were tuxedos. I've also seen sections of hobo camps that are all made up of boys who ran away from the hard times on their farms or got separated from their parents somehow. A lot of those kids look sad and lost. Unless they have a grown-up looking after them they might get taken advantage of. Have what few goods they've got taken, get beaten up. Some don't survive. But more and more keep coming. Pop showed me a story in a newspaper a few months back. It said that of the countless people now on the roads, there's thousands who are teenagers.

I'm glad to be with Pop, glad he chose to take me with him. And glad I am lanky and strong like Pop.

Pop says he's never seen anyone learn the ins and outs of being on the road as fast as I have. There're men who've been hoboing for years, he says, who haven't picked up as much as I have in the two years since Mom's passing. I feel proud about being complimented that way, but I don't tell Pop what I think may be the real reason I've absorbed so much in such a short time. It's not just that I'm a natural fast learner—as my teachers said back at school. It's that losing Mom left such a hole in my heart that I needed to fill it up as soon as I could. Otherwise my whole life might have run out like water from a leaky pail. But everything about being a knight of the road seemed the perfect way to plug up that aching spot in my chest. That and having Pop always by my side, as constant as the sun coming up every dawn.

The train is almost to us, not picking up much more speed because it is just hitting the uphill stretch that carries it over the hill. We're well concealed from sight by a mulberry bush thirty feet from the track.

Pop pats me on the shoulder. It means I am to go first, a few yards ahead of him. It makes me proud that I have his trust. I crouch like the sprinter I was during my last year in Garrison Elementary School, when my coach told me he never saw a boy with a faster start.

A real Jim Thorpe, Coach McGunty said.

I might be running for that school now and not getting set to run after a train were it not for the fact that it's no more. I love to run and I know I'm good at it. I would wager that I'd have won a few races. But Garrison closed down for good around the same time we lost our little farm. Our crop had failed right after Mom died. That meant we couldn't make the payments on the mortgage, and the bank was not willing to carry us. All we could do was watch as the marshals came and took everything—house and barn, tools and furniture, livestock and all—leaving us just the clothes on our backs.

Pop's decision for us to ride the rails together was easier to make then, both of us being so unencumbered. Me of school, Pop of what earthly goods he'd owned, and both of us no longer having Mom, the one loss that truly broke our hearts.

We had both cared for her the best we could.

"You two are my good luck," she would say, with that smile of hers.

Pop spent everything he could on the doctor and the medicines. But she just kept getting sicker.

"And here is my bad luck again," she'd say about that, shaking her head and making it sound like a joke.

Even when she was sick, Mom kept her sense of humor. She was beautiful, too. Tall, taller than Pop, with wide shoulders that—before her illness—seemed strong enough to hold the weight of the world. Strong as my father is, he always said that if it came down to a wrestling match she'd beat him. Sometimes when she hugged him she'd pick him right up off the ground. She had long dark hair that came to her waist and the biggest darkest eyes I've ever seen—eyes that could see into my mind and know when I was happy or hurting and then also know just what to say on either occasion.

"Those lovely, soulful Armenian eyes," Pop used to say, almost singing it.

Their being Armenian was the only thing Mom knew about her family—who died right after coming to America.

"My bad luck," she'd say about that.

Which was how she ended up in the New York Foundling Hospital and then, at the age of ten, on one of those trains that carried thousands of orphans like her west. There in Nebraska the Wilsons, an older Polish couple with no children, adopted her.

"And that was my first good luck," she'd say about them. "They were so kind."

I never met those adopted grandparents. The influenza of 1918 took them both when she was eighteen.

"My bad luck again."

They left her a little money. It was not enough for her to stay in school to be a registered nurse, but she did get work as a practical nurse. That was how she met Pop. She was working in the Veteran's Hospital when Pop—who'd been riding a train that crashed—was brought in.

"It was love at first sight," Pop would say.

"Mine first," Mom would add, "seeing as how your father's eyes were bandaged up when I first saw him. But I fell for that cleft in his chin."

"You and me we are getting married, mister," she told him the week the bandages came off. "And we are getting us a place."

And that is just what they did.

"How could I say no?" Pop used to say whenever they told me the story of how they got together. "She was bigger than me."

Then Mom would grab him by the arm or the shoulder and pretend she was going to beat him up before they ended up laughing together in a hug that always included me.

Mom's money added on to what Pop had managed to save while working odd jobs as he was hoboing was enough to make the down payment on our farm. And a year later I was born.

She tried to keep taking care of us. But then, halfway through doing something like making supper, it would happen. She'd

44

stop, press her hand against her side where it was hurting. Then she would have to lean against something.

"I wish my body could stay as strong as my love for you two," she'd whisper as Pop and I would come to steady her.

"My darn bad luck," she'd say then. "I'm such a burden now."

"No burden I would not bear," Pop would reply. "I would gladly carry you from here to France and back again."

Then Mom would smile and let Pop and me help her to bed.

"What now, Pop?" I asked as we walked away from what had been the only home I'd ever known.

Pop was silent for a good half mile. Then he began to pick up the pace, me right behind. Pretty soon we were running full out. Even though Pop limped as he ran, he was still faster than most men. It felt good to be running like that. It wasn't like we were running away from anything or running with any destination in mind. We were just running for the sake of running the way Pop and I had done since I was old enough to run. It was something he said was in his blood, something his own father used to do with him. Running. I loved it.

We went a good three or four miles before we slowed down to a walk. Neither of us was winded, but I could see that Pop had begun limping more. Plus I sensed he was ready to talk now. He stopped, sat on a log by the roadside and patted it for me to join him.

"There's one thing that comes to mind for us, Cal," he said. "At least for now."

"Whatever you say, Pop," I replied, lifting my head. "I am up to it."

"I believe you are," Pop said.

But now the sound of the engine passing pulls me out of that memory.

The engineer sees all of us from his elevated perch and nods. Like many of the men who drive those big machines he holds no grudge against those of us looking to ride. Keeping his train free of hoboes is not his job.

One after another, three passenger cars *clickety-clack* by.

"Now," Pop says.

I bolt from behind the bush half a second before all the others around us. Out of the corner of my eye I quickly count a dozen men rising up like those soldiers who grew from dragon's teeth in the old Greek story. I have always been quick at tallying up and taking note of such things. So it does not break my concentration as I focus on the rail I intend to grab. There's no competition for that handhold. Pop and I have got the jump on all the others. The other 'boes most likely will mass together at one or the other of the next boxcars with doors that'll be swung open by the first to arrive. Those who've hopped in first will reach out their hands for the rest. Helping one another. That's part of being true knights of the road.

My feet pounding on the loose stones along the track, I swing up my left arm—closest to the train—to grab the ladder side rail. A second later my right hand takes firm hold of the rail parallel to it. Then and only then do I lift my feet.

Never try to jump up with a single handhold. That was one of the things I learned during our first week on the road. Not having a firm hold is a recipe for being swung under those

46

unforgiving steel wheels that'll lop off a leg as easy as a knife cutting through butter.

My feet find the rung and I reach up one hand after the other, climbing the ladder quick as a squirrel scrambling up an oak, making space behind me for Pop to follow. Despite that lame leg, he's managed a swift seesawing sort of run, fast as most men with two sound limbs. The vibration of the ladder below me tells me he has caught hold and heaved himself up.

As soon as I get atop the car I take a firm grip with my left and reach my right hand back. Not that Pop needs my help. Offering aid is just the proper thing to do. He takes my hand, shaking it as much as using it to assist him onto the roof. Then, with the grace of a dancer, he spins down into a sitting position next to me.

We stay there for a while atop that car. The wind feels good in my face. Although the strongest smell that comes to my nose is the coal smoke from the engine five cars ahead of us, I can also catch another scent in that wind.

"Magnolia. Scent of the South," Pop says, reading my mind. "Almost as sweet as the prairie."

I nod, trying not to show any sadness in my face as I do so. Our little farm was far to the west of where we are today. Sometimes I miss that place so much it hurts. Though I would never say that to Pop. Out there in Kansas, the sky just goes on forever and you can hear meadowlarks singing in the spring. There is sage there and grasses you do not see in the East or the South, grasses the old buffalo herds grazed on before they were all killed off.

There were Indians back then following those buffalo herds. Pop says there are still Indians there. I never saw any around our farm or in the little nearby town. I suppose I have yet to meet one. The government keeps them cooped up on reservations to the north of where we lived, according to Pop.

Maybe, though, I might have seen an Indian or two and not recognized him. Pop says they don't look like the ones in the dime novels anymore. The government makes them dress like white folks and talk English.

"Indians nowadays," Pop says at times, a kind of catch in his voice for some reason, "they're hard to distinguish from sunburned farmers."

There were Indians, he told me, with the Expeditionary Force.

"Reliable," Pop said once. "Good men."

That leads me to believe that while over there he was friends with an Indian or two. But he's never said more about them and I've never asked.

Unless he starts reminiscing of his own accord, asking Pop anything about the Great War is not a good idea. Asking almost always produces one of three results.

First, which is least frequent—scarce as hen's teeth—is that he might actually answer. An answer usually short as a rabbit's tail, but a real answer nonetheless.

Such as, "It was shrapnel."

End of answer to my question about what caused the wound that left a thick line of red scar tissue wrapped round his knee like a snake.

Second result is nothing at all. No words, nothing. Just a silence so deep that you could drown in it. An uncomfortable silence, thick and heavy as a wool horse blanket that makes me wish I had kept my trap shut. Like the time I asked him about what it was like in the trenches.

Third result is the one I dread. It makes me bite my lip. That is when a certain look comes over Pop's face. It's followed by a curse escaping from his lips like a hurt bird bursting from a cage. Then a black mood comes over him, and he clenches his fists and turns away. He has never struck me, but seeing him like that makes me feel as if I have been punched in the gut.

The last time he got that way was when I asked him why he and other men who served over there didn't get treated better after they came back home.

That black mood can last a minute, an hour, or even a day. And woe betide any man who should cross Pop's path then and do or say anything that might be taken amiss. Like that one huge railroad bull back in Omaha a month ago who came out from behind a little shed, a shed that bore the sign reading **JOBLESS MEN KEEP GOING.** He raised his club to hit me. Pop—who had been two paces behind me—was on him like a hawk on a fat rabbit. It all happened so fast that to this day I cannot describe what Pop actually did. But he left that big bully out cold and bleeding, his broken club on the ground next to him. I think my father might have killed him if I hadn't grabbed his arm and yelled "Pop, don't!"

As soon as I did that, the look on his face changed. His shoulders drooped and his head dropped as he let me drag him away.

He seemed dazed, as if he didn't know what to do. It was almost as if for a moment I was the father and he was the son. When I told him we'd better hop the next freight, he just nodded and let me lead him across the yard over to the track where they were putting together a line of empty boxcars. We climbed into the last empty reefer humped off the main. Me taking care of him.

We ride the roof for a spell until the heat of the sun begins to get a bit much for us. Pop looks over at me, raises an eyebrow, and looks down. I nod. The two of us walk along the top of the boxcar till we are over an open door. Side by side, we both lean over to look inside. It's occupied, but there's plenty of room. Like circus acrobats, we each get a good hold and swing down to land light on our feet inside the car.

"Whoa!" says the 'bo closest to where we land. He's a man who appears middle-aged, with a neat little goatee and a clean white shirt. "Who might you gents be, falling from the sky like the winged Mercury himself?" His voice is pleasant and there's a bit of a chuckle in it as he speaks.

Before Pop can answer, a second man, bone-thin with pants so short they leave his shins exposed and a cigarette dangling from his lip, speaks up. "It's Injun Joe," that man says, his voice raspy from smoking.

Injun Joe?

I look over at Pop, who's now staring straight at the thin smoker.

"Boney," Pop says. That's all, but it's enough, especially when Pop uses that dangerous tone of voice.

50

The thin man takes a step backward, plucks the cigarette from his mouth. He holds his arms out to the side—looking even more like a skeleton when he does that.

"Sorry," he rasps. "Didn't mean nothing by it, Will. No offense?"

Pop says nothing. He turns to the older man with the goatee, holds out his hand.

"Professor," he says. "Nice to see you."

"Railroad Will," the professor says. "Couldn't make out your visage, turned away as you were when you came catapulting in. But I should have discerned it from the dramatic manner of your entrance."

Pop smiles, looks toward me. "You haven't met my boy, Cal."

I shake the professor's hand. His grasp is firm, but he's not trying to prove how tough he is by squeezing till it hurts. I make eye contact for a moment noting how clear and blue those eyes of his are, how amused they look because of the way Pop put Boney in his place with a single word.

I'm glad Pop did that. There is no way anyone should ever link my father with one of the worst characters in that novel by Mr. Twain. Injun Joe, indeed. How could anyone ever picture my pop as a murderous drunken half-breed?

"Pleased, sir," I say as I let go of his palm and step back.

"My, my," the professor says. "Quite the conversationalist, are we not?" Then he chuckles. "Take not my jesting in the wrong light, my lad. I am, indeed, pleased to meet you as well. Any son of your father's must be worthy of respect."

Pop rests a hand on my shoulder. "The professor," he says to me, "was indeed that before the war. A professor of literature."

"But now," the professor adds, "I am but another foot soldier in the growing army of the unemployed—one who found his place in the university taken by younger men."

The professor looks at me again. "There's the bright light of intelligence in this lad's eyes," he says. "Correct me if am errant in my judgment, Will."

"You could say that," Pop replies, a bit of pride in his voice. "And quite the reader. Never without a book in his bindle."

"But not in school," the professor says.

Pop shakes his head. I know that bothers him at times.

"A boy as smart as you, Cal, there's no limit to what you might do with the right education." That's what my father said more than once in the time we've been knights of the road together.

Then, what Pop usually does is just shake his head and say, "Some day, somehow. But I guess you're okay for now."

However, that is not how he answers the professor. Instead, he says something that surprises me. "Lately, Professor, I have been thinking about a way to remedy that."

I look hard at my father. Remedy that? How? My school is closed and gone forever. And from what I know of schools, they're for those who live near them. People with homes, not folks always on the fly. People with money go to school, not hoboes. It makes no sense.

But Pop says not another word and, as always, I do not attempt to break his silence.

52

We settle into one corner of the boxcar that's shared, in addition to Boney and the professor, by three other men. None of them know Pop, which is not all that surprising. There are so many of us riding the rails these days. Not just hundreds or thousands, but millions.

I lean back against the boxcar wall, combing my hair. The thrumming of the rails makes the wall vibrate against my back. The sound of the steel wheels beneath me is as familiar as the babbling of a brook is to one who lives by a stream. Pop's next to me, his shoulder warm against mine. His familiar scent is comforting to me as we lean against each other. It's a mix of wood smoke and soap. His body odor, even when he's all sweaty, somehow always smells clean. I close my eyes and start counting backward from a hundred as I always do at night. I'm asleep before I can get to ninety, comforted by the sound of my father breathing beside me.

Next thing I know I am back home. It is time for breakfast. I can smell Mom's cooking downstairs. It's bacon and eggs. Toast made from bread she baked yesterday. My bed is so warm and comfortable that I don't feel like leaving it. But now, for some strange reason it's vibrating under me. There's a sound of rumbling and rattling. I'd like to keep sleeping. But that grub sure smells good.

A light tap on my toe wakes me. Pop is leaning over me. I'm no longer home—back at that house that's no longer ours. Back when Mom was still with us. I'm on a train.

I feel sad for a moment. The dream that took me over this time was gentle, a place I'd rather not leave. But it's gone now, gone as that home where we were a family of three. I push it away, beyond the back of my mind. A man can't live in what's past.

It's not real dark inside the car now. The moon's shining in through the open door. As Pop pulls me up, I see another light coming from a corner. The flame of a portable stove. Little, but big enough to fry up whatever it is I'm smelling. Fried potatoes and bacon!

The professor, the apparent owner of both stove and pan, is bent over, stirring the mix.

"Care to share some of this repast?" he asks as we walk over to where he's cooking.

I nod my head. I'm always hungry these days—because I am growing like a weed, Pop says.

Pop holds out his banjo—the little frying pan he carries in his bag along with the trenching shovel. The professor spoons out a pile of steaming hot bacon and fried potatoes. I'm pretty sure the potatoes in the pan were my father's contribution—given him by Miz Euler. Pop and I pull out the metal spoons we always carry and dig in. Before I know it we're scraping the bottom of the pan.

Only the three of us share that little meal. The other four in the car stayed in their corner. Add to a meal, you get to share it. When you don't, you don't. Unless you're truly in dire straits. Rule number fifteen.

Help your fellow hoboes whenever and wherever needed; you may need their help one day.

The professor and I wash our food down with water from Pop's army canteen. Boney and the other 'boes are passing a small bottle around, but Boney knows enough not to offer it to Pop. My father does not object to the drinking of others, unless they get so liquored up as to be bothersome. But no alcohol ever passes his lips.

I make a pillow out of my coat and lay back next to Pop on the wooden floor of the car. There was a time, when we first took to the road months ago, when sleeping on a hard surface was not easy for me. I'd been pampered too long by having my own bed. But my body got used to the change. Plus being outdoors in the fresh air makes sleep come faster to a man. Now all I need do is close my eyes and listen to Pop's breathing. With him by my side, it's easy to drift off to slumber land. I wonder, just before I fall back asleep, if that dream of home is going to come back. I start counting. A hundred, ninety-nine, ninety-eight . . .

When I open my eyes, it feels like no time's passed at all. But it has to have been hours. Dappled morning sunlight is streaming in through the open door. That tells me we are heading southwest. Pop, sitting next to me, has that newspaper open and is reading it. As always I've just opened my eyes a crack. Nothing's moved but my eyelids so I do not think he knows I am awake. As I watch, he reads and then rereads the page he's holding up in front of him. He's looking at it so intently that it seems as if his eyes might burn a hole into it.

"Washington," Pop says in a whisper. He lowers the paper.

"You're awake," he says.

I sit up and nod.

"Good," he says. "Remember Joe Angelo, son? I told you about him last year?"

I nod again. I have a good memory, as Pop knows. Joe Angelo was a vet. Like Pop he survived the Great War. Mentioning him might mean Pop's about to share more memories about being over there. This'll be the second time this week that my father has decided to talk about the war. He doesn't do that often. But lately it seems to be on his mind a lot.

"Met Joe in 1918 after the big battle on the Meuse-Argonne line. He was in the 327th tank division. When their commander, Major George Patton, was wounded, it was Joe who dragged him to safety, patched him up, and then ran Patton's orders from one group of tanks to another."

Pop puts aside the newspaper he was reading. Then he reaches into his pocket to pull out the folded article he carries there next to his Compensation Certificate.

I've seen it before, but Pop wants me to look at it again. I unfold it carefully and read the headline.

VETERAN, WEARING MEDALS, JOBLESS, STIRS COMMITTEE

Below it is the picture of a skinny man wearing his army uniform, serviceman's cap on his head, eight medals pinned to his chest. His face is thin, starved-looking. His eyes are huge, dark, and haunted.

"He'd just testified," Pop says, "in Washington D.C., to the House Committee on Ways and Means, which was considering whether us veterans could take out loans against our

Compensation Certificates. Joe walked all the way from his home in Camden, New Jersey. Took him three days on shank's mare."

Pop takes the article back from me, reads what Joe Angelo said.

"'I come to show you people that we need our bonus. I represent eighteen hundred men from New Jersey. They are just like myself, men out of work. I have got a little home back there that I built with my own two hands after I came home from France. Now I expect to lose that little place. Why? My taxes are not paid. I have not worked for two years and a half. Last week I went to our town committee and they gave me four dollars for rations.'"

Pop looks at me, biting his lip. "Sound familiar, son?"

I nod.

Pop shakes his head. "Makes me feel as if I ought to do something. If one Joe Angelo could stir those congressmen, what about ten thousand of us? All of us in Washington and asking nothing more than to be treated fair and square for the sacrifices we made? Joe told them he was making good money—a dollar twenty-five an hour at the DuPont Powder Works. But he chose to enlist—not drafted like some—for army pay of a dollar a day."

Pop folds the article with the care of someone folding a flag. He slips it into his pocket and lifts up the newspaper. His lips are pressed together as he looks at it. We rattle on for another ten miles or so. Then he turned it toward me so I can see the headline.

VETS MARCHING ON D.C.

"Washington," he says, tapping the newspaper with one finger. "Men like Joe and me are going there now. Vets asking for a fair shake. They figure that if enough of us show up, Congress and the president will have to do something. They'll have to give us our bonuses! And me too."

Pop's voice has been getting more excited as he's been talking. He looks straight at me and says that name.

"Wash-ing-ton!"

Says it like a magician chanting Abra-ca-dabra before he pulls a rabbit out of his hat.

"Wash-ing-ton! Me in Washington? Can you imagine that, Cal?"

I don't say anything, but I can. I have one of those rare moments when I can sort of see the future.

There are all of those soldiers marching down Pennsylvania Avenue. Pop is marching with them.

But I don't see me there.

"Yes, sir," Pop says, bringing me back to the present. "Yes, sir!"

His voice is softer. He's talking to himself now. "That's it. I need to join my brother soldiers. One last campaign. One last march."

His mind's made up. Once Pop decides on something, nothing stops him. Not hell or high water. And now I am feeling excited, too. If Pop is going to Washington I'll surely be going there as well. Me taking care of him. Him taking care of me.

Washington, D.C. I've never seen that place, but I've read

about it and it sounds wonderful. The Capitol building, the big memorials, the White House, all sorts of museums, and the nation's biggest library.

But then Pop lowers the paper and looks straight at me. The expression on his face has changed. It's no longer excited. It's thoughtful.

"Son," he says, "I have been thinking."

The tone of his voice has changed, too. It's serious in a way that worries me.

"Now that *I* am going to Washington."

Now I am confused, especially because of the way he emphasized that one word *I*. Not we.

"I," I say. "Pop, won't we both be going?"

He shakes his head. "No, son. If this is going to be a campaign, then I have to go it without you. It might be dangerous and I want you safe while I'm gone. It'll be me and other vets doing this. It's time for you . . ."

He pauses, looking out the door at the trees and telegraph poles whizzing by. The train's going over a rough spot in the tracks. The two of us rocking back and forth with the motion of the boxcar.

"What, Pop?" I ask. "Time for what."

"School," he says. "I have been thinking about this ever since we hit the road. It's not right you missing out on schooling. You need to get back to being educated, Cal. And I know how to do it."

That confuses the dickens out of me. Back to being educated? Back to school? I cannot imagine any way on God's green earth that can be done. The school I was going to is closed. No other school is going to take in a hobo boy just hopped off a freight train. Nor do we have any money for such things as books and school supplies. And where would I live while going to school? It makes no sense.

"How?" I say. Then, because I am feeling so totally befuddled I say it again. "How?"

For some reason, that makes Pop chuckle. "Exactly," he says. He lifts his head to look straight at me. Then he does something strange. He holds out his left hand and strokes the back of it with the fingers of his right.

He's done sign language before, especially when it's been necessary for us to keep quiet—like when we're hiding from a railroad bull. Sign language comes in handy at such times.

But what he just did was a sign I haven't seen before. I don't understand it. It's not like lifting his index finger up and dropping it down for yes or holding out an empty palm for no.

"I don't know that sign, Pop."

He smiles, strokes the back of his hand again. "It means Indian," he says. "Pointing out how Indian skin is darker than that of a white man."

Indian?

Then he holds out his hands, side by side, open palm up. That's a gesture I understand. It means book. But I still cannot grasp what he is telling me.

Finally, as if it explains everything rather than making me even more baffled, he says two words.

"Indian school."

CHAPTER FIVE

INDIAN SCHOOL

"Indian school?" I stare at Pop. I'm so confused the words are spilling out of my mouth like water from a tipped bucket.

"Indian school? They teach you there how to be an Indian?"

Rather than giving me an answer, Pop starts laughing. So hard he throws his head back against the boxcar wall behind him.

BANG!

But it doesn't stop his laughing, even though he reaches up to rub where there's surely going to be a bump.

"Oh my," Pop says, getting enough breath back into his lungs to actually say something. "Wouldn't my old teachers at Challagi have a fit if they heard that? A school where they teach you how to be Indian?"

Pop lets out a short laugh like a horse snorting. Then he shakes his head.

"Nope, son. You could not say that. It is *au contraire*, as they put it over in France. Just the opposite. Understand?"

I surely do not. But I am not about to say anything for fear it will start Pop off on another bout of laughing. I just do what I usually do when I have a question. I look at him and raise my left eyebrow.

Pop smiles. It's not one of his happy smiles, but one that can best be described as rueful. "Of course you don't understand, son. How could you after the way you've been raised thus far?"

Raised thus far? That provokes the desire in me to ask what in blue blazes that might mean. But I hold my tongue. Pop is going to explain those strange remarks of his. All I need to do is what he said his own father—a grampa I never met—taught him.

If you want to hear something, don't talk.

So that is what I do. Or rather do not do.

Pop looks straight at me. That sad smile's gone from his face.

"Cal," he says, his voice so soft no one else in the boxcar but me can hear—especially those who turned their heads our way when Pop had that attack of guffawing.

"Cal, there's a lot of explaining I have to do. Your sainted mother and I agreed it was best to raise you . . . like we did. But the time has come for me to explain a thing or two."

I feel like I'm standing with my feet stuck in mud, with water rising around me. But even though I don't know what's going on, I can sense that my life is about to change. That scares me.

"Let me start," Pop says, "by explaining what Indian school is. Okay?"

"Okay," I reply, my throat so tight the word comes out as a hoarse whisper.

"There was a time," Pop says, "when this United States was at war with the Indian tribes. You been taught about that in school, right?"

I nod my head, remembering some of those stories. They told how this country was won from the savage Indian tribes who

62

were the enemies of civilization and progress until they were all subdued. Manifest Destiny. How things were meant to be.

But I'm also remembering how when I came home and told my parents about what I'd learned about Indians, Mom would get a funny look on her face. And Pop would say "There's more to it than that."

Then he'd tell me other stories. How when the first white settlers came to America, they were helped by the Wampanoags. How during the American Revolution nobody would assist General Washington at Valley Forge till the Tuscaroras and Oneidas brought tons of food and saved his army from starving to death. How the Five Tribes of the South—the Cherokees, Choctaws, Chickasaws, Creeks, and Seminoles—became so much like their non-Indian neighbors with cattle herds and their own schools, even dressing like white people. But then they were driven off their land and sent on the Trail of Tears to Indian Territory. How every promise made between the United States and Indian tribes was always kept by the Indians and broken by the government.

So, even though I never met any real Indians, I grew up feeling different about them than the other kids in my classes. My thoughts of them were always friendly-like.

Not that I said anything in class. Silent Cal was what I was called. But I did write an essay in fourth grade that led my teacher, Miss Knowlan, to ask me where I'd learned such things that were certainly not in any of my books.

"My pop," was all I said.

It resulted in two things. First was my paper getting a big red F scrawled on top of it along with the word "Ridiculous!"

Second was Pop paying her a visit after I brought that paper home.

I was by his side when he walked into the school, a book under his arm. Both my parents had been invited, but it was one of those days Mom was too sick to leave the farm.

I watched Miss Knowlan greet him. There was a bigger smile on her face than I ever saw in our classroom.

"Mr. Black," she said. "I am so pleased to meet a real-life war hero."

Pop said nothing, just held the door open for her.

I stayed in the hall, on the bench where students always had to sit when parents had conferences with her.

Pop nodded at me before he shut the door behind them.

I heard the chairs scrape as they sat down, followed by a question from Miss Knowlan.

"Now, where did your boy get those outlandish ideas?"

Pop started answering her then. His voice was so deep and low that I could not make out all the words. What I did hear clearly, when he paused now and then, was what Miss Knowlan said. And kept saying.

"Oh." Just "oh."

I began counting. She said that "Oh," fourteen times during the twenty minutes—by the hall clock—they were in there.

Then there was a moment of silence before Miss Knowlan came out of the room. She had the book Pop had been carrying in one hand and a handkerchief in the other. Her face was all red. She walked right past me without saying a word.

Pop was close behind her. "Let's go," he said.

That F got turned into a B. I can't say that Miss Knowlan liked me after that. Matter of fact, she pretty much ignored me. Which was fine by me and a whole lot better than being called ridiculous in front of everyone.

That memory takes no more than a heartbeat to go through my mind as I listen to what Pop is saying.

"There came a time," Pop said, "when it was decided that fighting Indians and trying to just kill them off was not the best idea. Part of it was that some white people were sympathetic to what they called the plight of the Indian."

Pop pauses. He looks up and to the left. That always means he is remembering something. He takes a breath.

"To be honest, though, it wasn't conscience that led the government to change its mind about what to do with Indians. Mostly it was money. You know how much?"

I say nothing. Pop's asking this question just to set up his own answer to it.

He presses his lips together. "One million dollars," he says. "Per dead Indian."

I cannot help but whistle at that. A million dollars. More money than I've ever imagined. No workingman could ever earn that much in ten lifetimes, even at a whopping two bucks an hour.

"So," Pop says, "they figured it was a whole lot cheaper to send them to school and educate everything Indian out of them. First place was this school called Carlisle."

"Jim Thorpe went there," I blurt out. I can't help myself, him being one of my biggest heroes. Like I mentioned earlier, I was even compared to him by my track coach in fifth grade before our school got shut down.

Pop nods. "Yes, he did."

My father pauses for a second to look up and away, lost again in some recollection before he resumes.

"It was rough at a government Indian school. Being taken from your family and shipped far away from home. First thing that happened after an Indian boy got off the train at Carlisle—and every other government Indian school that came after it—was that they cut off the long hair that the Creator gave him. Then they dressed him in a uniform, and taught him how to march like he was in the army. When the bugle sounded at five in the morning, an hour before breakfast, he had to be up and out on the drill field. Just imagine a little kid holding one of those great big Enfield rifles from the Spanish-American War and going through close order drill."

Pop holds up his hands as if he has a gun in them.

"Attention! Present Arms! Shoulder Arms. Forward March!"

Pop's voice has gotten loud, barking out those commands like he really was on a drill field.

It takes me back to one time when we were rolling through Kentucky. Pop and I had to hold a dark-skinned man named Lucius down. He thought he was back on some Belgian battlefield and was trying to jump out the door of the speeding boxcar. As he struggled he was yelling out words in a language Pop later told me was French.

Everyone in our boxcar cringes when Pop shouts out those commands. They're afraid he might get violent as ex-doughboys sometimes do. The other 'boes in the car may be thinking that Pop is having some sort of episode like Lucius did. Some of the men who ride the rails—even men who did not serve—are real fragile in their heads. They can hurt themselves or others when they have an episode.

Pop sighs and shakes his head. His voice drops down low again.

"Things were hard at Indian school. Idea was to get rid of everything in you that was Indian. Drill it out of you, teach it out of you, beat it out of you. Told you never ever speak Indian again. Punish you hard if you forgot, uttered even one Indian word. Just saying *hers'ce* would earn you a whipping or two nights in the guard house."

Hers-key? Where did that word come from?

"A simple howdy-do in Creek language," Pop says, as if hearing my thought. "Good word to know. Not as good, I suppose, as *mu-to*. That means thanks in Creek. *Mu-to.*"

Mu-to, I think. *Mu-to*. I feel the word lodge itself in my head, alongside of *hers-ce*.

It's always been that way for me. Say a new word and my brain just grabs it like a frog snagging a fly with its tongue.

But now I have to ask.

"Jim Thorpe was Creek?"

"Nooo," Pop says, speaking real slow. "I was."

67

CHAPTER SIX

HOPPING OFF

My mouth is wide open.

Pop smiles at me. "Trying to catch flies, Cal?" he asks.

I shut my mouth, but I am no less bamboozled.

Indian? Creek Indian? What is Pop talking about? That just makes no sense at all. Indians do not look like he does. They ride horses and live in tipis and hunt buffalo. They use bows and arrows and tomahawks, and they don't speak English. And they sure as blue blazes do not ride the rails or go hoboing.

Or do they?

I look Pop up and down. Not a sign of anything Indian in what he is wearing. Just the ordinary well-worn clothes any working-man might have on, not a bead or a feather to be seen. But then I look at his face. It's a face so familiar to me that I guess I've never looked at it that close. I see—as if for the first time—just how brown his skin is, how his hair that he always wears down to his shoulders is as dark as a crow's wing, how from the side he sort of looks like the Indian chief on one of those brand-new copper nickels, the ones with the buffalo on the back.

Then I think of what I have heard folks say about me—that I am the spitting image of my pop. I have the same hair, the same brown skin, the same bent-nosed profile.

No! I shake my head—like I was trying to clear it of spider-webs. No!

I'm not an Indian. No way, no how. Despite some of the things Pop said—like when he confronted that teacher of mine—there's nothing positive about being Indian. It's not me. Not him.

Every picture I've ever seen of an Indian, every image of Indians, has been either stupid or scary. I've seen them in movies, whooping and hollering and getting shot off their horses. I've never met a real Indian. I've never even thought about there still being Indians. Until Pop started his crazy talking about Indians I thought they'd all been killed off by the army.

I feel as if my body has been frozen in place. My head is aching now. I can hardly even think.

"Pop," I say, "you're kidding me. Right? You're not an Indian."

Pop shakes his head. There's no sign of a smile on that face of his. He makes the gesture he makes when he's saying an emphatic no, sort of holding his hand out palm up and swinging it out like he's tossing something away.

"Cal," he says, "I've got a lot of explaining to do."

He surely does. But I'm not sure if I want to hear what he has to say. What I truly want is for this to all be a bad dream.

And there's something else that is just as upsetting as what he's telling me about him being Indian. It's that he wants to send me away from him. Send me to school.

I've been just fine so far not going to school. Hasn't Pop said I've learned more about being a knight of the road in a year than most men do in ten? I like this life we've been living together. I don't want to go to school. I don't need to go to school. Not Indian school or any other kind of school. What I want is to stay with my father, go with him to Washington.

I've always trusted Pop in the past to do what's best for us both. But now I feel like my brain is split into two sides fighting with each other. One half is saying I have to trust my father like I've always trusted him in the past. The other side of my brain is just saying No! No! No! No!

"I know," Pop says, as if he's reading my mind. "We really need to talk, son. But we can't do that right now."

He jerks his head to the side, the way he does whenever he want to point something out to me, using his chin or his lips. Never a finger point the way most do.

I look that way, out the door of the open boxcar, and see what he means. The car's slowing down—the rattling rhythm of the train's wheels on the steel rails has changed. We're coming to a rail yard. A sign by the tracks tells us where.

FAIRVILLE, ARKANSAS

Arkansas. Three states since Virginia, which we left yesterday. There's no faster or finer way to travel than by rail. It's like one of those magic carpets I read about in the *One Thousand and One Nights*. Except there are no genies or magic lamps. Just bulls with clubs and pistols—and a hatred of hoboes.

I've never been to Fairville before. Pop has told me about it, though. There are towns like this all over the country. Not a lot of them, fortunately.

A good many towns don't pay that much attention to us wandering souls. As long as we stay outside the city limits, we're tolerated. Others are more friendly. In such places you'll find a cross carved into one of the lower boards on the wall of a church or a mission, meaning that you'll get fed after listening to a sermon. That same cross on a house, along with a smiley face, means there's a doctor inside who'll treat a hobo free of charge. Some cities, like Chicago, are known for being more understanding. They have soup kitchens where you can line up for free food and shelters where you can spend the night.

The message scratched into the lower edge of that Fairville sign indicates how far from friendly this town is. Two interlinked circles. Handcuffs. It means that any bum caught here by the law gets dragged off to jail.

Most hoboes avoid this place like the plague. But there are times when, headed one place or another, you have to end up here. It's a major intersection of tracks coming in from and going off to the four directions.

Don't get noticed. And don't ever go into town. Stay in the jungle deep in the woods far out of the town. That's especially true if your skin is dark. A white hobo caught for loitering—which means doing nothing more than breathing the air here, precious air—will spend a few days in jail. He'll probably be let go with nothing more than bruises from the beatings served up with bread and water each night. A black hobo caught here may never be seen alive again.

71

No time for any more talking. In less than a mile we'll be in the rail yard where this train comes off the main. To get where Pop wants us to go we have to catch another train headed west. That train won't be coming through until tomorrow.

The other men are already taking the lead. Leaning out the door to grasp a handrail, they're hopping out to go running along, then peel off into the heavy grass. The professor is just ahead of us.

"Geronimo!" he says as he lets go, rolls, and comes up on his feet like a circus acrobat. Quite a nimble feat for an old man surely no less than fifty years of age.

He turns back toward us and does a bow, then spins on one heel. I lose sight of him as he hurries away from the tracks.

"Your turn, Cal," Pop says.

"Wait," I say.

I've just noticed something out of the corner of my eye. Over behind a pile of boxes in the back corner of the car I've just seen something move. A booted foot?

I walk back to take a quick look. There's a man hidden back there, just as I thought. Sleeping with his face turned toward the wall of the car.

"Mister?" I say in a loud whisper. "Mister? We're stopping!"

The man turns his face toward me. The corner of the car is shadowed but I can see that he is exactly the same size as Pop and wearing the same cap on his head and similar clothes. What used to be part of an army uniform. There's even a pair of medals pinned to his chest. But I can tell from his hair and his brown skin—a shade darker than Pop's—that he's not a white man.

He looks surprised being roused, but has come totally awake in an instant. The way Pop always does. There's intelligence in the way the man looks up at me, as well as concern.

"Where?" he whispers back.

"Fairville," I say.

"Arkansas?"

I nod.

"Holy Mary, Mother of God!" the man says. He leaps to his feet like a big cat, takes two strides, and goes flying out the door of the car as my father slides aside to let him by. I look back down the tracks and catch sight of the man's back disappearing into a field.

Pop squeezes my arm. "You did a good thing, Cal. Now go."

I drop off. No fancy rolls for me, just an easy trot seeing as how the train has dropped so much speed. The screeching of the brakes against the wheels is so loud it about deafens me. Pop is already beside me. Bum leg or not, he hops off a train with as much grace as an able-bodied man ten years younger than him. It almost always makes me swell a bit with pride at how capable Pop is at just about anything.

But we're not in the clear yet. There's a man in a black uniform standing up on the platform fifty yards ahead. He hasn't seen us yet, but there's a mean look on his face and what looks like a gun holstered on his side.

We run low and fast back away from the rail yard. Awkward as his stride may be because of his stiff knee, Pop moves at a good clip. As do I. Despite my shorter legs, he doesn't urge me to keep up even once.

73

We pass a gray-shingled house where the professor turns off and we keep a-going. Round one bend and then another, we run a mile or more before Pop holds up his right hand. We've come to a place where the brush and trees are thick off to the left. He looks down and so do I. Most, unless they were fellow knights of the road, would not be looking for what I notice right away. Cut into one of the wooden cross ties is an arrow. Its point indicates a trail ordinary folks would never know was here.

We don't take it right away, though. Pop points ahead with his lips. I follow him fifty feet farther off the tracks uphill into a thick patch of dry brush and stunted trees. Little clouds of gray dust swirl under our feet as we scramble up the loose gravel. We crawl in under the bushes and crouch down, concealed by the low branches of a twisted cedar. Then we wait, making sure no one is following us—such as that mean-eyed man in the black uniform.

Minutes pass. A blue jay, unaware of our presence, lands on a branch two feet over my head, preens itself with its beak, flaps unhurriedly away. That, in itself, is sign enough that no one else is approaching. But we still wait longer, the sun moving a hand's width across the sky. Finally Pop nods and motions for me to follow him back to the hidden trail. He pushes a branch aside, we take a few dozen strides, and then the path appears before us.

Pop is a great tracker. As I think that, another thought comes to me. Is it because he's Indian that he's so at home in the woods? That thought stops me in my tracks. All the confusion and uncertainty I've been feeling since Pop told me about himself comes rolling back into my head like a fog.

"Cal," Pop whispers, "catch up."

I start walking again, hardly feeling the ground under my feet.

After ten minutes of walking, the trail opens up. There's a clearing in the thick woods. The narrow, twisting trail we followed is the only way into this hidden place. It's a spot that would be lonely were it not for the fact that we're far from alone. There must be at least forty men and boys in this hobo jungle that's been carved out of the forest. Rough shelters of every sort are scattered here and there. Cardboard boxes, cobbled-together lean-tos, even a few little cabins made of scavenged lumber. If this were a safer place there'd be fires going. But not here. Rising smoke might give away the fact that this little sanctuary exists.

A few raise a hand in greeting as Pop and I pass. They either know Pop from the past or are just being friendly-like. Pop nods to each of them, including one person I recognize. He's sitting on a rock next to a tree with no shelter of any sort. No surprise since he got here only minutes before us. It's the light-skinned Negro man I had to wake up in the boxcar. I still can't believe he actually dared stop over near this town that's the opposite of its name.

"Good to see you, Corporal Black," the man says, standing and holding out his hand to my father. His voice is deep and warm. "Didn't get a chance to thank the boy back in the car."

"Esom Dart," Pop says, taking the man's hand in both of his. "Good to see you, too, Corporal. This is my son, Cal."

Corporal Esom Dart shakes my hand. His palm is hard and

calloused from a life of hard work. "Thanks for pulling my fat out of the fire back there, Cal," he says. "It is a true pleasure to meet you."

"You, too, sir," I say.

He holds my eyes for a moment longer, long enough to make sure I know just how sincere his thank-you truly is. Then he lets go of my hand to turn back to Pop.

"Long way from the Marne here," Corporal Dart says.

"You could say that," Pop replies, "just not as friendly."

Corporal Dart snorts out a laugh as he looks back up the path.

"Never intended to end up here. Fell asleep in that car and missed hopping off a hundred miles and a whole state line back. I'll be flipping the first freight north tomorrow morning."

Pop nods.

The corporal notices me looking at the medals on his chest. He lifts his left hand to tap first one and then the other with his index finger.

"Know what these are?" he asks.

"Yes, sir," I say. "French medals."

"Right as rain," he says. "France Victory Medal and a Croix de Guerre."

I know what a Croix de Guerre is and why the medals he's wearing are not from the U.S. Army. At the start of the war black men were not allowed to sign up. So a group of them joined the French Army. The Harlem Hellfighters is what they were called.

Pop said those Negro soldiers he encountered over there were some of the bravest and most honorable men he ever knew.

"Well earned," Pop says.

"I suppose so," the corporal says, shaking his head. "But they have done nothing to make my row any easier to hoe. Medals do not get a man a job. Especially if his skin is brown."

There's a moment of silence between them.

For some reason, though I've never had that thought before, I'm thinking about the fact that Pop's face is just about as brown as Corporal Dart's. Indian brown? And that what the corporal said about himself not getting a job because of his skin color might be as true about my pop? That people would treat him different if they thought he wasn't a white man?

I shake my head a little, confused about the kind of thoughts I'm having that I never had before.

Finally, Pop nods, looks around. "Where do we go?"

"Over there's the mayor," Esom Dart says, pointing off to his left. "He's a good old gent, and a vet at that. I was directed to him right off, and he didn't hesitate about giving me permission to stay."

Pop and I both look. There, a hundred feet away, a gray-whiskered old man is sitting on a box in front of a little cabin made with mismatched boards.

As Pop and I approach, the elderly gent with the whiskers holds up his hands and claps them together.

"As I live and breathe!" the old man says, his voice raspy. "Be this me old pal Railroad Will a-coming my way? Been so long since I seen yeh, my lad, I was a-feared yeh was in the bone orchard after having greased the tracks."

"Nope," Pop says. "I have not caught that westbound yet, Cap."

"And who might this here road kid be?" Cap says, grabbing hold of my right forearm with an iron grip so tight it almost makes me wince. He shakes my arm, then lets it go.

"Tough nut, ain't he?" Cap says with a grin that discloses a number of gaps where pearlies once resided. "Guess that would make him yer boy, right?"

"My son, Cal," Pop says, putting an approving hand on my shoulder.

Cap nods, holds out his right hand. "Put 'er there, son."

I hold my own hand out, expecting it to be crushed. But the old man's grasp this time is as soft as one of my father's handshakes.

"Sir," I say.

"Pleased to meetcha," Cap replies. "Welcome ye both to Hard Times Township."

"You the mayor here?" Pop asks.

Cap grins even wider than before, slapping an open palm against his chest. "Me?" he says. "Well, there is some who might say that. Anyhow, no friend of mine—nor his boy—need fear any jungle buzzards while they be here. No yeggs be allowed in Hard Times Town. Yeh are welcome to be calling in, warm yerself by me fire, share the mulligan. No need to make the moon yer blanket tonight."

A FINE MULLIGAN

It's later in the day.

From the position of the sun in the sky, and by what Pop calls my internal timekeeper, I reckon it to be about six in the p.m. Time for dinner. Cap has dragged out a pot. He starts sloshing the water I just lugged in an old galvanized pail from the nearby creek he pointed out to me. When it's half full he hangs its handle on an iron tripod over the fire in front of his shanty.

This fire, burning brightly, has been made using wood so dry that no telltale smoke is rising up from it. The wood stacked around it has been just as carefully chosen. No wet logs whose moisture would turn into thick clouds of water vapor like the Indian smoke signals I saw in a western movie.

Cap sits back on his packing crate. That fire, the pot, the water in it, and a handful of salt is all that he plans to contribute. Pop reaches into his pocket and pulls out three potatoes.

"All right!" Cap says. "Earth apples is a great start."

Fine, firm spuds, like the ones he produced earlier in the boxcar to add to the professor's little frying pan. The rest of those given him by Miz Euler. They're good-sized and solid and red-skinned.

Pop doesn't peel them, just cuts them into chunks with his knife and plops them into the pot.

Another 'bo comes up to join us, holding something green in his hands. He leans toward the pot, but Cap puts up a hand to stop him.

"Show us what yeh got first, Shorty," Cap says.

Which is a good idea. I have, in the past few months, seen one mulligan stew nearly spoiled when a half-lit rum-dum 'bo tried to pour in a double handful of smelly dirt.

"Greens," Shorty says, opening his palms. "Green wild onions just pulled. Washed 'em good, Cap. Real good."

Cap gestures toward the pot, and Shorty dumps in his contribution.

One by one, others add to the stew. Esom Dart is among them. He hands Pop a number two can with twenty ounces of kidney beans. The next man contributes a good-sized turnip that Pop cuts into thin slices. A number three can of sliced tomatoes, then six carrots.

The mulligan is already smelling heavenly to me—though I suspect with the appetite I have worked up from not eating all day that boiled shoe leather might also seem appetizing. But it's not yet finished.

Cap reaches down under his crate and pulls out a bag of flour.

"Thickener," he says, stirring in a couple of sizable scoops with a big spoon he also produces from under his wooden seat.

"Would a bit of meat be welcome, good sirs?" a familiar voice asks from behind me. "Courtesy of my sibling's eldest offspring?"

I turn to look at the professor. He is holding up a ham hock, displaying it as if it was some sort of prize, which of course it is.

Every one of the seven of us gathered round Cap's fire express their assent.

"You bet!"

"Yessirree, Bob!"

"Ah-yup!"

"For sure."

"Indeedy-do."

"Thank you, Professor."

Those last words being, of course, from Pop. To which I add a hearty nod.

The ham hock boiled into the mix, the stew seems all set. But Cap adds a few more surprises in the form of spices. Like a magician pulling a rabbit from a top hat, he makes pepper and dill appear and artfully stirs them in.

My mouth is watering. But I remember my manners—as does everyone else. No one tries to dig in. Finally after half an hour has passed, Cal raises his wooden spoon like a baton.

"Time to test 'er," Cap rasps. He dips the big spoon into the stew and then, to my surprise, holds the full spoon out to me.

I blow on the spoon and take a taste. It's so good I feel as if I am about to faint. Somehow, I manage to hand the empty wooden spoon back to our gray-bearded cook without gnawing on the wood.

"Well, young feller," he says. "What be yer verdict?"

I hold out both my hands and do a double thumbs-up.

"All righty," Cap says. "Time to chow down."

Everyone starts to lean in, except for Pop and me whose lead I always follow.

"Hold yer horses," Cap says. He pulls out a series of mismatched cups, some chipped and cracked, but serviceable.

"Wash 'em in the stream once yer done," he states.

One after another, Cap fills the cups and passes them out.

Each of us refills our cups more than once until the last of the mulligan is gone.

"We'll clean the pot for you, Cap," Pop volunteers.

"Thankee, Will," the old man says, beaming a gap-toothed grin through his whiskers. "You are a blowed-in-the-glass 'bo, for sure."

I have to smile at that compliment. It's the highest one knight of the road can give another. To be called blowed-in-the-glass means being recognized as true blue, someone you'd trust with your life.

"We'll take all those cups, too," Pop says. "Right, Cal."

I nod and collect the cups. They're already near as clean as anyone might get them from using not just spoons, but index fingers to scoop out every last drop of the mulligan.

We shoulder our bindles as we stand up. It's not likely anyone would steal them while we are gone, But a 'bo who takes it for granted that everyone else is as honest as he is, is a 'bo who believes in mountains made of rock candy.

Despite the dark—which never bothers Pop or renders him near blind like most men confronted by a lack of light—we make our way sure-footed back to that little brook, which I hear babbling fifty yards before we reach its edge.

We have emerged from the shade of the trees, and with the

light from the moon, it's brighter here by the water. Near as easy to see as if it was day. The creek is no more than a few feet deep and ten feet wide. There's a flat rock by a small waterfall where I filled the bucket during my first trip to the stream. I kneel on it and rinse out each cup—after Pop has scoured it with wet white sand from the creek bed. Last of all, I lever the heavy pot—almost too big to lift—into the swift flow. I hold the handle with my left hand and run my right hand around the inside of the pot. Then, dumping out the water, I give up the handle to Pop who lifts the weighty pot effortlessly from the brook.

He piles the seven cups carefully into the pot. Then, instead of starting back to the jungle, he sits and leans back on his bindle.

I'm glad of that. This is a peaceful place. The music of the little stream is nearly as soothing to my ears as the rhythm of a boxcar's wheels on rails of steel. I could close my eyes and fall asleep here, secure that I'd be safe with Pop by my side.

I'm also glad because Pop sitting down means he is ready to talk. Maybe he's finally going to answer those questions that have been buzzing through my brain like bees most of the day.

Pop stretches his bad leg straight out in front of him. He rubs his knee with both hands. I am sorry to see that. It means it has been paining him. He never complains, but I've seen how his lips get tight when he does that.

"So," he says, straightening back up, "where was I?"

I do not venture an opinion. That was not a real question. Just what Pop says when about to start speaking on one topic or another.

83

"Where do I begin?"

Another question that isn't. So I wait.

"Well," Pop says, "you know a good bit of it already. What happened, that is, which leads us to where we sit at this moment in time. It's just you didn't know what my story was. Which, so to speak, is also your own."

When my father begins talking in this roundabout way, it might be frustrating to some. Luckily for me, I am used to it. It's the way he might begin if he were to tell me more about over there in the Great War. I take his verbal maneuvering as a good sign and settle back farther.

"I am talking," Pop finally says, "about my family. Our family. Your great-great-grandparents. They were full-blood Creek, as were my own parents. One of the Five Civilized Tribes. Forced to leave our homelands in Georgia, leave behind a good-sized farm where they had hundreds of acres of crops, herds of cattle, and a fine living. Leave for no other reason than they were Indian and white men wanted their land. Sent to Indian Territory. Which is where I grew up as Will Blackbird. Blackbird, not Black. That is my real last name and yours, too."

Blackbird, I'm thinking. I actually like that name better than just plain Black. Somehow it seems more right for Pop and me. But something else is happening. As Pop talks I'm finding myself somewhere else. I'm seeing people dressed in old-fashioned clothing, men and women and children, people with faces as brown as Pop's. Those people are calling out to one another in a strange language I almost understand. Men in uniforms and carrying long guns are pushing us out of our log cabins. Fires are burning. We're being driven from our homes.

I shake my head and I'm back sitting by my father's side. The light from the half moon is throwing a shadow across his face. Around us the forest is a dark haze. The sounds of the stream and the calling of night birds from the trees make this all seem as much like a dream as the vision I just had. Am I really here. Am I awake or asleep? Is my father, who I thought I knew better than any other person in the whole world, actually telling me this? He actually is an Indian? Why have I never heard this till now?

Instead of answering my questions, he's just adding on more. I have to ask something now. One question in particular. A question that's beating its wings like a bat stuck inside my head.

"Why?" I say. "Why didn't you tell me?"

Pop turns toward me. Because the moon is in the sky behind him, it casts his whole face into darkness. I can't see his eyes or his lips moving as he speaks.

"We did it," Pop says, "your mother and I, to protect you."

If any of the confusion in my head can be seen on my face I must look as uncertain as a deer caught in the headlights of a car. Pop reaches out to grasp my shoulder.

"I know, Cal," he says. "It's a lot to have to take in."

I nod.

"Thing is," Pop says, "it's not easy being Indian. People look at you different, treat you different. This may be the land of the free and the home of the brave, but when you are seen as a brave you are a lot less free."

I know Pop means that as a joke, but it's not really funny. I just nod again.

"There's too many out there who think Indians are stupid and backward, worthless drunks, dirty and uncivilized," he says, his voice soft. "It's not much different from how they see a man who's black. I wanted to get you away from that. No matter what you do, as an Indian you're never as good as a white man. In their minds it is only white men who are created equal. Not long ago, if you were Indian you couldn't vote. But you could fight for this country. Indians weren't even American citizens until 1924. But if people think you are white, it's different. White men have all the rights. If our family could pass—if you could pass—for white there might be no end of opportunities."

I've seen how black men are treated. Seen it more times than I'd like. I believe and have always tried to live by what Pop has told me ever since I could understand words. We all are the same under the skin. One man's blood is just the same color as the next man's. And you can never judge any person or any thing by how they look on the outside. Some of nature's deadliest creatures are really pretty to look at—like the black widow spider whose bite is poison.

"That's why, when I joined the army, I kept quiet about being Indian. I would have been treated different. That's for sure. I just told people who asked why I was so tan that it was my Italian blood." Pop chuckles. "Not that I had any."

"Did Mom know?"

Pop smiles. "I was never able to hide anything from your mother. The second thing she asked—right after asking me to

86

marry her—was about that. Except it was more a statement than a question. Sort of like her proposal. 'You are an Indian,' she said to me. Just like that."

Pop shakes his head, looking off to his left as he does when he remembers things. "Your mom had a gift, Cal. Seems like you have it, too. She had this way of knowing things no one else could know. Sometimes even seeing things before they happened. So I had to fess up to her about how I was passing for white."

Pop stays quiet for a long time.

"What did Mom say then?" I finally ask.

"She said she understood. How it was a little like being foreign or an orphan and having people look down on you. She also said that it was probably better for people not to know. If we were going to get a mortgage on the farm we were going to buy the bank would be more likely to give it to a white couple who are a tanned war veteran and a nurse and not an Indian and a dirty immigrant. We always planned to tell you some day, but we were so happy together. And we thought it would make things easier for you. Even though your mom could see things, she never saw the worst of what was going to happen to us."

Pop goes silent again. The way the moon is shining on his face I can see that his eyes are moist. I'm having a hard time not crying myself.

I understand now why Pop reacted that way when Boney called him "Injun Joe." I can see how it must have hurt him to be lumped in with that picture of an Indian as a murderous, drunken savage.

Okay, I think, so Pop is Indian.

Or rather he was Indian till he joined the army. And then he and my mom decided he should keep passing as white to get our farm.

Maybe I can accept that, though it's a lot to wrap my head around. But what does his being Indian, even former Indian, make me? Indian, too? Half Indian?

I look at Pop, about to ask another question. But he beats me to it.

"Why now?" Pop says. "Is that what you are wondering, Cal? Why tell you now about your blood?"

And why talk about Indian school? I think.

Pop nods. I suspect that nod is as much to himself as it is to me.

Somewhere back in the forest an owl *whoootooluls*. Pop cocks his head in that direction. Pretty soon, another owl answers farther off to our left. I've always liked hearing the call of an owl, though it can startle you some. That's what it's meant to do if you are something small an owl likes to eat. Make a mouse jump, rustle the leaves enough so that owl can swoop in on silent wings and grab it.

"My grampa," Pop says, "told us that an owl calling like that might be a bad omen. A warning that something bad was about to happen. At Challagi they taught us that an owl was just an owl."

Pop shakes his head. "Challagi," he says again. "Hah! You should have heard the stories the older boys told us about owls

88

and witches when none of the teachers or disciplinarians were around. Especially the Cherokee boys. Those scary stories made you pull the covers over your head once you were in bed. Mason Bushyhead—he was eastern Cherokee and fifteen years old. He told us little boys about something that happened in House Four, the dorm where the younger boys lived back then. It happened back when he was my age, which was eight at the time.

"He said something woke him up in the middle of the night. It was the sound of someone eating. He peeked out from under his covers and what he saw chilled him to the bone. There was a green light hovering over Charley Cornsilk, four beds down from him. And he could see a shape floating in the middle of that light, a person it was. And that person was holding something bloody in its hands and chewing on it. Then that witch, for that was what it had to be, reached a bony hand down, shoved it into little Charley's side, and pulled out another piece of his liver.

"Mason said he screamed then. He couldn't help himself. And as soon as he let out that scream, that witch turned into an owl, shot up right through the ceiling and was gone.

"His scream woke everybody up. They lit the lanterns, but there was nothing to see. Except that Charley Cornsilk was real pale and sick and so they took him to the infirmary where he died two days later."

Pop goes silent as soon as he finishes that tale. He's told me other stories in the past, but never one like this. Most often they have been tales about animals acting like people and doing foolish things. Not Indian boarding schools or witches. It was like hearing someone else other than my father talking. Even his voice as he told that story was different.

It scared me because I found myself in that dormitory as my father was talking. I was taken over as he told it, seeing things he was not mentioning. Like the way one boy's boots at the bottom of his bed had fallen over. Or that the boy three beds away from Charley Cornsilk was crying in the darkness. Or that the lantern they lit had a cracked glass. Or that the letters *C.C.* had been carved into the side of the low rafter over Charley Cornsilk's bed.

Pop shakes his head. "I don't know why I told you that story, Cal. I didn't even know I remembered it. Funny how things come back to you when you start talking about the past. I ran my train way off on a sidetrack, didn't I?"

Pop laughs, a little one that sounds almost like he's clearing his throat.

"Why talk about being Indian now when I hid it ever since I married your mother and we decided it was the way to make a better life for our family?" Pop's voice is dead serious. "Son, it is because of where we are now. Just look at us. Now I do not mean there is any shame about this hobo life. Especially when a man follows the ethical code. But I am the one who chose this way. Not you. Cal, this was not your choice."

I'm still upset about what I saw as Pop told that story. Why is it that I keep finding myself in other people's memories? And why is it that they always seem to be dead people? I can't talk to Pop about that. It would worry him. But that's not the most important thing right now. What's important are Pop's plans for me. Maybe I can still change his mind.

"Pop," I say, "I'm happy being a 'bo. I think my life is fine now."

My father shakes his head, turning it just enough so that the moonlight shines on his face. I make out that there are tears in his eyes.

"Son, a man needs the chance to make choices. I thought my making the choice for you of being white would be the best. But that was before this whole country went to hell in a handbasket. There are no opportunities now unless you were born a rich man. Doesn't matter now whether you are white or red. When you are without a job and you have no food and no idea about where to go, you are not better or worse than an Indian. And that is how they treat you when you are down and out. Including those of us who fought in Flanders Fields to make this world a better place. But now I do have an idea about someplace to go. Two ideas, that is. One idea for each of us."

Pop slaps his chest and I hear not just the thump of his hand against his rib cage, but a flatter sound. Paper, maybe? Sure enough, when Pop reaches into his coat he pulls out that newspaper he was reading.

"This is my idea," he says. "I've been thinking about it. It's an idea for both of us. Let me tell you about it and then you can tell me if you'll agree. That's important, because if you do not agree then there is no way I am going to force you."

I nod to that. "Okay," I say. "That's the code."

Pop nods back. Rule number one.

Decide your own life, don't let another person run or rule you.

"Remember Joe Angelo?" Pop asks. "What he did?"

That confuses me some.

"No," I admit.

Pop smiles. "Sorry, Cal. I'm jumping the gun a bit. Too many things going through my head right now. You know who I am talking about, though?"

"Yes."

He's the vet who walked to Washington. That I do understand.

"Okay. What Joe did was to put himself on the line. He spoke up for all of us who served. Spoke up about our bonuses. But he wasn't the first to do that. Last year, back in December, a bunch of men went to Washington and staged a hunger strike. Then this priest from Pittsburgh led a whole army of jobless men to agitate for help for the unemployed. And now," Pop raises his hand and makes a circle, "there's talk of more of us going there from a man named Walt Walters, a veteran himself. His idea is that we can be an army of peaceful warriors asking that the Congress and old President Hoover treat us fair and square and give us our bonus money."

Pop's eyes glisten in the moonlight, as if lit by a fire from within.

"Think of that, Cal, thousands of men camping out in the very heart of the nation. Asking the nation to open its heart to those of us who fought for freedom. And if we do get our bonuses," Pop puts his hand on his pack, where his own Compensation Certificate is carefully stowed away, "then I'll have enough

92

money for us to get a little place of our own and a good life. A federal mortgage, vocational training. All that could happen. I could get us a house, really settle us in again."

Part of me likes the thought of that. The bonus money coming through. A whole thousand dollars. Us back on a farm of our own.

But part of me is wondering if that is really possible. Young as I am, I know that President Hoover has a heart of stone as far as poor folks and veterans go. All he cares about is the rich. No matter how many men go to Washington, he is not going to change his stripes any more than a hyena is going to change into a horse.

I can't say that to Pop, though. I have to repeat what I said before.

"I like being on the road, Pop. It's aces being a 'bo. I like being with you. We already have a good life."

Pop looks at me with a bit of surprise. That was a long statement for me to make.

He reaches out and pats my foot. "Cal," he says. "Cal, Cal." Then he sighs. "You are going to be a good man, son. But our life is not good right now. We are getting by, but that is about all. This is not the way I'd choose for you if it was up to me. Now I did decide to lead this sort of life after I ran away from Indian school the last time. Riding the rails was freedom to me. About the only freedom I could imagine for an Indian kid with no family. And then it was the army. But when your mother and I met, when we were able to have a place of our own, when we had you. Son, that was a good life and I want us to have it again."

Pop picks up a stick and starts scratching it on the earth that would look as red as blood in the daytime but is dark in the moon's half-light. But there's light enough for me to see what he is drawing. It is half of a circle.

"This is what I think," he says, tracing partway around the circle. "This is the way I have to go now. To Washington."

Then he moves the stick back to the starting point and tracing partway around in the opposite direction.

"And this is the way you have to go while I'm gone."

He lifts the stick and looks up at me. "Just while I'm gone," he says. "Because you can't go to Washington with me. I'm not saying it'll be dangerous, but it'll be an army and you are not ready yet to be part of any army. And you cannot be riding the rails on your own. A boy your age alone? No, sir. I want to know you'll be safe with three hots and a cot."

He looks at the stick in his hand. "I never wanted being seen as Indian for you, Cal. I thought you knowing about your heritage would do you no good. And I sure as blazes never thought back when we had our farm that an Indian school would be in your future. It's taken me a lot of time and a lot thinking to come to this, son. But the way things are—in this country and in our lives—I just can't see another way. If there was any other road, I'd take it. But I cannot think of any place other than old Plains View that would give you not just an education but also food every day and a roof over your head."

Pop pauses. "Then again," he says, "you will be also joining a sort of army there. You'll get you a uniform and learn military discipline." He chuckles. "One thing they teach you for sure at Indian school is how to answer the bugle and march in formation, just like soldiers."

Having a uniform and being like Pop was in the army sort of interests me. But it is still far from anything I'd choose if it was up to me.

Pop turns back to the shape he's scratched in the dirt.

"Anyhow, Cal, it won't be for that long," he says. "Just till I am done in D.C. and I can come back and get you."

Coming back to get me.

That's the first totally good thing I've heard in everything Pop has been telling me. But, for the first time in my life, a part of me is wondering if I can trust him. I've never ever mistrusted my father before. Now, though, I just don't know.

Pop looks at me. I have no doubt he is seeing the uncertainty on my face as obvious as a question mark painted in the middle of my forehead.

"Now, look," he begins moving the stick on one side and then the other of his rough drawing, completing the circle. "See how the two halves come back together again? That's us, son. We'll just be apart for a while."

I open my mouth to say something. I'm not sure what.

But whatever I was going to say is forgotten as soon as we hear the gunshots.

CHAPTER EIGHT

GUNSHOTS

Most folks, Pop says, when they hear the sound of a gun, turn and run.

Soldiers run, too. But they go toward the sound of the guns.

"Stay back of me," Pop says.

Leaving the pot and cups behind us, we start running.

There's a way to run a trail through the woods at night, Pop taught me. Don't run headlong. Jog along, feeling the path under your feet. Don't just look down toward your feet. Look up. There's a faint line of light above the length of a trail, especially when the moon is bright.

No more shots. That might be good. But when we begin to see the light from a fire ahead of us it's burning much bigger than a cooking fire. That's not good.

We pause at the edge of the clearing, staying low to the ground. We're behind the trees, faces not lit by the fire. A man's face is the first thing an enemy sees. Just putting your head down and not looking up makes it hard for anyone to notice you. It would have been better if we'd darkened our faces with mud. No time for that. But leaning forward, long hair falling over our faces, is almost as good a way to hide eyes and cheeks that might reflect back the light.

Pop and I are unseen, but what we are seeing isn't good.

The clearing is so well lit because of the fire consuming

one of the wooden shelters. Not Cap's. At least not yet.

Armed men with torches have invaded the hobo jungle. One's holding a hound by a leash. That explains how they found their way here.

They've lined up all the 'boes, forced them to kneel with their hands behind their heads. That first shot was likely fired into the air as a warning. I am just about certain who pulled the trigger.

It's the mean-faced man in the black suit. He's sporting a big badge on his chest, holding what looks like a .45. He raises it high above his head, points it at the half moon.

"Where is he?" the man with the gun says. "Where you hiding that . . ."

BLAM! He fires another round up into the sky.

Some of the kneeling men cower lower. But not Cap. He's looking straight at the man with the gun.

"That is a right nice weapon you have got there, Sheriff," Cap says.

"Y'all want a closer look?" the sheriff says, in an even voice that's a-heavy with menace. He lowers the gun, presses it against Cap's forehead, and pulls back the hammer with his thumb.

This time Cap says nothing.

The sheriff uncocks the weapon and pulls it back from the old man's forehead. "Now, listen," he says, "I am a reasonable man. I been tolerating you white bums jungling up here just as long as you don't do no stealing. But I will not tolerate the likes of that man I saw get off the train. Not in my town. No vagrant Negroes are going to be allowed to come in and stir things up with their ideas. We get along fine with our own coloreds who know their place. They all know Sheriff Dan Boyle is a fair man."

Sheriff Boyle makes a circling motion with the gun. "Now I am not saying I'm going to shoot all of you. No, sir. But if y'all don't tell me what I want to know, we are going to burn down every single one of your rotten little shacks, strip the clothes off your backs, beat the bejesus out of every one of you, and then send y'all down the road barefoot and naked as jaybirds."

Some of the frightened 'boes are looking in our direction.

There's a slight motion off to my left. Someone under a long pile of leaves is starting to move. I have no doubt who it is. Corporal Esom Dart. About to give himself up.

"No!" Pop hisses. "Stay there." As he rises to his knees, his hand reaches out and presses down on my back. "You too, Cal."

I don't want to, but I do as he says.

Pop reaches up to pull back his long black hair and tuck it under his cap.

"Don't shoot," he shouts. "I'm coming out."

Hands raised above his head, he steps out into the light.

All seven men, including Sheriff Boyle, have turned at Pop's first words. Their guns are pointed in his direction as he stands there, totally still.

"Yew?" the sheriff barks. He grabs the torch from the hand of the man closest to him, steps forward and holds it close to Pop's face, who stays as motionless as the Statue of Liberty. He looks Pop up and down, from his boots to his cloth cap. "Yer the one I saw hop off'n that train?" he snarls.

"Yes, sir, Sheriff," Pop says. "But I am no Negro, sir. Though I am a Black."

Pop smiles as the sheriff lifts his torch again to study my father. From the look on the lawman's kisser, he's confused. Did he make a mistake because he was so far away? Pop's height and build and even the clothes and cap he's wearing match those of the corporal. With his long hair tucked up, the brown of Pop's face, close to that of a light-skinned Negro, is visible.

"What are you then, boy?" the sheriff says, his voice still hostile. "Mulatto?"

"No, sir, Sheriff," Pop replies. His voice is soft, conciliatory. "Easy mistake to make, sir, but I am Indian. Full-blood Creek out of Muskogee, Oklahoma."

Pop lowers one hand to take off his cap. Long black hair falls down to his shoulders.

As Pop drops that hand holding the cap to his side, the hound that was sitting back on its hindquarters, stands up. It walks forward as far as its leash will allow. It touches its nose against the cap, then licks the back of Pop's hand, whimpers, and starts wagging its tail. That's no surprise to me. Pop has this thing about him when it comes to dogs. Even the meanest mutt responds to my father as if he was a long lost friend. A bit of that seems to have rubbed off on me, as well.

The sheriff is looking a bit more at ease. "Yew got a name?" he says, his voice no longer a harsh growl.

"William Black, sir. Veteran, sir. Army papers in my pocket got my name on them."

99

"Take 'em out."

Pop slips his hand into his jacket to pull out his discharge papers and his Compensation Certificate.

Sheriff Boyle takes them, reads them, nods.

"So why you here, boy?" he asks. This time his words sound more like an actual question than an accusation.

"Just stopping over for the night, sir," Pop says. "On my way to Oklahoma, up near the Kansas border. Taking my son to Indian school there."

I may be wrong, but it seems as if I can see the hint of a smile on the sheriff's face.

"Challagi?" he says. "Old Plains View?"

Pop nods.

Sheriff Boyle laughs out loud. "That's it, for sure," he says. "Every year I catch me a nice little batch of runaways from up there. One year it was a whole group trying to get back East to their own little reservation in the South."

Sheriff Boyle grins, showing white teeth that look as big as tombstones.

"Nice manners on 'em, I have to say. None of them Challagi boys ever puts up a struggle nor gives any lip when I catch 'em." He grins at the thought.

He squints toward the woods where Pop came out. "So where's that boy of yours at? Hunkered down in the brush? Bring him on out."

"Cal," Pop calls.

I stand up and walk into the clearing, stop by my father's

side. I reach up for my own cap, take it off, and hold it in both hands in front of my chest.

"My son, Cal," Pop says.

"Sir," I say to the sheriff, bowing my head as I do so and keeping my eyes on the ground.

"Off to school, huh?" Sheriff Boyle says.

"Yes, sir."

"You look just like your pa here."

"Yes, sir."

"All right, then."

He hands Pop back his papers, turns to look around the clearing at the kneeling men, all of whom look considerably less terrified.

"Now, you bums," Sheriff Boyle says in a loud voice, "you all just take a lesson from this man and his boy. They might be Indians, but they know their place, nice and polite. Just remember, you do see any strange Negroes, you come and tell me right quick, you hear? And be glad you have such a fair-minded man as me keeping the law hereabouts."

He waves a hand over his head. "Let's go men, we done here."

Pop and I stand stock-still, not moving a muscle as the sheriff and his posse of torch-bearing men depart. Nor do the other men of the camp stir from their places on their knees until the bobbing light of their torches can no longer be seen through the trees.

Cap is the first to stand.

"Buckets!" he yells, pointing at the little shack set on fire by Sheriff Boyle.

Men go scrambling in every direction, grabbing pails and

101

throwing the water already in them onto the burning remains of what once was a bo's home. Too late to save it, but soon enough to keep the fire from spreading to the other nearby shelters.

We pitch in to help. It takes a while, but eventually the last embers are out.

Through it all, there's been no sign of Pop's old war buddy.

"Go get the corporal?" I ask Pop as I stand combing the ashes out of my hair.

He tilts his head toward the woods. "You can try. But I expect he won't be where you saw him. He's used to making his way through enemy lines."

When Pop says that, I get a quick glimpse of the future. I see Corporal Dart walking through the night. He's moving fast, making his way cross-country with no hound on his trail. He'll catch a northbound freight five miles away before dawn.

"You're right, Pop," I say.

"What's that?" he says.

The bright half moon is at just the right angle now to light the spot where that pile of leaves and debris concealed the corporal. From the limb of an overhanging shrub there's a glint of metal.

I walk over to look. The moonlight is bright enough for me to see what's hung there. The France Victory Medal that was pinned on Corporal Esom Dart's chest. I free it from the branch. It's cool in my palm.

"Did he lose it?"

Pop shakes his head. "Nope, Cal," he says. "Knowing Esom, he left it there for you. You helped save him. It's yours now, son."

UPSIDE DOWN

We've managed to catch the very train my father was hoping we would. The two of us are possum belly on the roof of a westbound passenger car. We're on our way to Challagi. Just one stop farther along the way according to Pop.

Normally I'd enjoy riding this way. It's a fine sunny day. The air is warm and fresh as it washes over us. You have a great view from the top of a train car. But I can't take any pleasure out of this ride right now. Not when my mind is going even faster than this train.

What I had overheard of the conversation Pop had with Sheriff Boyle last night has put unanswered questions into my mind. They're all about Challagi, the place Sheriff Boyle mentioned and also called Plains View. What is it? Why did my father run away from it? Those questions and a dozen more are elbowing one another inside my head. There was no time last night to ask any of those questions, though. And this morning we had to hustle to make it in time to flip this ride.

Now, though it is just the two of us together, this is still not the time when I can ask questions. What with the train doing a good forty miles an hour, the wind whipping past us is too strong for any conversation at all.

I reach over and grasp my father's arm. He turns his head to look at me. There are these hand signals he taught me, a whole bunch of them. Ones I guess he must have learned when he was over there in the war. I use a couple of them now. First, I tap my chest. That means me or I. Then, I hold my right hand up, palm out, and sort of waggle it back and forth. That means a question.

I have a question.

Pop lifts his own right hand, sticks out his index finger, and drops it down.

Yes.

He points with his lips behind us, where there's a string of boxcars.

We make our way back, hop off our passenger car onto the one behind it, careful to land soft enough to not make any thumping sound that might attract the attention of a conductor. Most conductors don't mind men hitching a ride. That is especially so because nearly all hoboes stay true to rule Number Eleven of the code, to always ride your train respectfully and never interfere with the operating crew.

But there are some conductors who have a mean streak in them and will kick off even the most polite of us. So we try to go unnoticed as much as possible.

The first boxcar we reach has its door shut tight. As does the next. But the third car's right side door is half open. Even better, it is empty. The straw in the stalls and the lingering scent of live-stock tell me horses were recently transported in here. So we watch our step as we make our way over to a couple of wooden boxes to sit on. Sort of like Cap's packing crate, though all that's under our seats are loose hay and a scatter of oats.

Pop looks at me, waiting. But now that it's quiet enough to talk I feel hesitant.

I take out my comb and run it back through my hair a dozen times on each side. You never need put a drop of oil on your hair if you just comb or brush it regular. The natural oils in your scalp are all you need. That is what Mom taught me.

I put the comb away, rub my hands together. I have never been much for words—as far as saying them goes. Right now it's harder than usual to speak. Finally I just blurt out what's on the top of my head.

"So I'm Indian?"

"Half," Pop replies. "As you know, your mom was Armenian, though that was about all we knew, what with her being an orphan. You are half Creek Indian." Half Indian? What does that even mean? It feels like a rock I didn't know I'd swallowed is stuck in my gut.

Some things are making sense, though. Like the stories Pop told me—stories that he said I shouldn't ever share with anyone else. Were those Indian stories? Or all the things Pop knows about plants and nature, things he learned from his parents. Those must have been Indian things. Creek Indian, he said. And the sign language he taught me that was supposed to just be shared between the two of us. Was that Indian, too? It's all too much for my brain to hold all at once. I can feel my heart pounding.

I breathe in and out real slow, trying to calm myself down. Maybe I should just focus on where Pop said we're headed.

"Challagi?" I finally ask.

The great thing about talking with Pop is that I never need to say much for him to understand me. Just speaking that one word is enough.

"Challagi Federal Agricultural Indian Boarding School," he says. "Some call it Plains View. Challagi's how you say Cherokee in Choctaw. Sort of an insult—seeing as how it means cave dwellers. Folks without real houses." Pop shakes his head. "Naming a school for the way one tribe insults another? Just what you'd expect from Washington."

He picks up a handful of hay from the floor, selects three long pieces, and begins braiding them together.

"It was founded back in 1890. Idea was to teach us useful trades. Academic classes half the day, and the other half of the day industrial. Farming, barbering, harness making, printing, baking, masonry, and the like for us boys. Domestic trades for the girls such as sewing, housekeeping, and cooking. Boys and girls brought from more than forty tribes, mostly from Oklahoma. Every age from first graders to high school. Though now it is mostly seventh grade and up. Which makes it all right for you, Cal, seeing as how you finished sixth."

I take a deep breath.

"Why'd you run away?"

Pop takes a long look at me.

"Good question, son. No, it was not at all perfect. I'd say that most of us didn't really want to be there. Running away was something a good many did or planned to do one time or another. Me, I ran away three times during the five years I was there.

First time was right after I got there. They caught me that time and brought me back. Second time was during my third year there. That time, though, I came back on my own. My family was all gone by then, and I realized that what family I had by then were the friends I'd made at Challagi. Those boys in our Creek gang were some of the best buddies I ever had. The third time I ran, I joined the army—and found another sort of family there."

Pop pauses, but not to make sure I'm listening. He knows I'm hanging on his every word. It seems to me he's pausing because talking about this is bringing it back to him. He's not enjoying it any more than he enjoys digging up the memories of his time in the trenches.

"Why did we run?" he repeats. "A good part of it was the discipline." Pop places his hand on my arm, the way he always does when whatever he says has special meaning. "I doubt it's that bad now since the Meriam Report."

What kind of discipline? And what's the Meriam Report.

"Some white folks," Pop says, "work at Indian boarding schools like Challagi because they want to help us. They care about Indians. They may look at us as ignorant savages, sure. But they're good-hearted—even if their eyesight is not so hot. And some teach things we can really use, especially about farming."

Pop shakes his head and a new tone comes into his voice, one I seldom hear. Anger.

"But real bad things were happening. A government commission investigated the Indian schools. Indian schools were supposed to civilize us, make us like other Americans. At some schools they were killing us. Indian kids were being starved. Freezing in poor housing. Getting beat almost every day. In some Indian schools there were more names on the school gravestones than the rolls of those who graduated. That's what the Meriam Report said."

Pop pauses. He looks far off, not at the landscape whizzing by or at anything in particular. Just staring into space as he does at times when he's upset and trying to calm himself. Then he clears his throat and looks back at me.

"Cal, I never planned having you go to an Indian boarding school."

He shakes his head. "But now . . ."

He looks back into that distant place his mind goes when he is thinking or remembering. "You're tough, son. You've seen a lot."

He pauses, letting more miles go by before he clears his throat and continues. "Even now, though, I sure as hell would never ever send you to one of those schools if you were a little girl, Cal. There was this one teacher who would go into House Three—that was the little girls' house—late at night and wait in the halls for any girl foolish enough to get up in the night and try to go to the toilet. His name was Mr. Fetterman, taught English. But behind his back the girls all called him Mr. Chi-Chi man. Mr. Boogeyman."

Pop stops talking again, looks out the door of the car at the wide expanse of plains we're passing through.

My face didn't show it, but a shiver just went down my back. The story about the Chi-Chi Boogeyman is one he told me years

108

ago. But this time what I see in my mind is not an imaginary monster. It's the face of that white man. It's because I see that man. Mr. Chi-Chi man. I'm in that past where my mind takes me. He's so close I don't just see his face and his long bony hands. I also smell the chewing tobacco on his breath. My hands are tied together.

No! I bite my lip and shake my head to clear it of that vision. I blink and I'm back in the railcar.

Pop has not noticed. He's busy taking those deep breaths he does when he's seeing something painful from the past. He wipes his hand over his face.

"Sorry, Cal. Hard remembering this. Some complained, but no one listened to those little Indian girls. After all, Mr. Fetterman was a white man and a teacher. An employee of the sacred Bureau of Indian Affairs. Only ones who listened were the other Indian students. It bothered us all. But what could we do?"

Pop holds up the grass string he's been braiding together, adding more strands as he goes. He grasps it in both hands, pulls it tight so that it makes a snapping sound but doesn't break.

"One night when Mr. Chi-Chi man was sneaking through House Three, he didn't notice something strung across the top of the stairs. A jump rope left there by accident. And he tripped over it. Said he might have seen someone just before he fell. Couldn't say who it was. Just a dark shadow. Superintendent decided that was just Mr. Fetterman's imagination. A man with two broken arms and a fractured skull sometimes has a hard time remembering things . . . or even putting words together. A sister of his came out to take him back home. He was never seen again."

Pop smiles at me. I smile back. I just saw who was hiding in the shadows—ready to give a push if it was needed.

"But getting back to your question, son, as to why we ran? Sometimes we just had enough of the military discipline. After all the drilling and training we went through at Challagi, boot camp in the army was a breeze. There were the long days and being punished for talking Indian or breaking the rules. Then there was the bad food that we also never had enough of, the stiff clothes and the heavy clodhopper boots they gave us that fell apart, the bathrooms that were never clean and stunk to high heavens."

Pop pauses and looks off to his left. "But that discipline was not the worst thing. Homesickness was the biggest reason why we ran. Being away from home was hard. Missing our families."

"Like I'll miss you."

I've blurted those words out without thinking. I am sorry as soon as they're said. A hurt look comes over Pop's sensitive face.

But it lasts no longer than a wisp of cloud crossing in front of the sun. Pop shakes his head. "No more than I'll be missing you, Cal."

His hand is on my shoulder as we watch the land whip past us backward. Mile after mile being left behind.

Pop lets out a long breath. "This is the right thing to do, son. Get you back in school. That way you can make use of your time while I'm in Washington—which is no place for a boy to be." Pop smiles. "Even boarding school's better for Indians than D.C."

Better for Indians.

Indians. That's how Pop is now referring to him and me. Is Indian what I am? It's not what I've ever seen myself to be.

"How am I going to fit in?"

Pop looks at me. "You mean with them all being Indian and you having been raised to think of yourself as white?"

I nod.

Pop smiles. "First of all, Indian or not, those Challagi students are people. People, human beings. You know what I've said about that?"

I nod again. All human beings bleed the same blood, breathe the same air. Our heartbeats all sound the same. It's not how a man looks but what's in his mind and heart that counts. That's sort of what it says in the hobo code. Knights of the road help one another, no matter a man's skin color.

"You worrying about not looking Indian? Not being able to speak Indian?"

I bite my lip. Pop's right. I'm probably going to stand out like a sore thumb.

Pop holds up his left hand, sticks out his little finger. He does that when he's about to start counting things up.

"First of all," he says, "there'll be Indian kids there who don't know much Indian at all. Even back when I went to boarding school there were Indian kids who spoke nothing but English. Their own parents went to boarding school before them and had the language beat out of them. By now there'll be even more who hardly know a word or two in Indian."

111

Pop's now holding up the finger with the golden wedding band he never takes off.

"Second, there's not just one Indian language. There's one for every tribe. The students at Challagi are from a passel of different tribes. Cherokees, Choctaws, Chickasaws, Creeks like us. Cheyennes, Arapahos, Comanches, Delawares, Kaws, Poncas, Pawnees, Potowatamis, and more. So even if they spoke Indian, not a one of them would know all those different languages."

He adds another finger to those first two.

"Third thing is that at Challagi Indian School you're not supposed to speak anything other than English. When I was there, say one word in Creek you get your mouth washed out with lye soap."

Pop lifts his gaze and looks off to his right.

"The boys in my gang," he says, "would talk Creek when none of the teachers or disciplinarians was around. Then there was Danny Tiger." A small smile flits across Pop's face. "Danny was a real rebel. Set the record for running away by the time he was thirteen. One day he walked right up to the head disciplinarian, and said *hers-key*. Like I told you, that's Creek for hello. Then before the man could say anything, Danny reached into his pocket, pulled out a bar of soap and took a big bite of it. That earned him a whipping. But when I sneaked up to the guardhouse to toss a candy bar through the window, Danny said it was worth it just to see the look on that man's ugly face."

Pop turns back to me. "Cal, I've been itching to share some of those stories with you. Tough as it was there, I never had any friends as good and true as those at Challagi, even in the army. Makes me smile to think of them. Now that I've started remembering it's hard to stop."

Though it may be just the way the light coming through the boxcar door is hitting his face, his eyes look moist.

Pop uncurls his pointer finger.

"Fourth thing," he says. "You'll learn. I've never known anyone to be a faster learner than you, Cal. You're always listening and you remember things first time around."

Pop chuckles. "You'll learn a lot if you hang out with a Creek crew. Out of earshot of the teachers us Creeks talked Indian as much as we could. Weekends we'd go way out in the woods, make a fire and stomp dance. This one full-blood boy, Lincoln Bigfox. His family lived in Oklahoma City. Both parents went to Carlisle. So he was raised with not a word of Indian. When his mom and dad broke up he ended up getting sent to boarding school. He was only at Challagi for one year before his parents got back together and brought him home. But by the time he left he knew half a dozen stomp dance songs and was able to speak pretty good Creek."

Pop holds up his thumb.

"Fifth thing is that back when I was in Challagi about a quarter of the kids looked no more Indian than Bette Davis or Laurel and Hardy. You'd see blue-eyed blondes and boys and girls with pale skin. Only thing they all had in common was Indian blood in their family and being poor."

Pop pauses, dropping his hand. "It ought to be easier for you, Cal, than for those kids. There was always a lot more bullying

113

of kids who looked white. And you don't. You look as Indian as I do."

I think about all the times Pop and I have almost been taken for Negroes because of our brown skin. Times I wished I were blond and fairer. But now it's going to be an advantage? The whole world seems upside down.

"I was lucky," Pop continues. "I got taken in right away by the Creeks and the older boys looked out for me. It will likely be the same for you. When you arrive they'll probably take one look at you—the other kids, I mean—and lump you in with the full-bloods, seeing as how your hair's black and your skin's brown. They'll see you as Indian."

Indian. Just like that?

My world is upside down now for sure. I guess I'm going to have to get used to walking on the ceiling.

CHAPTER TEN

HORSES

The train is slowing down. I peer out the partially opened door. We're coming to a rail yard dominated by what looks like barracks and stockyards. There are corrals with fine-looking horses in them. Their hooves are kicking up dust as they run back and forth behind the fences.

There are men, too. All are either wearing the blue army uniforms of cavalrymen or dressed like cowpunchers. I look back at Pop.

"Stay put," he says.

The train stops. Voices come from outside. I step back from the boxcar door. With a whirr of metal wheels it's pulled open. A man with thick black hair and a handlebar mustache is standing there next to the burly crewman who just opened the door. The black-haired man strokes his mustache, nods his head, then shows his teeth in a wide friendly grin.

"Indians?" he asks.

I don't know how to reply. No? Yes? Maybe?

"You could say that," Pop says.

"All right! Know much about horses?"

Pop raises an eyebrow. "Only everything."

"All right," the man says again. "They's bound for Challagi.

Retired cavalry mounts. Some is a bit skittish, though. Help us load 'em and then ride on with 'em? We'll give you and your boy a square meal. Deal?"

"Deal," Pop says.

A ramp is brought up. The crewman moves aside so that it can be fitted onto our boxcar. Pop helps settle it into place and then the two of us walk down to join the others. We follow them to a corral holding eight big horses. The two largest ones, a bay and a pinto, are galloping back and forth, tossing their heads.

Retired they might be, but far from worn out.

Pop leans over to me. "Been a practice of the army to retire its horses at Challagi. There's plenty of room for them on the eighty-six hundred acres around the school and more than enough hands to care for them."

There's a smile on my face for the first time since Pop started talking about the Indian boarding school. Horses! Any place with horses can't be half bad. Galloping along on a horse's back is even better than riding the roof of a passenger car. Our three horses are one of the things I miss most about our farm. Aside from Mom's death, the saddest thing I remember is watching them being led away.

The first six are easy enough to catch with the help of the two wranglers assigned to the task. Four mares and two geldings.

As Pop puts the bridles on he checks each animal's teeth, he pulls back their lips, feeling their back molars for the signs of wear that show their age.

"Not a one over fourteen," he says. "Lots of miles left on these babies."

Leading them up the ramp one by one to their stalls is no problem. I take two all by myself.

"Boy's good with horses, ain't he?" one of the cowboys says. His dark skin may mean he's either part Mexican or Indian himself.

"You could say that," Pop replies. I can hear the pride in his voice, and it makes me feel fine.

"But now we got them to deal with," the second cowboy says, gesturing with his thumb back at the remaining horses, the bay and the pinto—in the corral. "Names are Dakota and Blackjack, we was told. Ought to be Trouble and Damnation far as I am concerned."

Both of them are wild-eyed, whinnying, rearing up, baring their teeth, kicking up a fuss, and looking to fight.

"What do you think, Arjay?" Cowboy One asks.

"Seems to me, Eljay, like we have got us a couple of hellions there," Cowboy Two answers.

"Nothing that a bullet in the brain won't cure," Eljay adds.

I suppose they're only joshing about killing those skittish horses. But the thought of putting an animal down like that bothers me.

"Pop and me can get them," I blurt out.

"Well, I'll be," the wrangler named Arjay says. "You hear that, Eljay? It turns out the boy can speak after all." He steps back, one hand on his heart, the other held out palm up like I saw a doorman in a movie do while opening a door for a man in a tuxedo. "Go right ahead."

117

"Be our guest," Eljay adds, copying his friend's gesture.

Pop and I go into the corral. They close the gate behind us.

"Want us to get a broom and dustpan to sweep up your remains?" Eljay asks.

Arjay chuckles. Then, in a serious voice, he says, "You two take care. That bay there, Blackjack, he broke a man's arm yesterday."

A small crowd has gathered outside the fence to watch, including the black mustached man who first saw us and a bunch of cavalrymen.

Pop and I pay no attention to the onlookers. Our minds are on the pinto and the bay. We don't move at first, though. We just stand there for a while, letting them get used to us. It doesn't take that long. These aren't wild horses, but cavalry mounts. They're just upset because they're being separated from the people who rode and took care of them. They don't know what's going to happen next.

What happens next is that Pop starts singing. Soft at first, barely loud enough for a person to hear. What he calls his horse song. Every morning when we'd go into the barn to hitch up Austin, our plow horse, or Humken and Hokkolen, our matched pair of bays who pulled our wagon, he'd be singing it. There's no real words, just sounds that are soothing.

"Ho-ho-yeh, hey-ey-yo."

The two horses prick up their ears. They stop rearing and turn toward us. We walk their way, our hands down at our sides. Pop is singing a little louder now.

118

"Ho-ho-yeh, hey-ey-yo."

The horses stand still, watching as we approach. The big muscles in their thighs are still twitching, but they're getting calmer. We stop about twenty feet away. Pop is still singing. Me, I'm just keeping my mind calm and friendly-like. Horses sense when a person is nervous or angry around them.

Finally, the horses look over at each other and nod their heads like folks reaching an agreement. They walk up to us, lower their heads, and nuzzle our chests as we stroke their necks.

"Well, I'll be," I hear Eljay say.

"You can open the gate," Pop says as he slips the bridles over each of the horse's heads.

We lead the two horses out past the awed cowboys. I go up the ramp with the pinto named Dakota, Pop with the bay named Blackjack. We secure them in the two last stalls, then come back to the door. The crowd that watched from outside the corral is now at the bottom of the ramp.

As soon as we appear they start clapping.

Pop waits until the applause stops. Then he touches two fingers to his cap in a little salute.

"Mealtime now?" he asks.

CHAPTER ELEVEN

AN INDIAN HANDSHAKE

We're on our way again. I'm leaning against the rough pinewood wall of the stall where Dakota is standing. Every now and then he whinnies soft-like and I give him a handful of hay. A mound of that sweet-smelling grass was forked in with us before the call of *All Aboard*.

After our dinner, which was real fine—pot roast with onions and carrots, potatoes, and enough thick brown gravy to float a battleship—we'd been offered a better ride.

"You can join us in the caboose," Wilkie, the mustached man told us. "You earned that."

Pop shook his head. "Horses'll be happier having us with them."

Plus Pop needed more time alone with me before we got to Challagi.

"Classes won't be hard for you, Cal," he says.

The train is rolling across an endless expanse of brown and yellow plains. Not a patch of green to be seen. Off in the distance are big black clouds—no doubt chock-full of dust. Not headed our way, though. Fixing to dump a few thousand acres of Oklahoma soil into the Gulf of Mexico.

We study those clouds a bit before Pop turns back to me.

"No," Pop says, "academic classes ought to be easy. You learned a lot from your old school. More than most high school students at Challagi did in my time. Matter of fact, unless they got a better batch than when I was there, you may find you know more than your academic teachers do as far as your three Rs go. At Challagi the big emphasis is on industries. The agricultural side of things there is top-notch, modern farming in fact. There's where you can get an education. Pay attention, Cal, and you'll learn a thing or two we can use when we have a farm again."

Pop pauses. He looks off to his right as he does when he's visiting someplace in his memory.

"The first thing they are going to do is boil you up. Strip you, scrub you clean, run a metal comb soaked with kerosene through your hair to get rids of nits and lice. Even though you don't have any." Pop looks at me. "They'll cut your hair, too. Real short. Can you handle that?"

I nod, but I feel like I've been gut shot. Cut off my hair? I resist the impulse to pull out Mom's comb or run it back across my head. I know that might make Pop feel bad.

A man can stand almost anything as long as it's not forever.

That's what I tell myself. I have to come to terms with this. It'll be over before all that long. Just a few months. Pop will get his bonus money, come back and get me. I'll grow my hair back then. We'll start a whole new life on a new piece of land. A hundred acres with a barn, a team of horses, a cow or two to milk, and chickens to give us eggs. Out in the country, but not so far from a town that we can't go in on a Saturday night to a

121

movie house and see the latest Tom Mix serial, maybe go to an ice-cream parlor and . . .

"You hear what I just said, son?"

I focus my eyes away from that dream and look at Pop. He knows I have been off somewhere in my mind. I would never lie to him.

So I shake my head no.

Pop smiles. "I was just saying you better be prepared for three things, Cal. First is to start marching come tomorrow. They'll have you in a uniform and bugle you up before dawn.

"Second thing is when they feed you, don't hold back. No such thing as table manners at Challagi. Grab what you can as soon as it hits the table. Otherwise you are sure as shooting going to get thin."

Pop pauses again and looks at his hands. "Last thing is that you've got to be prepared to fight. The big boys won't pick on you. It'll be the ones your age."

Pop holds up his hands, makes them into fists. "Unless things have changed one hell of a lot, they won't be pulling knives or using any weapons. No biting or eye-gouging or hooking. No ganging up or kicking while you're down." Pop smiles. "They won't fight like white men. They'll fight fair. But they will be trying to get their licks in. So you fight hard, too. Think you can do that?"

"Yes," I reply, which is not exactly the truth.

Pop has tried to teach me boxing. But it's not something I learned all that well. I don't like the idea of hitting anyone.

At my old school I only ever got into one fight. It was during recess with a bigger boy a year older than me. He was bullying the three second graders, keeping them off our one swing. When

I told him to stop he cocked his fist and threw a punch at me. I knew in my head what I should do. Step aside and let the punch go by me like Pop taught. Then maybe throw a left hook.

Except I just froze. All I did was stand there. Luckily for me, what he punched was my stomach and not my head. Unluckily for him, what he hit was my belt buckle. So it hurt him a lot more than it did me, especially since it was a pretty big buckle and I've always had strong stomach muscles. That blow just pushed me back a step and I stood there looking at him.

"Oh man," he groaned, shaking his fist. "I'm done. I give."

It all only took a second and was over before any of the teachers saw anything. So I didn't get in trouble. That was only a month before our school got closed down forever.

Pop settles back. Both of us are sitting in the open boxcar door, knees drawn up to our chests. You don't want to let your legs dangle outside a fast-moving freight. It's a good way to get yanked out if there's a post or a signal near the track. More than one beginner's seen their hoboing career come to an end that way.

Behind us, the horses are making soft sounds. Every now and then one knocks a hoof against a stall as they move about. They're just shifting their positions. Contented and quiet. I take a deep breath, The scent of horses is something I've always loved. Being here with them should make me feel at ease as the miles go rolling by.

But it doesn't. I don't feel right. It's almost like just before I came down with the chicken pox. My head is throbbing and there's a sensation like a knotted rope in my belly.

123

Pop says I'm Indian. But I've never felt like an Indian, never thought of myself that way. I just want to be myself. Just Cal. Not something strange as the other side of the moon. What I am is a gentleman of the road. A man with an ethical code. My pop's son. I don't want to be a stranger surrounded by folks who are likely going to despise me.

I close my eyes, trying to shut off my thoughts. I count backward from a hundred. I do it twice, but I'm still awake. I try listening to the rhythm of the train's wheels. It's a metal melody that's soothed me to sleep hundreds of times over the months we have been on the road.

Clickety-Clack, Clickety-Clack, Clickety-Clack, Clickety-Clack, Clickety-Clack, Clickety-Clack . . .

But this time the lullaby of the rails is different. What I'm hearing is not the whir and rattle of steel on steel. Instead it seems to be saying:

You're White, You're Indian, You're White, You're Indian, You're White, You're Indian . . .

And then somehow, though I'd thought it impossible, I must have slept. When I open my eyes we've almost stopped. The half-light of that time just before dawn is sifting in through the boxcar door. Pop's not by my side. His warmth is missing as well as the sound of his breathing, his familiar scent.

A noise comes from behind me. It's just the horses, stirring in their stalls.

For a minute I panic. Where's Pop? Did he leave me already?

"Cal."

The boxcar door slides farther open. It's being pushed by Pop, who wasn't visible in the shadows.

"We're here," Pop says.

We're pulling into a small railway station. **ARKANSAS CITY,** the sign reads. The depot clock says it's five a.m.

"Where's the school?" I ask.

Pop chuckles. "This is as close as the train brings you to Challagi. We're not even in Oklahoma yet. This is Arkansas." He looks to the south. "State line's that way. It's a four-mile walk from here to the school."

A square-built, spade-bearded man is waiting on the platform. He's walking toward us.

"I am E. Wimslow," he says in a booming voice, not even waiting for the train to stop. "My company has been delegated the responsibility of receiving those mounts I was told you two would be accompanying."

It seems they've telegraphed ahead. So Pop and I are not treated like bums. Instead, we help unload the horses, bringing them down the ramp with no trouble at all. They've gotten to know us real well in the time we've spent with them. Sleeping with a horse in its stall tends to relax it, make it feel like you are sort of family.

As we lead them down the street, Mr. E. Wimslow never stops talking. Most of what he says is just idle chatter until he puts up a hand as we reach a stable.

"My two hands and myself," he says, "will be handling it from here. We have the government contract with the school. We will check the horses over, make sure they are sound, then stable

125

them here for the night. This being Sunday, the Lord's Day of Rest, we shall not be bringing them to the school till the morrow. So, I thank you for your help."

I guess this is where it ends for us as far as those horses.

It's a disappointment for me. I feel so at ease with them. They're like old friends after our train ride together. I had this image in mind of Pop and me riding in to the school. Everybody watching with their mouths open as we gallop up, whooping like wild cowboys. That kind of entrance might make it easier for those people I've never met to see me as somebody special. Like Hoot Gibson or Ken Maynard. Not some random nobody who doesn't know who he is anymore.

But no. We'll not be arriving at the Indian school on shank's mare.

Mr. E. Wimslow is shaking both our hands. He's grasping mine so firm I feel like my fingers are being crushed. However, I do not wince or show any sign of pain.

"Here, my lads," he says releasing me from his iron grasp. He reaches into his breast pocket, pulls out two coins, slaps the shiny silver dollar into Pop's hand and the fifty-cent piece onto my own aching palm.

Then he turns and closes the stable door, leaving us on the outside.

Pop leans over my way. "One more thing to remember, Cal," he says out of the corner of his mouth. "Notice how Mr. E. Wimslow grabbed your hand in that vise grip of his?"

I look at my hand, wiggling my fingers to make sure they still all work.

"White man handshake. One way white men show how much power they've got. In the white world you always have to prove yourself. Everything is a competition. Not like it is with old-time Indians who knew sharing was more important than wealth or power."

I bite my lip as Pop says that. Ever since he's told me his big secret there's been a change in the way he talks about things. Like talking about white folks as if they're different from him and me.

Pop holds out his right hand. "Show me how I taught you to shake."

I reach out my hand and grasp his, just firm enough to hold on, our hands relaxing together, neither of us struggling for control.

"You see," Pop says. "You shake hands like someone who trusts the other and doesn't have to prove he's better. That's an Indian handshake."

PART 2

AT CHALLAGI SCHOOL

CHAPTER TWELVE

UNDER THE ARCH

We've reached Challagi.

Yet we are not really there. We're just at the entranceway. Dropped off by a farmer who was kind enough to let us hitch a ride on his buckboard wagon, seeing as how he was passing by here on his way to his farm ten miles farther down the road.

All I can make out of the buildings of this Indian boarding school is that they look tiny—like those in a kid's toy town. They're so far away down a dusty red road.

"Over eight thousand acres," Pop says. "Imagine that."

Around us, in every direction, is rolling prairie. It's easy to understand why they called it Plains View. There's a plain view here for sure.

Above us is a metal archway thirty feet high. **CHALLAGI,** the big metal letters twisting across the top read. Below it, in smaller letters maybe a foot high each, are the words **INDIAN BOARDING SCHOOL**.

There's also a design perched on top in the center. It's some sort of cross with each of its sides twisted. It makes me think of a whirlwind.

As I look at it, something starts to happen. The world spins around and then I'm somewhere else. I'm on a broad avenue with big white buildings. There are people all around me, mostly men, marching along. Some are in uniforms, others in civilian clothing. They're carrying signs I can't quite read. People are watching and calling out encouragement. Everyone is happy and excited. Except me. I know something awful is about to happen. I look around for my father. I have to warn him. But I can't find him. And now I'm hearing the rumble of tanks coming toward us.

"You all right, Cal?" Pop says.

I nod, but I'm not okay.

For just a moment I feel angry at my father. Angry and worried both. Then I feel angrier at myself. I can't give in to my feelings of uncertainty. I can't let myself be held back by what was probably just a daydream because I'm feeling so anxious.

I take care of you, you take care of me.

Right now, taking care of Pop means making it possible for him to do what his heart is telling him he has to do. And the battle he plans to fight isn't just for himself. It's for me and him. And it's for every other doughboy now being neglected by an ungrateful nation.

I have to try to do the best I can. Pop is counting on me.

I straighten my back and step out. Pop marches beside me, our feet raising little dust clouds from the bone-dry road. I start counting cadence to myself.

Hup, two, three, four.

Hup, two, three, four.

We've gone at least a mile. The air's less dry now. We're passing between two small lakes, one either side of the road. There's a bridge in front of us to cross. Far off to the left is the dam that created these shallow lakes from a creek.

The smell of the water around us is sweet as summer rain.

Water's a blessing, something no farm can live without. We had plenty of water on our farm thanks to our deep well and a brook that ran year-round. It flowed down through the lower forty where our two cows and our horses, grazed. It hurts remembering that, so I turn my mind back to counting.

Hup, two, three, four.

As we continue, the buildings growing larger, I see there's more of them than I realized. The most distant ones are big, finely built white structures with red roofs. Those must be the houses Pop told me about where the Indian students live. This road leads directly to the front of the biggest one. White limestone, four stories tall, with wide steps that lead up to an elevated porch. It looks more like a governor's mansion than how I imagined an Indian school building would be.

Hup, two, three, four.

And there are more buildings to either side of us. They surround a big open area only partially visible through the closest building.

"Print shop," Pop says, nodding to the right. "Tailor shop next to it, then harness making and shoe repair." He looks to the left. "Academic Hall there."

He looks beyond them, farther to the left. "Stock barn."

The stock barn is way off. I can barely make out its wavery outline in the heat already building up, though it's not yet midmorn. The shapes that look tiny as ants must be horses or cows in the pasture behind it.

So far, though, we've seen no people. Is it because this is a Sunday? Does everyone leave the school on the weekends?

As is often the case, Pop senses what I'm thinking.

"Once a month you get permission to go in to town," he says, pausing to stretch his stiff leg. "But today's Sunday. Might they be inside at services?" He looks up at the sun. "Nope. About eleven a.m.," he says. "We missed Sunday School. Every one of us not Catholic had to go to it. Catholics always had their worship an hour earlier. So I expect they are getting set for Parade."

Parade? What's that?

Pop offers no further explanation. He just starts walking again. I set off behind him, trying to keep up.

Hup, two, three, four.

I continue the count in my head as we get closer to that big open area.

HUP, TWO, THREE, FOUR.

Whoa! Those shouted words were not in my head! We stop walking and turn toward the sound of tromping feet.

From around the corner of the academic building comes a whole company of marching soldiers. More than forty of them.

HUP, TWO, THREE, FOUR.

That cadence is being counted by the officer walking beside them, watching with an eagle eye to make sure no one is out of step.

HUP, TWO, THREE, FOUR! RIGHT!

They turn to swing past us. They're close enough now for me to see they're all about the same age. Maybe three or four years older than me. At first they look the same. All in military attire, hair cut short, caps low on their foreheads. Only their brown faces suggest they're Indian. Though I see some among them whose skins are as pale as a white man. Plus a few whose complexions are as dark as a Negro's.

DOUBLE TIME, MARCH!

Their feet start moving faster, so perfectly in step they might be one giant many-legged being. Not a face turns our way as they pass.

My mouth has fallen open watching them. It's a stirring sight and also a little disturbing. Is marching like that what I'll be expected to do?

LEFT MARCH.

They turn as one toward that big broad expanse of brown grass.

No sooner have they passed than I hear the approach of another company. As they round the corner, they're moving just as smartly as the first group we saw. And others are coming into view behind them. Company after company goes marching past. The student soldiers are getting progressively smaller as each company passes us. The youngest ones, who look like second or third graders, are fewer in number. They are having some trouble staying in step—which makes me feel a bit better.

HUP, HUP, HUP, HUP, HUP.

Finally the last group passes us. I didn't try for an exact

count, but I'd guess they numbered more than four hundred.

Pop and I follow those marchers. It's not clear where they were coming from, but it is dang sure obvious where they're going. The open area ahead of us, the center of which looks to be a football field.

As we get closer I hear the sound of drums and horns. They were barely audible over the thudding of those hundreds of marching feet moving in time to that music.

"John Philip Sousa," Pop says. "Best marches ever written."

I nod my head. I have to admit it makes my heart beat a bit faster.

At the far end of the field are bleachers. In front of those stands is the source of that stirring music. It's a big band, made up of Indian students dressed in uniforms much more colorful than those of the marchers. Some are banging on drums of all sizes. Others are playing horns, including a gigantic tuba twice as big as the boy blowing into it.

Just behind them is all the rest of the people. Those bleachers are filled with more seated spectators than marchers. So many it makes my head spin. I've never been around so many folks all at once. It makes me feel small.

Half of those in the stands are females. Most dressed alike. From the smallest little girl to the biggest young woman they're wearing baggy long dresses with vertical stripes and ribbons in their hair. About the same number of girls as there were marching boys.

In the very center of the stands, set apart from those female students, are adults. They stand out because their clothing is not all the same and far from military. Some of the men in suits look as dignified as foreign dignitaries. Among the women are ladies whose bright dresses and big, feathered hats make them look like exotic birds.

"We're in luck," Pop says to me as we approach the stands, staying well to the side. "Got here just in time for the weekly dress parade."

Though none of those marching students turned an eye our way, that's not true of the folks in the stands. We've been noticed, for sure. Some of those grown-ups are staring at us.

We slip our packs off our shoulders and take seats off to the side of the bleachers.

"Just look at that, Cal! My, oh my!"

I turn toward the direction Pop's indicating.

Some of the squads of marching boys and young men are performing intricate maneuvers. The youngest ones, who had made some pretty obvious missteps as they passed, have now halted. They're all standing at attention to the right of the parade ground.

"The older boys are competing for privileges," Pop explains. "Extra desserts, maybe release from some duties. Plus the best squads get advances in rank. They might even still be giving medals like they did in my day."

It seems to me as if every single person in those competing companies is perfect. But Pop's practiced eye is sharper than mine.

"Ooops," he says. "That second company there. Third from

135

the left just took a wrong step. Plus the boy behind him has his cap at the wrong angle. No rewards for them today. Those two are going to be in hot water tonight with their fellow squad members. Never mind what the drill master thinks. Last thing you want to do is let your company down. Ten to one they'll have to stand at attention till midnight in their dormitory."

I do not think Pop even realizes how nervous everything he's saying is making me. I don't show it, of course. Nor do I say any-thing. But I can imagine myself as the one who takes a wrong step, trips, and brings the whole line down on top of him. They'll likely stand me up in front of a firing squad for that!

I'm ready to run away from Challagi Indian School before I've even spent my first hour here.

"How do you like the music?" Pop asks.

The maneuvers are being done to the music being played by a good-sized marching band standing directly in front of the crowd. They are mostly playing drums, though now and then some horn players join in, including one with a tuba about twice his size. I have to admit that I do find the sound stirring. It almost makes me move my own feet.

"Now look there, Cal," Pop says.

He indicates with a turn of his chin a long-nosed, hatless man in a light brown suit who is standing at the front of the stands on a small raised platform. He's tall and his posture is slightly stoop-shouldered, almost like a heron that's just waded into a pond looking for frogs. His right hand, which seems unusually large, surrounds a microphone set up in front of him.

"Know who that is?"

It's not really a question for me to answer. I know Pop is going to tell me.

"That is the superintendent, Mr. Morrell," Pop says. "He was the head ag teacher when I was here. Only classes I ever gave a hoot for. I heard he got promoted. Smartest thing they ever did, putting him in charge."

Pop pokes me in the side with his elbow. "And he is the main reason why I am sure you'll be let in, even if it is halfway through the school year."

"Why? Cuz he knows you?"

Pop raises an eyebrow at me, maybe a little surprised at my speaking up like that. Then he shakes his head.

"More than that," he says.

The band suddenly stops playing. The marchers come to a halt, ranged in a dozen ranks that spread in a wide line facing the spectators. Each company is separated from the next by ten feet or so. The company farthest to the right is so close to us that I can see the sweat on their brows.

A sound like a hammer hitting a nail comes out of a loudspeaker.

Pop and I both turn to look back toward the center of the stands where most of the adults are gathered.

Superintendent Morrell taps the microphone again with one long finger.

"THIS ON. . .ON. . . ON?" echoes across the crowd. A smile crosses the superintendent's face. "Yes, I guess it is," he says.

137

He scans the crowd. He's taking everything in. Including Pop and me. His eyes rest on us for a split second and he nods. Then he holds up an enormous left hand. Everyone gets quieter.

"I want to thank our student companies for their excellent performance this Sunday morning," he says in a deep, mellow voice. "Shall we give them a round of applause?"

The assembled crowd—including Pop and me—all start clapping. There's also a fair amount of shouting from the girl students. Not exactly shouting, though. They're making an echoing sort of call. It's nothing like the catcalls or sarcastic hooting I've heard from the stands during the few baseball games I've seen. There is something old and strong about it.

It stirs me even more than that drum music did, makes a shiver go down my spine. Some of the young men at attention in the drill squad closest to us are shifting their shoulders. Standing up even taller.

That's especially true of one boy two rows back from the front. I'd already noticed him because he looks sort of familiar. A scar twisting down his cheek from his ear to his chin makes him memorable. Despite that scar, his face has a friendly look to it. There's also the hint of a mischievous smile there.

Superintendent Morrell clears his throat when the sounds die down. Along with the rest of the crowd, I turn my attention back to him.

"I wish to welcome you all here today to see this fine display of discipline and wholesome competition, principles that Challagi attempts to ingrain in our boys and girls as we mold them to meet a world so different from that in which their savage forebears lived."

"Hmmpf!" Pop says, a sound he may not even know he's making. I've heard it before when something doesn't sit well with him—like a man mistreating a horse. That "hmmpf" is usually followed by Pop stepping in to give that person what for. All he does now, though, is cough loudly into his hand.

"Bullrggh!"

The only one, aside from me, who seems to notice is that boy with the scarred face. His eyes flick toward us and his lips move—just for a moment—into an actual smile. Then he winks at us.

"So," Superintendent Morrell continues, "the moment you have been waiting for. My judges and I . . ." He looks back at two other people seated behind him who nod their heads in agreement. ". . . have decided that today's honors go to the eleventh graders of Blue Company."

He gestures toward the squad of boys two ranks to the left of us.

"Step forward, men."

"Two steps forward, HUT!" the drill master barks and the eleventh graders of Blue Company move as one.

A group of girls stand up from the front of the bleachers. They pass out ribbons to each of the boys, who accept them with their right hands while keeping eyes front. In a few cases, though, some of those boys briefly grasp—as if by accident—the fingers of the girls who've given them those honors.

Pop chuckles. "Just like when I was here. They may try to

keep the boys and girls apart. All sorts of rules and penalties if you're caught fraternizing. But we'd still find ways to get together."

The girls retreat to their seats, but not without quite a few of them glancing over their shoulders at particular boys—all of whom are attempting to look impassive.

"Thank you all," the superintendent says. "You are dismissed."

The loudspeaker distorts his voice into a loud squeak at the end. It's like a signal for the ranks of uniformed boys and young men to disintegrate into a disordered crowd. Caps are removed, jackets unbuttoned. Some boys start scuffling playfully. New groups are being formed as friends join one another.

None of the adults, their teachers and advisers, seem to be concerned about the roughhousing. Most are heading off on their own. A few men, though, who look like they might be Indian themselves, are talking and joshing with the boys themselves.

"Former students," Pop says. "Challagi likes to hire back its best graduates."

Despite that atmosphere of ease among the boys, order is being kept among the female students. Older women are herding them away from the boys.

Pop notices me watching all this.

"House matrons," he says, smiling. "But they can't keep watch all the time. You can't count the number of marriages that have come out of old Challagi."

He studies the groups of male students now moving away from us in all directions. "I see another thing hasn't changed much," he says. "Those boys there look to all be full-bloods. And over there . . ." He nods toward a group of young men with much lighter hair and paler faces. "Ten to one, those come from families so mixed that they are less than one-eighth and don't know a word of Indian, speak only English at home. You can bet they get called *stahitkey*."

"Stah-what?" That word was strange. Even the way he pronounced it was unlike anything else I've ever heard from his mouth.

"*Stahitkey*," he says again, saying it slower so I can get it. I notice that his lips don't move as he says it. "It means white man."

I don't have a white face. But until two days ago I thought I was white or *stahitkey* as Pop called them. Is that what the boys in the school will call me?

"White man," Pop says again. "*Stahitkey.*"

As he speaks that word, a shadow falls across our feet.

"William Blackbird? Is that you?"

We turn to look up at the man who spoke. He's standing with the rising sun directly at his back, so bright it is hard to make out his face. But I know who it is, having heard that voice of his so loud and recent. It's the superintendent.

Pop moves his pack off his lap and stands up. Superintendent Morrell holds out his arms, grasping Pop's elbow with his left hand as he vigorously shakes with his right.

"It is you, isn't it?"

"You could say that," Pop replies.

Superintendent Morrell turns to me, releasing Pop's hand

141

from his huge paw. "And who might this be? No, do not tell me. Your son from the look of him. The very image of his father."

"My boy, Cal," Pop agrees.

"Sir," I say, nodding my head.

Then I hold out my hand, ready to have it crushed. To my surprise, though, the superintendent's big mitt makes mine disappear right up to the wrist, his pressure is firm but light.

"Young man," he says, "am I correct in assuming your father has brought you here to join us? Although it is . . ." his voice takes on a teasing tone ". . . far from the start of the regular school year?"

"Yes, sir," I reply.

Superintendent Morrell nods down at me. "Good manners," he says. "Excellent."

He's so close I can smell something on his breath.

Mints, I think.

My conjecture is proven right away. He reaches into his coat pocket, extracts a red-striped lump, shucks off the cellophane, and pops the candy into his mouth.

"Your father," he says, sucking on the mint, "had quite a record here at Challagi. Unforgettable, some might say. A fair student in the academic realm, but top-notch in agricultural skills. Promising—when he was not running away. Two times in four years, was it?"

"Three," Pop says, "if you count when I enlisted."

Superintendent Morrell smiles broadly, disclosing a gap between his two front teeth.

142

"I do not," he says. "Answering the call of duty to one's country cannot be called running away. Rather running to. From what I heard, you acquitted yourself quite well as a soldier, William."

"You could say that."

The superintendent nods, then gestures at me with an open left hand. "So," he says, "why now?"

My father breathes in and then out, the way he does when he means to make his words count.

"We had a farm," he says, his voice slow and clear. "Lost it to the bank. Cal was in school. That got closed down when there were not enough kids left. I have hopes now to get my bonus money and get us another farm. Until then I want Cal to be back in school."

The superintendent nods his head up and down when Pop finishes speaking, looking even more like a heron as he does so.

"Ah," he says. "Good enough. We are a bit down in numbers. There could be room. If he is a good student . . .?"

"He is," Pop says.

"And a hard worker?"

"That, too."

"Then, we may find a place for him here. Interested in agricultural science, young man?"

"Yes, sir," I reply. Then, seeing more of an answer is expected, I force myself to add, "I like farming."

The superintendent slaps his hands together, producing a sound so loud I almost jump back. "Excellent. As your son, an enrolled member of the Creek Nation, there's no question that the government will subsidize him." He shakes his head. "You

143

might be amazed at how many—unlike your boy—have sought a place here in recent years with no degree of Indian blood or claim to being Indian . . . Negroes in particular. Unlike your years here, the number of full-bloods has declined greatly. Less than half. Your race might be bred out of existence before achieving the full benefits of civilization."

I wait for Pop to mention that I am already fully civilized, a gentleman of the road, and half-white. But instead he just sighs.

"Are we set then?" Pop asks.

"There are certain forms," the superintendent replies.

"Can I fill 'em out now?" Pop asks. "Hoped by coming this early I could settle my boy in time to catch a train."

Superintendent Morrell nods. He turns and makes a broad gesture toward one of the big-hatted women who'd been seated to his right. She's a bone-thin lady, with brown hair framing an angular face that looks washed clean of all expression. She's wearing white, from her hat to her calf-length dress, stockings, and shoes. She was watching us the whole time the superintendent was talking with Pop, sort of expectant. Soon as he gives her that wave, a purposeful look comes onto her face. She nods, stands up, straightens her shoulders, and strides off.

The superintendent pivots back our way.

"My office," he says, popping another mint into his mouth. "We shall do the paperwork—despite it being a Sunday. I think the Lord will forgive us."

Then he turns and begins striding long-legged across the grass oval, us tagging along behind him.

He didn't notice the look I'm certain is on my face right now. I'm dizzied by how fast things are happening. I want to grab Pop's hand and ask him not to leave me. But I am not going to make it harder for him to do what he's decided he has to do. Even though I feel like I'm carrying a ton of weight.

We have not walked twenty feet, though, before Pop puts an arm around my shoulders.

"Cal," he says, his voice is kind. "This is a lot for you to absorb all at once. You going to be all right?"

"It's okay," I say, somehow keeping my voice calm. "I'm ready."

CHAPTER THIRTEEN

THE TOUR

Our walk across the wide oval is more or less in the direction of the big central building made of white stone. It's where the smaller of the boys in uniform headed when they were dismissed. The others continued on to two other sizable buildings beyond that one.

Those uniformed boys are disappearing into those three structures. Maybe to change out of those stiff-looking uniforms. Those duds seemed much too heavy for a hot, sunny day like this one is becoming.

None of the girls went in the direction of the boys, though. Kept in tight order, they were herded along by the house matrons to three other buildings far off to the east.

Like Pop said, keeping the boys and girls as far apart as possible is the order of the day here.

As soon as I think that, Superintendent Morrell speaks up.

"Boys' dorms ahead of us, Houses Two, Four, Six," he says. "Girls, Houses One, Three, and Five off over to our right."

"East is east and west is west and never the twain shall meet," Pop says.

"Very good," the superintendent says, nodding in approval. "You've kept your Kipling."

As we continue along, the superintendent points out more

things. "Power plant. Laundry. Harness shop. Print shop. Dining hall." He stops and a big smile splits his face as he gestures with both arms. "And there, there are our livestock barns."

There's a note of genuine pride now in his voice.

"The finest herd of Herefords in all of Oklahoma! Percheron horses that are the envy of the state fair. And our chickens, all Rhode Island Whites, are so many and such reliable layers that we now have at least one egg a day for every student."

"Better than when I was here," Pop whispers to me as the superintendent strides ahead of us, unwrapping yet another mint and tossing the cellophane off to the side. "Back then I was lucky if I saw an egg a week in the dining hall." Pop chuckles. "Though we did liberate quite a few eggs and more than one fat chicken from the henhouse at night and cook them at our camp back in the catalpa grove."

We're beginning to run into groups of male students, changed now into work clothes. Sunday makes no difference to cows that need milking, chickens that need feeding, and clothes that need washing. More and more boys are heading off to their daily chores in the barns, the laundry, and other work buildings.

All of them politely greet the superintendent, but none speak more than a word or two. Good morning and then a *Yes, sir* or *No, sir* to any question he asks.

None show any interest in me other than the quick glance of an expressionless face. As far as I am concerned that's aces. I would just as soon not be noticed. Being invisible would suit me just fine. Being anywhere but here would be even better.

I also want to know more of what it was like when Pop was here. But everything is moving so fast that my head is spinning. I'm not going to get the chance to ask him anything.

Pop has seen me taking notice of the other boys. And maybe he can see what I'm thinking as he so often does. He leans in my direction as we keep walking.

"Sunday," he says to me in a low voice that goes unheard by our enthusiastic guide still striding ahead of us and praising the civilizing virtues of his institution. "Sunday was always my favorite day. After morning service, drill, and taking care of chores, we were left on our own. No way they could keep an eye on us all." Pop chuckles. "We went hunting in the woods, sneaked off and had our own fun. Like those boys you just saw there. Five'll get you ten they're planning some mischief."

"Now here we are," Morrell says. "Building One."

We've come around to the broad steps of that big white building. Those steps are so wide at the top I'd bet every student in the whole school could sit on them all at once. Up top to one side is a small screened-in porch. It looks empty.

But as we ascend the stairs, our long-legged leader two steps above Pop and me, I see a slight movement off to the side, inside that porch. Its screens are heavy wire mesh. A closed, bolted door leads into the wooden box of a room that's no more than six feet wide and ten feet long. Someone, staying in the farthest shadowy corner, is locked in there.

"One of our recalcitrants," the superintendent says, looking

148

back over his shoulder. His voice is matter of fact. "Another day to go in there for that young man."

"Not using the guardhouse anymore?" Pop asks.

"Certainly not," Morrell replies. "Discipline, of course, is still needed. But not in such uncivilized ways. Those unenlightened days are past at our school."

Then he walks on into the building.

CHAPTER FOURTEEN

POSSUM

Feeling like a lamb being led to the slaughter, I enter the building where the superintendent is waiting. He's sitting at a square oak table, that mild smile on his long face.

To my surprise, Morrell's not alone. There's an Indian boy with him. He looks to be about my age—maybe twelve or thirteen. Taller, though, and a good bit skinnier. To my further surprise, he's someone I recognize. Even though he's now in bib overalls and black sneakers rather than an army-style uniform and boots, I've noticed the scar on his sun-browned face. It's the boy who was two rows back from the front, the one who winked at me.

"Charles Aird," Superintendent Morrell says, pointing his finger like a gun at the boy's chest. Then he points back at me. "You will be in his class."

He swings his mile-long finger back in the scarred boy's direction. "Mr. Aird, this is Calvin Blackbird. You will show him about. Make certain he is properly prepared for tomorrow."

Charles Aird replies with a nod of his head. "Yes, sir," he says, clicking his heels together. "Superintendent Sir! At your command, Sir."

His face is dead serious. Somehow, though, the way he said

those few words was almost as funny as if he'd just cracked a joke.

Superintendent Morrell shakes his head. "None of your tom-foolery, Aird. Just do as you are told."

"Yes, sir, even if it means I die trying."

"The boy thinks himself amusing," Morrell says. "Still, he is reliable." He turns to Charles Aird and his voice takes on a firmer tone of command. "Now, take our new recruit about. The infirmary first."

"Yes, sir, Superintendent Sir," Charles Aird says.

Then, as the superintendent looks down to take another mint from his pocket, Aird leans his head close to mine to whisper one word.

"Ouch!"

I look at my father.

"Go ahead, Cal," Pop says. "It'll take me a bit to fill out the forms. I'll see you before I go."

Before I go.

Those three words hit like arrows shot into my chest. But I don't let it show. I just nod.

I'm steered out the door by Charles Aird.

Halfway down the steps, he turns and says something to me.

I do not understand a word.

He says it again. Once again it makes no sense. I just look at him.

"Hmmm," he says. "Looking the way you do, I thought you might talk it. Your pappy never taught you?"

I still don't understand.

"Indian," Charles Aird says. "You never learned to speak Indian."

Oh.

Should I tell him until only a day ago I never even knew Pop was Indian? How can I explain that to him when I don't really understand it myself? So I just keep my answer simple.

"No," I say.

Charles Aird nods. "Okay," he says. "Lots here never got taught nothing but English, especially if their folks went here. Even some who look as Creek as you do."

I follow him down the steps. At the bottom, he jerks his chin off to the left.

"Come on," he says. "This way."

I look in that direction. There's another slightly smaller building a hundred yards away. It's not built of stone like the one we just left. It's wood, painted white as snow.

"Building Four," Charles Aird says. "Scalping shop. Infirmary's in there, too. First stop." He lifts his right hand, opens and closes his index and middle fingers. "Snip, snip. No barber today, but nurse'll do as good a job of chopping off that long hair of yours." He runs his palm back over his own closely cropped head. "Can't have none of us looking like wild Indians and scaring the teachers."

His short laugh is more like a snort. "Ready to get shaved like a sheep?"

He studies my face as he says that. Looking to see if I show any signs of anxiety about being shorn like Samson in the Bible

152

story. I knew this was going to happen. But now that time is almost here, that gut shot pain is back. However, I keep my face impassive and merely nod.

"Talkative, ain't you?" Charles Aird says with a chuckle. He starts walking, me half a step behind. We don't go far before he looks back over his right shoulder.

"Cal?" he says. "That what your old man called you?"

I nod my head.

"Well, you might of heard my name back there as Charles Aird, right?"

I nod again.

"Okay. But that's not what any but the teachers call me. Possum. That's my moniker. Possum."

He stops dead in his tracks, spins on his heel, and favors me with a grin so big it about splits his face. It does sort of look like a possum's wide, tooth-baring smile. I almost laugh.

Charles . . . Possum, that is, raises an eyebrow, still waiting for a reaction. He doesn't get one from me. I just stand there looking down at the ground.

"Jeezum Crow," he says, letting go of that grin. He starts walking again. I follow behind like a condemned man being led to the gallows.

"Cal," Possum says to himself. He presses his lips together and shakes his head. "Nope. That don't sound right. Jay Bird's more like it. Seeing as how Jays are always squawking. Just like you." He turns again to make a face at me. "Man can't get a word in edgewise with you around. Can he, Jay?"

This time I can't keep a smile from curling up my lips. It's not just that it's funny in an ironic way—like giving a giant the nickname of Tiny. It's how he says it. The way he keeps changing the expression on his rubbery face. Plus I've always, like Pop, had a special fondness for birds.

"Okay!" Possum chuckles. "So that face of yours ain't made of granite after all. Even if I do have to keep up both ends of this conversation. My grampa, Big Rabbit, he claimed the best way to get a man to talk was to say nothing. I reckon he would have liked you, Jay Bird. You being living proof."

We've now reached Building Four. Four good-sized elm trees grow up in front of it. There are only eight steps here, nowhere near as steep as those of Building One. But they're still long and wide enough to seat a small army. Doing things on a grand scale seems to be the rule at this place.

Before it was closed down, the folks of the Kansas county where Pop and I had our farm were mighty proud of their four-room school. It was so much larger than the one-room schoolhouses in the adjoining counties. But every building I have seen thus far at Challagi makes my old place of learning look like a henhouse in comparison.

Possum cocks his head to squint up the steps at the big double doors.

"Hunnerd and eleven of us in here," he says. "You will make it an even one hunnerd and twelve. But first you got to get mowed and pincushioned."

He points his lips at a normal-sized door set to the left of the steps on ground level.

The word **INFIRMARY** is printed in black letters above it.

"Yup," Possum says, that big grin on his face again. "As many inoculations as any man could want. All free of charge." He plucks my shirtsleeve. "Nurse'll be waiting. Old Man Morrell sent her to get ready."

He gives me a gentle shove. "Go right on in. I'll be waiting till she's done with you."

I look at my pack. Possum took it from me as we started our walk. It's slung over his shoulder.

He nods. "It'll be safe with me, Jay. You can trust me."

The joking tone that's been in his voice since we met is gone. And somehow I know two things. First, that I can trust him. Second, that I've already found a friend.

Possum grins. "Don't keep her waiting too long or she just might make it worse for you."

I grasp the door handle, turn it, and try to pull the door open. I pull harder. Nothing happens.

Possum reaches a hand past me to tap his index finger on the word written right in front of my face on the door.

PUSH

Possum chuckles. Then he pats me on the shoulder. "Won't be that bad," he says. "Go on."

I push the door open and step inside.

CHAPTER  FIFTEEN

INFIRMARY

As soon as I pass through the door I'm greeted by the strong reek of alcohol. Not the drinking kind. It's what you smell in hospitals, like when I was seven and Pop took me to one after the scythe fell off the barn wall while I was trying to hang it up.

Remembering that makes me look down at the white scar that winds across my right forearm like a snake. Twenty stitches. But it doesn't remind me of the pain. It reminds me of how much I miss the life we had.

"Young man!" a woman's voice snaps.

How long have I been standing here, lost in memory, someone in a fog? Long enough for that voice to sound impatient.

Standing in front of me, tapping her foot, is the person who must be the nurse. The bone-thin woman who was studying Pop and me while we were talking with Superintendent Morrell back at the parade grounds. She's still wearing white, but has on a long white coat, like the doctor in that hospital six years ago. There's gray in her hair and frown lines across her forehead. Around her neck is one of those instruments that hospital doctor wore. Stethoscope, my dictionary told me.

"Yes, ma'am," I say, making my voice as polite as I can.

Her severe expression lightens a little. Good manners can do that when you meet someone for the first time.

"I am Mrs. Wilting," she says. "Coat off."

I take off my coat.

Mrs. Wilting nods. "Good. You speak English. Easier for me."

She tosses my coat over her shoulder onto a small cot behind her without even watching it land.

"Hmmm," she says, looking me up and down. "Fairly clean."

Her voice is as sharp as her features. Clipped, precise. Almost mechanical.

So is everything else in this room. It is all hard edges, white, so white that it hurts my eyes. Every object in here, medical things for which I do not know the names, seems hard and cold. Being an infirmary, this is where people get fixed up when they're hurt. But there's nothing comforting about it.

Mrs. Wilting raises her right hand in a fist. She pops up her index finger. Then she drops that hand so fast, like throwing a dart, that her wrist makes a clicking sound.

"Over there. Sit!"

I go over. I sit in the hard, metal chair she's just pointed out.

As soon as I'm down she steps behind me and grabs my shoulders. Her fingers dig in like a hawk's talons.

"Straighten up," she commands.

I do that right quick.

"Now," Mrs. Wilting says, sweeping a sheet around my neck and pinning it so tight in back I can barely swallow, "I am no barber. But no barber is needed for this."

I catch a glimpse out of the corner of my eye of the large, shiny shears she now has in her hand.

"Eyes straight. Do not stir unless you wish to lose an ear."

I don't move a muscle as she begins to chop. She does it methodically, grabbing a handful in her left hand, yanking it straight, then lopping it off with those razor-sharp steel shears.

SNIP!

A hank of my long black hair is carelessly tossed into the basket in front of the chair.

SNIP!

More of the hair I've never had cut before is sheared from my head.

SNIP!

Mom loved how black and shiny my hair always was.

SNIP!

Even though Pop wore his hair the same, saying that the Creator meant us men to have long hair, it was Mom who showed me how to wash it clean.

SNIP!

It was her who ran the comb through it, humming as she did so, her hands firm but careful not to hurt me, not jerking my head back and forth like Mrs. Wilting is doing now.

SNIP!

That thought of Mom's gentle hands, of the song she hummed as she combed my hair, is making a lump form in my throat. It's like losing her all over again. I feel tears forming at the edge of my eyes. I press my lips together. I'm not going to cry.

"Done."

There's a metallic click from behind me as the nurse puts down the shears. I start to lift one hand toward my head.

"Stay still!"

She grasps my head on either side, turning it roughly one way and then the next as she peers closely. Her hands are cold. It's as if her fingers were touched by the winter wind.

"Hmm," Mrs. Wilting sniffs. "No sign of little beasties. But we do not take chances at Challagi. Hold this!"

I free my hands from under the sheet, grasp the can she's thrust at me. There's a metal-toothed comb in it. The can's half filled with clear liquid. Kerosene, my nose tells me.

"Eyes shut!"

Pressing down so hard I wonder if she's drawing blood, she runs the kerosene-soaked comb over every inch of my skull.

There are actual tears coming out of my eyes when she's finally done. The combined result of the sharp scent of the kerosene and the pain of her scraping away nonexistent critters.

She unpins the sheet, whips it off me. Plops the steel comb into the can that she plonks onto a shelf.

I need to wipe my eyes. I start to reach into my pocket for a kerchief.

"Did I tell you to move?"

I drop my hands back into my lap.

Mrs. Wilting steps back, studying me again.

"Roll up your left sleeve."

I do as she asks. She grabs my wrist with one hand, pushes

my sleeve farther up with the other. Then she presses her finger against the rough circular scar on my upper arm.

"Hmmm. Vaccinated for smallpox?"

I nod my head.

"Good. Easier for me."

And me, as well. If this nurse gave me a smallpox inoculation she'd probably scrape a hole to the bone.

She moves over to a cabinet on the wall.

"Typhoid," she says, picking up a syringe with a needle on it big enough to kill a bull. "Then diphtheria . . ."

She rattles off the list of injections I'm about to get. Possum was not exaggerating when he said I was going to get mowed and pincushioned.

One needle after another goes into my left arm. Efficiently, if not gently. It's hard to say which hurts worse now, my burning scalp or my arm that feels as if it was hit with a baseball bat.

"Now for the physical. Stand up."

I do that. Somehow manage to avoid falling forward on my face from dizziness.

"Open your mouth."

I do, but not fast enough or wide enough to avoid her grabbing my chin and prying it down as she shoves in a stained, flat wooden stick to depress my tongue.

"Say AH!"

"Aggghhh."

"Good." Mrs. Wilting tosses the stick back into the cabinet.

She rams her stethoscope against my chest, sticking the listening pieces into her ears.

"Hmm," she says. She moves it to my back.

"Cough!"

I cough.

"Good. Lungs clear. No tuberculosis to share with the other boys and girls."

She grabs a card from atop a table, sits down, and picks up a pencil.

"Name?"

"Ma'am?"

"I thought you spoke English. *Your* name."

"Cal Black . . . Blackbird."

"Blackbird, Calvin." She slowly prints my name at the top of the card.

"Born?"

"Twenty-fourth of June, nineteen twenty."

She writes that down, too.

"Race?" she asks.

When I hesitate, not sure what to say she looks up at me and nods.

"Indian," she says, writing down the word that now defines me.

"Father's name?"

Railroad Will, I think. Knight of the open road.

"Name?" her voice impatient.

"William Blackbird."

161

"Hmmph! Of course. That roughneck boy! I should have recognized him from all the times he spent in here being patched up." She looks down at the card as she prints his name. "Tribe?" she says.

Then answers her own question. "Creek. And . . .?"

She looks at my face and makes her decision by what she sees. "Full-blood."

I don't try to correct her as she prints it on the card. I just want this to be over with.

She taps the card with her pencil.

"Father's occupation?"

I pause again, but not long enough for her to form a conclusion of her own this time. "Farmer," I reply, hoping it'll again be true.

"Mother's name."

"Mary," I say.

"First name is enough. Alive or deceased?"

My throat feels like it's still being choked by that sheet. I swallow hard.

"She . . . died," I manage to say.

"Deceased it is."

She puts down the card, taps it again with her pencil. "This is not my job," she says. "But the school registrar is away this weekend. So I am filling in."

She stands, wipes her hands down the front of her coat several times as if brushing away dirt.

"Done," she says.

"Ma'am?"

She walks to the door, opens it, and points for me to go.

I grab my coat off the cot and barely make it through the door before it is authoritatively slammed shut behind me.

CHAPTER SIXTEEN

GOOD ADVICE

Possum's waiting. He's well away from the infirmary door, leaning back against one of the elm trees by the steps.

"Any survivors?" he asks, walking forward to help as I struggle to pull my coat over my aching arm.

I almost say no. I'm pretty sure that would get a laugh from him. But nothing seems funny right now, not even the way he is scrunching up his face at me. Getting my hair hacked off and needles stabbed in me was no picnic. But the truly painful thing for me was answering questions about my family to someone as cold and uncaring as Mrs. Wilting.

If that's what everyone's like here at this place, I'm ready to run away right now.

I blink, fighting back the tears that are ready to flow like a river.

"Jay Bird," Possum says. His voice is soft. He puts one arm around my shoulder. "I know. When you first get here, it feels like the end of the world. Right."

I have to nod my naked head at that.

"But don't you worry," he says. "From here on in . . . ," he pauses. "From here on in it just gets worse."

That does make me laugh. Possum is laughing now, too.

He leads me over to the elm tree and sits me down against it.

"Just breathe," he says. "This old elm here's my favorite tree. It'll help you some."

It's the sort of thing Pop would say. It does make me feel better as I lean my head back against the rough bark and close my eyes.

When I open my eyes again, Possum is still here. He's squatting down in front of me, his back turned, tossing bits of twig at a fallen leaf. I appreciate him doing that, giving me some space to recover while standing by to help if need be.

I remember one of the three words Pop said to me. He only said it once, but it stuck in my mind like a burr caught on wool pants. I speak it slow so as to get it right. *"Mu-to."*

"Holy cow!" Possum says, turning his head around so far on his neck that he looks like an owl. "So he can talk? *Ehi?* Yes? And talk Indian, too, after all?"

I nod, then shake my head. I look down, running my right hand back over my prickly scalp.

"Yup," Possum says. "Can't get you to shut up, can I?" He favors me with that wide grin. "Seriously, though, you always this quiet, Jay Bird?"

That's a good question. And the answer is that I've never been overly talkative. Most times, I'd rather listen. However, over the last couple of days I have been much more—what was that word I read in my dictionary? Taciturn. That's it. I've been taciturn ever since Pop sprung it on me that he was Creek Indian. Which meant that I was sort of Indian, too. And that, he was leaving me at a new school. An Indian school. This Indian school.

Possum is still waiting for my answer. It's hard to start talking—other than grunting out a word or two—when you've been silent for a while. But he deserves an answer. He doesn't even know me, but he has been acting like a real friend. Not that I've ever really had one. In all my years at my old school I never did find anyone I felt as close to as I'm feeling toward Possum after just meeting him. So instead of staying silent, like I always used to do, I answer him.

"No," I say. "I usually talk more."

"Jehosaphat!" Possum says. "The seas are parting. Five whole words in a row."

I smile at him. "I can do better than that," I say, counting off the words on my fingers for him. Six this time.

"All right," Possum says, slapping my shoulder in a friendly way.

I grit my teeth. That slap would have felt a whole lot friend-lier if that was not the side where I just had those inoculations.

"Ooops," Possum says, seeing me wince. "Forgot about that."

"It's okay," I reply. I stand up, sling my pack over my other shoulder.

"Hold on," he says. "Is that pack all you got?"

"Yup," I say.

"What's in it?

I slip off the pack and sit back down, cross-legged, with the tree at my back.

I take everything out, place it on the ground between me and Possum, who's squatted down to his heels. He pokes the three

166

books—Bullfinch, Dictionary, London's novel—with his fingers. Then he picks up *The Call of the Wild.*

"This a good one?" he asks.

"Real good."

"Can I borrow it? Library here ain't worth an owl's hoot."

"It's yours," I say. "I read it three times."

His right eye twitches when I say that—which makes the scar on his cheek stand out more. What I just said surprised him, me offering that book. To be honest, I've surprised myself. Just a few days ago I never could have imagined myself parting with one of those books. But things are different now. Maybe I'm even different myself. And I can tell just how much having that book would mean to Possum. So I am okay, for certain, with letting it go.

"Really! You sure?" he says.

"Ehi," I say.

"You might not know it to look at me," Possum says, "but I love reading adventure stories—there aren't many in our library. It seems as if when I am reading such that I'm no longer here."

Like me, I think. The last time I read *The Call of the Wild* was just after Pop and I took to the road and I was missing Mom real bad. But reading it every night for a week straight helped me out of that sadness.

He looks up at me. "Ever read that *Treasure Island* book?"

I nod and hold up four fingers.

Possum chuckles. "I read it twice before it disappeared from the library here. Wasn't a student took it. The old superintendent

167

figured it was giving us boys the ideas about running away and all that."

He picks up the book with both hands, touches it to his forehead, then slides it into his shirt. He touches his chest, bows his head, and says real soft that second of the Creek words I know. *"Mu-to."*

He turns back, picks up a small stick. He uses it to lightly touch the remaining items exposed to view. Canteen, spare shirt, extra pair of well-worn cotton socks, my extra drawers. Mom's forlorn comb. Just about all my belongings.

Possum picks up the comb.

"Won't need this now, will you?"

He drops it back among my pitiful possessions.

"That," he says, speaking each word slowly, "is . . . all?"

"Yup."

"Left everything else back home?"

"Nope," I say. Then I add, just to make it clear, "No back home."

"No back home," Possum says.

"Had a farm."

"Bank took it?"

I nod.

Possum touches each of my possessions a second time with his stick.

"There's nothing else you own?"

"Just this."

I take out my jackknife, the French war medal, the shiny

quarter Miz Euler gave me, and another twelve coins. The fifty cents the cowboy gave me plus a few I've picked up off the ground as we traveled. I've always kept my eye out for the glint of metal as Pop and I have trudged along.

Possum gently taps the medal with his stick. "Your pop win this"

I shake my head.

"Somebody else? He give it to you?"

A nod is all that's needed.

"I'm guessing you did something for whoever that was."

"You could say that."

"That medal," he says, "you need to keep safe. Not from the other boys, mind you. We don't abide no sneak thieves. Especially in our gang which is all made up of straight shooters. It's more from some of those who run this place. Leave something like this around, it'll vanish like snow on a sunny day."

Possum tugs the shoulder of my shirt. "Now, far as the clothes you got, those they'll just throw away." He chuckles. "No big loss there. Far as personals go, I reckon that medal's the only thing you'd mourn the missing of."

He looks back toward Building One. "I heard about a bunch of Navajos was shipped here years back. Every one of them arrived wearing turquoise and silver jewelry. That got snatched away soon as they got here. Just to keep it safe, they were told. It was put into the strongbox in the office of Mr. J. I. Taykum. Superintendent before Morrell got here. That jewelry of theirs surely was safe—so safe those Navajo boys and girls never saw

169

none of it again. But Superintendent Taykum got him some fine new suits and a brand-new Model A Ford he drove off in when he left here."

Possum straightens up and jerks his head off to the left.

"Follow me."

I put my things back into my pockets and my pack.

We walk back behind the building a hundred yards till we get to a hedgerow.

"You'll have your own locker at the foot of your bed," Possum says. "Those two books of yours—they'll be fine in there. But you want to keep that medal safe. . . ."

He ducks through the hedgerow and slides down a slope. I follow close behind. Another hundred yards ahead is a small grove. Possum heads straight to the biggest tree at the far end, an old live oak with wide, spreading branches.

"Okay at climbing."

"Yup."

Possum swings up into the tree. He hops from one limb to another, agile as the animal he's nicknamed for. I follow close behind, just a hair slower but no less sure of myself. I practically lived in a tree like this back on our farm. It feels good to be off the ground, pulling myself up, branch after branch. Almost as good as being atop a fast freight.

Possum stops short of the top, the highest branches still some thirty feet above us.

"Here," he says, tapping an irregular slab of bark that's about a foot wide and two feet high. Leaning closer, I see that it's been fastened to the oak with an old hinge so rusty that it's lost its shine. It looks as much a part of the tree as that piece of bark.

Possum sticks two of his fingers under the side opposite the hinge and pries. The slab swings open. It's a door, cleverly made to blend in.

That's interesting, but what's more fascinating is what's inside. The cavity isn't quite large enough for a person to fit in, but it's plenty big to hold a passel of interesting-looking objects. Different shapes and sizes, all are wrapped in leather or cloth.

"Possum's personal hidey-hole," he says, a pride in his voice.

"Wow!" I reply.

Possum grins. "Just what I said when I found this here hollow. Took me a day to make my door just so. Not that the making was all that hard. I could only work on it when the shop teacher wasn't looking." He flicks an index finger against the hinge. "That was in the blacksmith's barrel of scrap to be melted down."

He grabs a branch over his head with one hand. His long fingers wrap all the way around it. He lifts his feet off the branch we're on and he dangles there, looking even more like a clothes-wearing version of an American marsupial.

"Jay Bird," he drawls, "you're the first I've showed this to."

"Why?" I ask.

Possum swings back and forth, reaching up his other hand to scratch his chin. "Well, you appear to be a man who can keep a secret."

He lets go, dropping back down so lightly that the branch

we're on hardly moves. "Being dead honest," he says, "it's on account of something my grampa Big Rabbit said. Sometimes you can recognize a friend on first sight. Came to mind when I first seen you and your old man in the stands."

He spits on his right palm and holds it out.

"Friends?" he says.

I spit on my own right palm.

We slap our palms together and shake on it.

"Okay," Possum says, turning back toward the hollow in the tree. "Lemme show you some of what we have got here."

He pulls out a long object rolled up in cloth with a string tied around it. Even before he finishes unwrapping it, I know what it is. An unstrung bow.

"Osage orange," he says, holding it out to me. "Best wood to make a bow."

I hold it in my left hand, feeling how well it fits there. I hand it back.

"You know how to use a bow?"

"Not really."

"That's okay. You'll learn. Got me plenty of arrows in here. Come next weekend, we can string it up and I'll show you how."

He wraps the bow back up and slides it back into its place. The next thing he brings out is almost the shape of the bow, but a little bulkier. It's wrapped not in cloth, but leather.

"Smoke-tanned this myself," Possum says as he rolls open the soft, light-colored hide. "Best to keep deerskin around it. Won't never rust. Grampa Rabbit once found a musket inside a hollow tree outside Okmulgee. Must have been stashed there about the time of the Trail when our folks got sent to the Indian Territory from Mississippi. The stock was eaten away, but the barrel was as shiny as when it got put in there a century ago."

He hands me the gun. "Winchester," he says. "Model 51 Imperial. Single shot .22. Made in 1919."

"Bolt action," I say, opening the breech to check that it's unloaded. I close it and sight down the barrel at a fox squirrel that's poked its head out from behind the trunk of the hickory tree fifty yards away. Then I hand the gun back.

"Okay," Possum says. "Grampa Big Rabbit said you can tell a lot about a man from how he handles a gun even before he shoots it."

I nod. His grampa must be a lot like Pop. "Treat every gun as loaded," I say. Words I've heard my father say a hundred times.

Possum nods as he gently rewraps his rifle. "Betsy here," he says, "is one fine squirrel gun. You like squirrel stew with gravy?"

I nod my head, feeling my mouth water as I do so. It's mid-morning and I've yet to put food in my belly. My empty stomach chooses that moment to growl loudly.

Possum squints his eyes at me. "You eat anything today?"

I shake my head, a little embarrassed at how loudly my stomach voiced its disapproval about being neglected.

"Here," he says, holding out a greasy paper bag he's lifted from a tight-lidded tin box from his hidey-hole.

I open the bag and the scent that rises makes my mouth water even more.

"Jerky," he says. "Me and the gang made it from some beef we liberated from the kitchen. "Take a piece. Heck, take two or three."

I do just that. Holding two of the leathery chunks of cured meat in my left hand, I lift the third piece to my mouth, tear off a bite with my side teeth, and start chewing it. It's tough, but tasty, smoky, and a little sweet. I swallow and take another bite.

"We added some brown sugar," Possum says. "Good innit?"

I nod. *"Mu-tu,"* I say. Then keep eating. I'm happy being fed like this, but something Possum just said is giving me pause. Two words. The gang.

That's the second time he's mentioned them. Who are they? And what are they going to think of me? Getting along with just Possum seems like something I might be able to do. But with a bunch of other boys, all of them strangers?

"Now this," Possum says, putting away the jerky and taking out yet another cloth-wrapped item from the hollow, "is what we come here for."

What he discloses is a cedar box, not much larger than a book. He opens it and holds it out so I can see the treasures he's placed inside it and names as he takes each one out and then replaces it.

"One 1899 silver dollar, my grampa's gold watch, this arrowhead I found, wing feather from a red-tailed hawk, and, best of all, this here Cherokee rose."

He hands me the last thing he's named. It's not really a rose, though it sort of looks like one. It's a piece of red sandy stone.

"Ever seen one before? You know the story?"

I shake my head.

"You know how us civilized tribes got forced out of the South?"

I nod.

"Of course you do. Story is that near the end of the trail, the people's feet were all bloody from the walking. And as they walked along this one part of the Arkansas River, every drop of blood they lost turned into one of these. So they called them Cherokee roses. And you can find them to this day along that stretch of river."

As he speaks those words it starts to happen. I'm walking along that river, looking down at my feet. Except they're not my own. They're too big to be mine. They're aching from all the endless miles of walking, miles that wore out my shoes. Now, even though it's cold, they're just wrapped in rags. Where the rags don't cover them there are cuts and scars. But I am not paying much mind to myself. I'm too concerned about the old man next to me. I'm helping him along because he's so weak. His own rag-wrapped brown feet are leaving bloody footprints. He's bent over, his long white hair falling across his face as he limps along.

He turns to talk to me and even the words he speaks are not in English, somehow I understand.

Leave me, Grandson, he says. *I am done.*

No, I say, picking him up. *You carried me when I was little. Now I will carry you.*

I blink my eyes and that vision is gone.

175

What I see instead is Possum reaching out to take the Cherokee rose from my palm.

He returns the stone to the box, slides down so he is sitting, leaning back against the tree trunk. Then we just sit there for a time, neither of us speaking. He looks at me, his head to one side, as if he knows something just happened. But I don't say anything about what I just experienced and he doesn't ask.

"You want," he finally says, holding out the open box, "you can use this here for safekeeping."

I nod. There's no better place I can think of than in the company of that red stone.

I hand him my France Victory Medal.

THE DORM

We walk back up the hill from the grove where Corporal Dart's France Victory Medal is now keeping company with Possum's hidden treasures. I am feeling a little better, better than at any time since Pop told me he was leaving me here. True, my arm is aching like it got kicked by a mule. But I'm not going to be isolated here at this Indian school. Marooned on a desert island like Robinson Crusoe.

Or maybe sort of like Robinson Crusoe, with my new friend Possum as my Man Friday.

Then again, this is far from a desert island. How many boys did Pop and me see marching on that field? Four hundred or more. And there were just as many girls in the stands.

Counting teachers and all, there's more than a thousand.

A thousand!

I've never before been around so many people. Every day I am going to be surrounded by folks I don't know. And now that knot's back in my stomach.

We've reached the back of Building Four. I start to walk around toward the big front steps. Possum stops me.

"Good time to show you this. No one else being around."

He jerks his chin toward a huge vine growing up the side

of the building. Pretty much covering the whole back. It's been growing there for years. Some of its branches are as big around as tree limbs. It's fastened itself firm, tendrils digging in like fingers into the stone and wood. It's like a part of the building itself, reaching all the way up just short of the roof.

"Virginia creeper," Possum says. "Our private stairway. Nice, innit?"

He grasps a thick branch of the vine and starts to climb. I'm expected to follow. Which I do.

We scale that vine until we reach a window it encircles. Old, dried scars on the vine show where it's been cut back to keep it from covering the opening.

Possum's already opened the window and slid inside.

I peer in to see what I am about to enter. It's a long, low-ceilinged space with cots off to either side. The narrow aisle between them leads to a door at the far end of the room. Thirty narrow cots are crammed in here, fifteen to each side. All but one of them made up, sheets and blankets tucked so tight a dropped penny would bounce. Each bed has a small metal trunk at its foot.

But that's not all I'm seeing. I've been here before in my vision as Pop told the story about Charlie Cornsilk. A chill runs down my back as I stare into this all-too-familiar room.

Possum's already sitting on one of the cots, two beds down from the window.

"Come on in," he says, waving at me. "Welcome to our home sweet home."

178

He looks down the aisle. "One there in the middle," he says, indicating the one unmade cot. "That'll be yours."

I slide over the sill. The room's cramped, small for the number of people sleeping here every night. Last time I saw it, though, in that vision or daydream, there were even more cots.

"Middle of the room," Possum grins, "at's where the new boys get to sleep. Smells get the worst there in the night—'specially when they serve beans for dinner, which is every other night."

He pats his cot. "Not like mine, near to the window."

I walk over to the narrow cot. Mine tonight. And night after night after that. The room seems even smaller. Though I've tried not to show it on my face, Possum might have noticed I'm feeling anxious. He doesn't know the half of it. I reach up to the rafter that slopes down low over the bed. With my right index finger I trace the faint letters carved into the wood.

C.C.

Just like in my dream.

Possum walks over to sit down on my cot. He bounces up and down on it a few times, the springs creaking under his weight.

"Not bad," he says. "Some are so worn out you might's well be in a hammock."

I'd rather be in a hammock. Or on the wooden floor of a boxcar. Anywhere but here as long as I was with Pop. I picture the two of us together. We're walking down a country road, wind in our faces, birds singing from the trees.

"You missing that home you lost, Jay Bird?"

I shake my head.

"No?" Possum says. He looks a little confused at my answer. Surely he expected I was feeling homesick. He's been so kind so far that he deserves a better answer.

"I'm missing the road."

"The road?" Possum says. He looks really confused now.

A few words aren't going to do it this time. I take a breath while he waits.

"Knights of the road," I say. "That is what Pop and me were."

A light seems to come on in Possum's eyes.

"Hoboes?" he said. "You guys were hoboes?"

I nod.

"How long?"

"One year," I say.

"Holy jeezum," Possum says. "Jumping freight trains?"

I nod again.

"Sleeping out under the stars?"

Another nod.

"Oh man, I bet you got some stories."

"We do," I say.

"Tell me some? But not now." He stands up, looks over at the window. "They may run our lives in the day here. But not after dark."

I'm not sure what he means by that. I don't have time to ask. I've just noticed, as he has, the sounds of feet coming up the stairs outside the door. I think of bolting for the window, climbing down the vine and running.

Possum grabs my arm.

"Hold on," he says. "No heading for the hills. They'd just catch you and drag you back."

"In here." The door is opened by the person who just spoke. Superintendent Morrell. My father's right behind him.

My father looks straight at me, taking in my shorn dome. A sad look comes over his face, but he doesn't say anything.

The superintendent, though, is anything but silent.

"Excellent," he says. "You already appear much more civilized, young man. A lad of this century and not the benighted long-haired past. Next we shall rid you of those rags. Get you into proper clothes."

His gaze turns to Possum. "Showing our new recruit his quarters?"

"Yes, sir," Possum replies, straightening up to attention.

"Excellent, indeed." He turns to Pop. "As you can see, with the addition of our new house since you were here, we no longer crowd so many into each room. Further, each cadet . . ." he taps one of the metal footlockers with his toe, ". . . has a place for his personal items."

Morrell looks down his long nose at me. "I assume you are impressed with our facilities. Especially the addition of the washrooms down the hall. No longer must our lads traipse outdoors to use the outhouse as they did during your father's tenure with us."

Morrell doesn't notice Possum squeezing his nose and looking up at the ceiling at the mention of those indoor toilets. Pop does, though. A little smile creases his mouth.

"Now then," the superintendent says, gesturing broadly, "back downstairs. Your father needs to take his leave since he has—I believe—a ticket for this afternoon's train. One of our agricultural science teachers is driving in to town and can drop him at the depot. You can say your farewells before Mr. Aird escorts you over to obtain your uniform."

We follow Morrell down the stairs, waving his hands as he goes on about something or other all the way. But I am not hearing a word. All I can hear is a voice in my head.

Pop is leaving me, Pop is leaving me.

At the bottom of the stairs, Morrell stops talking for a moment. He takes my father's hand and looks into his face.

"You have done well by yourself and our nation with your service," the superintendent says. "Leaving your lad in our care is a wise decision. We shall make a gentleman farmer out of him, a credit to his race."

Pop nods and lets out a breath.

"I just hope," my father says, "my boy'll do well."

"Indeed, indeed," Morrell says, smiling benevolently. "Adieu, then."

He strides away, leaving us standing there. Possum walks over to study the bark of one of the smaller trees fifty feet away. I'm alone with Pop.

For the first time in my life I feel awkward around my father. I do not know what to say or do. The two of us stand side by side, looking out over the broad lawn that stretches in front of the big imposing buildings of the school.

"You going to be okay, Cal?" Pop asks, not turning my way.

No, I think. *I'm not.*

But I know what Pop wants to hear. Needs to hear. Since he explained his plan he's been happier. Going to Washington and getting his bonus money can get us back a farm again. There's only one answer I can give him.

"Yes," I say. I reach into my pocket, pull out Mom's comb, hand it to him.

"I'll take good care of this, son," Pop says as he places it in his pocket, his voice a little hoarse.

"I know," I say.

Then I bite my lip and look down at the ground.

Pop turns to hug me.

Hug me one last time.

CHAPTER EIGHTEEN

NEW DUDS

Possum comes back from that interesting tree. He stands beside me as we watch my father walking away. Pop does not look back. When you've said good-bye, after the first step you're already gone. Looking back just confuses things.

"You okay, Jay Bird?"

"No," I say. No point in not being honest with him.

"That's all right," Possum says. "None of us are ever okay when we end up here. But you know what the best part is from here on in?"

"It just gets worse?"

Possum slaps me on the back. "You got it," he chuckles. "Now let's get you some new duds."

The campus of the Indian school is so vast. It's as if the place was built to instill a sense of awe in those sent here. Make them feel small and powerless. That's what it's done to me.

Huge as the school grounds are, though, everything is—as Mom used to say—neat as a pin. Not even a single fallen leaf anywhere on the ground.

"Cleaner than your ma's kitchen counter, ain't it?" Possum asks. He's noticed me gaping at everything. Like some country hick seeing an elephant for the first time.

"Yup," I admit.

"Easy enough when you got over eight hundred slaves to do your bidding." A humorless chuckle follows his words. "On grounds duty you dang well make sure every blade of grass is cut the same height or there's hell to pay."

We walk past Building Two. Possum jerks his chin toward the two buildings far to our right.

"Girls' Dorms over there," Possum says. "Don't get caught too close. That's a hanging offense."

We turn left. Ahead of us, down the gravel road, are the smaller buildings where the superintendent told us carpentry and harness making and the like are taught.

There are other boys around. We've passed quite a few as we've been walking. Some alone, some in groups. Some our age, some younger and some older. Though none have actually come up to us, all have raised a hand or spoken a word or two in greeting to my guide.

Possum's answered each of them with that grin of his, a wave, an easy reply.

"How's it going?"

"Okay."

"Hey, Possum."

"Hey, Deacon."

Me, I've said nothing. And none of the boys have asked "Who's that with you?" It's almost been as if I'm invisible.

That's strange. In my past experience, everyone's curious about a new kid. Some want to meet you. Others want to make

185

friends. A few want to feel you out to see if they can bully you. But not here.

Maybe they think I'm not worth knowing.

Whatever the reason, I'm sort of grateful for it. I don't want to meet anyone. I don't want to be friendly. All I really want is to not be here.

Possum's been easy to be with. But is he really my friend? Am I fooling myself? Maybe he's just putting up with me. This school is his place, not mine. Tomorrow, when the routine here kicks back in, he's not going to have time for me. I'll be on my own. He'll be back with—his gang.

I'll be on my own, without Pop to guide me and be by my side every day and every night. I'll be alone in a crowd of kids who have nothing in common with me.

As we walk along, I notice something. Set back a ways behind those buildings is an ugly low flat-roofed stone structure that looks out of place. While the other buildings have had at least a few people around them, this one is totally deserted. It's not just dark in color, it has an air of darkness around it—as if bad things happened there—were meant to happen there.

I squint my eyes and study it further as we walk. I've always had eyesight that is keen. Like a red-tail hawk, Pop says. So even at this distance I can see that the heavy door at its front is padlocked and the place looks abandoned. Set up high on the one sidewall that's visible is a window with iron bars.

Possum stops again, once more knowing where I'm looking. "Draws your eyes, don't it?"

"It does."

"We don't go there anymore. No one does. No one goes any-where near there. That's the old guardhouse. One of the good things Old Morrell did was close it down soon as they promoted him to superintendent. Now they don't lock you up in there when you break one of their hunnerd thousand rules."

Something is happening to me as I'm looking at the old guardhouse. It's as if a part of me is leaving my body, passing through that padlocked door.

And now, somehow, that's where I am. I'm trapped in here. There's the strong smells of mildew and urine. On one shadowy wall is a plank bed and a wadded up blanket. I make out in the faint light that the floor beneath my feet is packed dirt. I look up at the barred window. No sunlight is shining through. It's the ghostly beam of light from the full moon that is enabling me to see what's around me.

"Jay Bird, where you at?"

I shake my head to clear it. Possum is staring at me. I don't know how long I've been in that vision. So I do what I always do whenever I get taken over. I do not let on that anything unusual has happened to me.

Then Possum surprises me.

"Does that happen often?" he asks.

"What?" I say. Maybe a little too quick.

"Seeing," he says. His tone is matter-of-fact, "Had me an aunt who was *heles-hayu*, a medicine person. She used to do that. She'd have that same look on her face when she was *seeing* something. *Hece.* Maybe something in the past, maybe even seeing something in the future."

"Oh," I say.

I'm standing still, my mind going a mile a minute because of what Possum just said in such a matter-of-fact way. There's others like me? And there's even a name in Indian for seeing past events through other people's eyes like I do sometimes. And what was that he said about seeing things in the future?

"Want to talk about it?" Possum asks.

I shake my head. I'm not sure if it makes me feel better or worse that others can have the same kind of experiences I've been having. I haven't even talked about my seeing things with anyone. Even Pop. And I'm sure as blazes not ready to start blabbing about it now.

"Okay," Possum says. Then he points again with his chin at the old guardhouse. "Anyhow, like I said, they don't use that no more."

"They use the lockup on the porch now, right?"

Possum nods. "You don't miss much, do you, Jay Bird? Good thing 'bout being there—up on the porch—is everyone knows you are there. No one can do anything to you without someone else knowing. They may have you on moldy bread and stale water, but there's no way they can beat you bloody in secret. Morrell does not stand for *that* kind of beating."

"*That* kind?" I ask.

"Well," Possum grins, "some of us boys get real stubborn. So they got to do something now and then to put the fear of the Lord in us, right? You do not want to see our dorm matron when she has got a switch in her hand. She is a true believer in that part of the Bible that says spare the rod and spoil the child."

I have never been hit even once in my life by Pop. Mom was just the same—firm in what she expected, but gentle with her hands.

I keep walking, my eyes on the ground, which is also where my heart is right about now.

"Your Pa ever hit you?" Possum asks.

"No."

"Mine neither." His left hand touches the scar on his cheek. "I never got this from him."

"Who?" I ask.

Possum shakes his head. "Far as anyone save me and one other knows, I got this two years ago here when I was alone in the barn and fell on the sharp edge of something. The one who did it was sorry once he saw how deep I was cut by his ring. Just meant to slap me cuz I'd sassed him. Got me right to the infirmary. But that would make no never mind to my pa. If my pa ever found out it was no accident, there would truly be hell to pay. He'd come here with his gun and end up hanging for manslaughter. So you forget I ever said anything. Promise?"

"Promise," I agree. Then, seeing how serious the look is on Possum's face, I add "My word as a knight of the road."

Possum shakes his head. "No point dwelling on the past. Can't get back water once it's under the bridge. Right?"

He doesn't wait for me to nod my head. That familiar grin has returned to his face like the sun coming out from behind a bank of clouds.

"All right," he says. "Now let's get hustling. Get your government issue from the tailor shop and your bullhides at the harness shop. If you're in luck, you might get something halfway close to your size."

The tailor shop is neat as a pin inside. There's a small assortment of clothes on the first table as we walk in the door and a box off to the side. Behind that table is a serious-looking, stocky boy. He's shorter than either of us, but twice as broad. If I had to guess at his age, I would say he was a year older than me. His dark face is as impassive and round as the moon. His brows are so thick they look like big caterpillars. He raises both of them as we approach that table.

"Possum," he says.

"Skinny," Possum replies. He looks over his shoulder, taking a quick glance toward the door. No one else anywhere close.

"*Mu-to*, brother," he says in a low voice.

"*Mu-to,*" Skinny replies just as soft, his face impassive.

Possum grins.

"Skinny here may have a redneck drawl, him being from Mississippi, but he is just as Creek as you and me, Jay Bird. Brought us three new songs we had never heard before when he first came here two years ago. At our stomp dances he takes the lead from Deacon now and then."

Stomp dances? What are those?

Possum nods his head toward the clothes spread out on the table. "Looks like you dug out all the fancy duds."

A hint of a smile has come to Skinny's face. He reaches out

190

one hand, his fingers fat as sausages, to pick up a pair of overalls.

"Sized him up from a distance," Skinny says, his voice a slow drawl. "I guessed these here might fit."

Possum turns to me. "You're in luck, Jay Bird," he says. "When they give you your outfit at the start of the school year there's a hunnerd in line. They just toss you whatever's closest to hand whilst they herd you through. Sometimes you get overalls so short in the leg they look like knee britches. But Skinny here has a fine eye for a man's size."

The overalls are followed by cotton underwear, two pairs of wool socks, two shirts, a denim jacket.

"Work clothes," Skinny says. "Won't need the coat much now. Come winter when you are out afield and a Blue Norther is a-blowing you'll be grateful you have got it."

I nod, even though I'm thinking that next winter I'll be far from here with Pop on our new farm.

Possum reaches up to slip my pack from my shoulder. "Strip your old duds off," he says. "Toss them into the rag barrel there." He turns his back. "Skinny and me won't look."

I slip off my shoes and socks, throwing my old things into the barrel as I do so. I'm not embarrassed about taking my clothes off with others around. I've had to do it often enough when Pop and I were soaked by the rain and, once the downpour stopped, stand naked in front of a fire. But I'm going to miss my old clothes. The shirt and pants are worn so soft that they're like a second skin—despite the many places they were sewed back together and patched.

The cotton underwear is scratchy. The new overalls and shirt are stiff. But I have to admit they're in way better shape than what I was wearing. The first new clothes I've had in over a year. Some tramps manage to dress fine by stealing off of clotheslines. But such behavior is below true knights of the road such as Pop and me.

"You decent or still naked as a jay bird?" Possum says, chuckling at his joke. He turns around before I can answer him.

Skinny nods his head. "Y'all shows some improvement," he says. He adjusts my shirt, tightens the shoulder straps of my overalls. "All set for picking rocks in the fields. Or maybe a-swamping out the horse stables."

He looks at my face as he says those last few words. Likely to see if it changes any due to his mention of hard chores. But stoop labor has never bothered me. I just look back and nod. He grabs one of my hands and turns it palm up. He feels the callouses there with a meaty finger twice the size of any of my own.

"Done some work, y'all?"

He slaps his wide hands against my shoulders.

"Hmm," he says. "Pretty sound. Might make a good tackle if he gets another year and some more weight on those bones."

"Skinny here," Possum says, "is the center on the school football team. Next season's co-captain. Last year we went seven and three."

Skinny smiles for the first time, showing a set of teeth as wide and white as marble tombstones. "Ah-yup," he says. "Would of won the Haskell game if'n the referees had not been a-paid off."

He turns toward me. "Come by the field next fall if'n you've put on another twenty pounds."

He holds out his hand and we shake. But he doesn't leave it at that. As he releases my hand, he slides his arm forward to grasp my forearm just short of the elbow. Without much of a pause, I grasp his forearm that same way, squeeze it once as he does mine. Skinny then opens his hand, slides it back, slaps my open palm and then grasps my hand with our thumbs linked, our fingers on the back of each other's hands. It's a series of moves easy to follow, so I have no trouble doing it.

"All right!" Possum says.

I'm not sure why Possum looks so impressed. But I nod my head.

Skinny lets go of my hand, ducks down below the table, and comes up with another pile of clothes. All neatly folded, they're a far cry from the everyday work duds I have just donned. I recognize that they are parts of uniforms I've seen on hoboes such as Pop who are vets.

"Government surplus," Skinny drawls. "Ever-thing from the high collar to the wrap leggings. Keep 'em clean and neat, Jay Bird. Wear only to drill."

He looks down at my feet. Though I have on one pair of my new socks, I slipped my old shoes over them.

"Shoe and harness shop next," he says.

The shoe and harness shop is a hundred feet from the tailor shop. We can get there in two shakes of a lamb's tail. But Possum stops me halfway.

193

"Here," he says, holding out his hand. Then he does with me that entire routine of arm grab, slap, and interlinked thumbs I went through with Skinny.

When we're finished, he raises an eyebrow. "Done that before?" he asks.

"Yup," I say.

Possum slaps his leg. "I thought so. Who taught you? Your pa?"

I shake my head.

"Who then?"

"Skinny," I say. "Five minutes ago." Then I laugh at the expression on his face.

"Dang," Possum says. "You got a sense of humor after all, Jay Bird. You really learn that fast?"

"You could say that," I reply.

Possum shakes his head. "I surely could. Most folks like you just as soon as they meet you, don't they?"

Not really, I think. But then again, though I've never thought about it before, it seems as if Possum might have a point. I try to keep to myself, being quiet and all, but some of the people I meet do act right friendly.

"Well, I guess you could say that," I reply.

Possum's grin actually gets wider.

"You know what that was?" he asks. "That handshake I just gave you?"

"Nope."

"The Challagi Creek handshake," Possum says. "Made up right here at this very school. Only done one Creek to another.

194

When somebody like Skinny does that with you, Jay Bird, it means you're accepted in as one of us."

That's good, I suppose, being accepted and all. But how long will it last when folks find out who I really am? Which is what? An Indian passing for white? A white boy who now has to be an Indian? It makes my head hurt.

Possum pokes me in the ribs.

"Turn round," he says.

I plant my left foot, put weight on my trailing leg, and pivot into a fast About Face. I've already sensed the presence of people coming up behind us.

Six boys. Arranged in a V formation like a flock of geese in flight. They're all wearing sweaters. All but one of those sweaters are gray. Only one is red. It's on the biggest boy at the head of their formation. The head goose. His face looks like it was carved of stone. He's set his course straight toward me.

Possum starts to say something. The red-sweatered head goose raises his right hand to shoulder height, palm forward, then quickly curls it into a fist. Possum shuts his yap. Then the red-sweater boy stops dead in front of me.

I wait for him to speak a word of greeting. Maybe in Indian, there being no school employees around. But he just stands there as the other boys arrange themselves in a circle around me.

I can guess what's coming next. Every school has its own groups that stick together. These boys make up what Possum's called his gang. Head Goose here is the leader. And now I'm about to be tested, like newcomers are at any school.

I should be nervous. But I have just plumb used up all my nervousness.

So I just wait.

As does he, looming half a head above me.

I keep looking off a little to his right and not saying a thing.

No ganging up or kicking while you're down, Pop said. They won't fight like white men.

More silence.

Then someone farts.

Not me. Nor Possum or the big boy in the red sweater. It's a long-limbed, wide-lipped boy with big ears that stick out from his head.

"Little Coon!" the head goose snaps, putting a load of seriousness into his voice.

"Sorry, Bear Meat," Little Coon drawls. Then he giggles.

He's not the only one amused by his unintentional breaking of the serious silence. That long drawn-out fart of his broke whatever tension the head goose was trying to build. All of the boys gathered around me are trying not to laugh. But not with much success.

"Hush up," Bear Meat growls. He turns his attention back to me.

"You!" he says, his voice purposefully deep.

"Me," I reply, my voice so matter of fact it surprises me.

I wouldn't normally make a joke out of being confronted like this. But I'm not in the mood right now to be buffaloed.

I smile at Bear Meat. He shakes his head.

"You don't look like much," he snarls.

"Ehi," I agree.

196

Possum laughs out loud. The others are holding back smiling. But no one's coming up yet to slap me on the back and welcome me into their gang.

"What you got in your pockets?" Bear Meat rumbles.

I push one hand into the pockets of my pants so new they crackle like heavy paper. I grasp my few coins, open my palm so he can see them.

I halfway expect Bear Meat to command me to give the coins to him. Instead he shakes his head.

"Put that away," he says. "Other pocket."

I bring out my jackknife.

"Nice knife," he says. "You want to give that to me?"

"Nope," I reply.

I stand there, my closed knife on my open palm. I brace myself to be pushed or punched. But that does not happen. Bear Meat furrows his brows and looks into my face.

"No?" he says. "How come?"

"Give a man a knife," I say, "you cut off any chance of him being a friend."

Bear Meat looks over at Possum, who shrugs and spreads his hands open.

Bear Meat grasps his chin with one hand, resting his elbow in the other hand.

"Tell you what," he says, "I'll rassle you for it."

He's bigger than me and likely just as much stronger. I don't want to lose my jackknife. But what else can I do?

I nod.

Possum holds out his right hand. I put my knife into it.

The other boys have moved back from us. The one called Little Coon is scraping a twenty-foot circle around us in the dry red soil with a stick.

"Loser's first one to say give or get throwed out the ring," Little Coon says in a slow drawl.

Bear Meat drops into a low stance, hands held out in front of his body. Each of his broad mitts is a size bigger than mine.

"Dirt Seller," Bear Meat says to the bowlegged boy to Possum's right. "You give the go."

"Okeydoke," Dirt Seller replies. He raises his right hand high in the air.

Out of the corners of my eyes I can see that our group got considerably larger while Bear Meat and I were confabulating. All kids—whatever their skin color—seem to sense when a brawl's about to happen. They're drawn to it like flies to molasses. Where there were nine of us minutes ago now there's dozens.

Unlike a fight in a white school yard, though, this crowd is pretty quiet. No one is screaming or yelling for Bear Meat to kill me. Everyone's mostly just watching. Not that they're totally quiet.

"Who's he?" I hear someone say.

"New kid," another person answers.

"Jay Bird," Possum corrects him.

"Pancake right quick," a fourth boy opines.

"GO!" Dirt Seller yells, chopping his hand down like an ax splitting wood.

I thought I was ready, but Bear Meat moves fast for so big a guy. Before I know it he's grabbed my arm with one hand and swung his foot to hit my leg and knock me off balance.

That kick to my left shin hurts, but I manage to pull free and avoid being thrown out of the circle. My well-worn shoes, not yet traded in for a new pair of bullhides, now has one sole that is loose. As I hop to one side, it catches on the ground and almost trips me.

"Nice try," a thin-faced boy who was one of the original five says. "You get him next time, Bear."

Bear Meat has stepped back, measuring me now that his first attempt to throw me failed. We circle. He's so much bigger than me that my strength's outmatched.

Watch what a man does and keep doing.

That's what Pop told me.

Bear Meat tries to grab hold of me. I duck back. When I do that, he crosses his legs as he circles. That's the third time he's done that.

Okay.

As his legs cross a fourth time I dive in. My shoulder hits his knees hard and I wrap my arms around his legs.

But he doesn't go down. Hitting him is like tackling a tree stump. I just about dislocate my shoulder. Then he drops all his weight right on top of me.

WHOOMPH. The air goes out of my lungs. I'm stuck on my belly with him on top, though I am still holding tight to his knees.

"Aitch-dee!" someone calls out in a loud whisper.

Though I can't breathe and feel three-quarters dead I recognize it as Possum's voice.

"Head disciplinarian," someone else says.

Bear Meat's weight suddenly lifts off me.

"What is going on here?" a harsh voice demands.

Boys are being pushed back in every direction. A white man so big he makes Bear Meat look like a pip-squeak is thrusting his way toward us. The head disciplinarian.

Bear Meat reaches a hand down and pulls me up to my feet. Though I feel like I have just been run over by a steamroller, I straighten my back and square my shoulders as the head disciplinarian reaches us.

He stares at me. "What happened, boy? Somebody knock you down. Point him out!"

There's no sympathy in his voice. He is just itching to have the excuse to punish someone.

"No, sir," I whisper, using what little air is left in me.

"WHAT?" the man bellows, leaning so close that the hot air from his lungs washes over my face and about chokes me.

I turn my face to the side, inhale a deep breath, then tilt my head back to look up at him.

"No, sir," I say. "Nobody pushed me. I fell." Which is pretty much true, though I do omit the part about someone falling on top of me.

The HD looks skeptical, so I point to my right foot. "My shoe's broken."

I reach out and put my hand on Bear Meat's arm. "He helped me up."

The big man stares around the circle.

200

"That is the Gospel truth, for sure," Little Coon says, "Mr. HD, sir."

The HD glares at him. "Shut your trap, Oliver." He stabs me in the chest with his thumb. "You're a disgrace like your father."

As he walks away I feel as if I should have said something.

My pop is not a disgrace. He served in France while you were here bullying little boys.

But I didn't. And I am feeling lower than a snake's belly.

Someone grabs my shoulder. It's Bear Meat. We are still standing in that circle Little Coon scratched into the red soil. Is he about to try again to throw me? Let him. I don't care. There's no way this day could get worse.

But instead of throwing me, he slides that arm around my shoulders.

"You're all right, Jay Bird," he says.

The other boys in the gang are coming up, shaking my hand in the Creek way. Possum places my jackknife in my palm after he shakes it. I start to hand the knife to Bear Meat.

He shakes his head. "Naw," he says. "Keep your knife." He slaps me on the shoulder. "You sit at our table for mess."

CHAPTER NINETEEN

MESS

Mess. Mess is the military word for a meal, in case you don't know. Like a lot of things here at Challagi—the marching, the uniforms, the strict discipline—the army is supposed to be the model for much of what goes on here.

Here, though, in the mess hall, it seems as if a good part of that discipline has just flown out the window. Though I am not saying there are no rules.

Possum is spelling them out to me as we march into the room and scramble to get to our tables. As he talks, Possum steers me toward the one by the west wall that belongs to our gang.

"Talking's okay in here. Jes' no hooting and hollering. Stay at your table until the old bugle blows. Then, exit the mess," he says. "Most important, eat as much as you can before we got to get up and go."

The smell of meat and potatoes is greeting my nose even before we've reached our gang's table. But there's no eats there. As I slide onto the bench, all I see are metal plates, dull-looking pewter forks and spoons, and empty mugs. No food at all. I turn my head to make out where that aroma of food is coming from.

Deacon, who's sitting on my right, chuckles. "Settle down, Jay Bird. Food's still in the kitchen," he drawls.

Little Coon's across the table from me. "You a-feeling hungered?" he asks.

I surely am. My belly is growling and my mouth is watering. Aside from Possum's jerky, I haven't eaten anything all day. My stomach is about to move in with my backbone. Last time I tasted victuals was after Pop and I loaded in those horses. Since then I've walked and gotten a ride, been poked with needles, scalped, stripped, and practically turned into a pancake in my wrestling match with Bear Meat—who's sitting at the head of our table, knife and spoon held ready in his hands.

"Get set for grub, son," he says to me.

"Ah-yup," Little Coon says. "Food's terrible here and there's not enough of it. So y'all be ready."

I look around the huge room. The biggest I have ever been in. Big enough to fit every one of the eight hundred or so students with room to spare. Big enough to leave a sizable aisle between the tables where us boys are sitting and those far to the left occupied by the girls. Matrons are standing to keep watch on that space between the sexes.

Possum points with his lips at the line of demarcation.

"That there is no-man's-land," he chuckles. "Everything but land mines and barbed wire."

There are better tables around the outside of the room. They have cloths on them unlike our bare wood ones. Teachers and school staff are at those fine tables. Far away as they are, my eyesight's keen enough to see that they have glassware, not mugs. Their silver knives, forks, and spoons glitter.

They're already being served by student waiters coming out of the doors to the kitchens in back.

Little Coon leans toward me. "Now that there's a job I would not mind having," he says. "Waiters and kitchen workers are about the only ones can get fat here. Specially working the tables where staff sits. Always lots of leftovers on their plates."

"BOW YOUR HEADS!"

That command has just come from the tall man standing up at the head of the biggest table. Superintendent Morrell.

Everyone's head goes down, but it's not dead silent. The rattling of dishes from the kitchen, the shuffling of hundreds of pairs of student feet on the floor drown out the grace spoken in a normal tone by Superintendent Morrell who's standing, hands raised, palms out, like a surrendering soldier. All the assembled multitude hears is his final word.

"Amen!"

It's echoed like a rumble of thunder from everyone's lips, mine included.

"AMEN!"

"Here she comes," Little Coon says.

I look where's he's gesturing with his chin. A stream of waiters is exiting the kitchen. Some hold big pitchers. Others have serving plates on their shoulders.

Our table's among the first. The pitchers are brimming with fresh buttermilk, white and foamy. As soon as the pitcher is plopped down on the plank table Bear Meat grabs it and begins filling the mugs passed to him one by one. Out of the corner of my eye I can see things are not as well organized at other tables. There, many hands are grabbing for those pitchers.

But then the plates of potatoes and meat are slammed down by the waiters. The potatoes look overcooked and lumpy. The beef's nearly gray in color and ribbed with gristle. But it makes no matter how this food looks. It's like tossing a rabbit into a pack of wolves. Even Bear Meat, head of the gang though he may be, can't control the chaos of spoons and forks stabbed at the food from every direction. My own included. Pop's warning about what happens at Challagi mealtimes is fresh in my mind.

It's amazing no one gets a hand impaled. And mighty sensible, I now realize, that we've not been issued knives for our meals. If we were, we'd likely end up with mangled mitts after chow. As it is, I check my plate to make sure no one's finger has ended up in the mess of tough meat and half-cooked spuds that's about to be my midday meal.

Possum eyes the sizable helping I got. He pokes me in the ribs with his elbow. "Jay Bird," he asks, raising an eyebrow, "you sure you never ate here before?"

It's a question I don't answer, being too busy forking food into my mouth. Chewing beef that would make shoe leather seem tender is not conducive to talking.

Possum chuckles and turns his attention to his own plate.

As I eat I look around the table at the faces of the Creek gang. Though I've only known them for a day they already look familiar. I never wanted to be here, but being accepted like this—a strange thing for me—makes me feel less abandoned than I did when I watched Pop walk away. Plus it feels good to stuff my gut. It's the fullest meal I've had since the dinner we ate on the train.

Little Coon looks up from his plate at me, grins, and then belches. To his left, Bear Meat follows suit, belching even louder, followed one by one by the others at our table. I can't help but smile as I take a breath and then let out a burp as loud as any of theirs.

My mind and my spirit may not be pleased about being stuck here at Challagi but my stomach sure doesn't mind.

"Biscuits!" Little Coon yells, and everyone's attention turns toward grabbing at least one or two from serving plates that are empty before they even touch the table.

IN STEP

I sit up in bed, confused about everything. Where am I? What was that earsplitting sound that just woke me up? And why am I hearing other people moving and talking all around me?

I rub my eyes. There's hardly any light to see by.

"Pop?" I whisper.

Someone grabs my shoulder and shakes it.

"Wake up, boy! Didn't you hear the bugle?"

The face thrust in front of mine is not my father's. It's a younger man. His dark eyes are deep-set and close together. His broad brow is knitted above his thin eyebrows. His earth-colored cheeks are scarred with the pocks from a bad case of chicken pox as a child. His lips are thick, his chin broad, and there's a gap between his front teeth. When he speaks it's with a lisp. But despite that seemingly unattractive catalog of features, the face staring at mine is a pleasant one.

C.B.

His name comes to me at the same time I realize where I am. Where I've been for over a week now.

Challagi Indian School.

C.B. is the boys' adviser for House Four. He's Cherokee, graduated from this school seven years ago. His room is one floor down.

"Blackbird," C.B. says. His voice is firm but not unkind, "Am I gonna have to dowse you again to get you up?"

Like he did the first morning I was here and refused to stir. I just kept trying to dig further into my dream of riding a fast freight to California by Pop's side.

When nothing else roused me—not Possum tickling my nose with a feather, or Deacon prodding the sole of my bare foot with a stick—C.B. knew what to do. He heaved me up over one broad shoulder, carried me outside to the horse trough, dropped me in, and worked the handle of the pump so vigorously that I near drowned in the torrent of cold water.

"No, sir," I say.

I sit straight up and throw off my covers.

C.B. laughs.

"You slept in your uniform?"

"Yes, sir."

I pull on my boots, quickly put on the wrap leggings that were so much trouble for me to figure out six days ago.

I don't have any hair to comb, so that morning task's not needed. I didn't drink water before climbing into my cot, so I don't need to use the latrine down the hall.

Thank goodness for that!

I've had enough of that latrine to last a lifetime. First job I was assigned was to clean it several days ago. Walking in there, kerchief tied over my nose, brought to mind something I read in my mythology book. *The Labors of Hercules*. But Challagi Creek, the stream that runs through the school grounds, is half a mile away. No way I could divert it to flow away the stinking mess in that boys' room the way the world's strongest man ran a river through the Augean Stables.

No latrine for me.

Each night I follow the lead of Possum and Deacon and the others. They climb out the window after dark, go down the vine to use the old outhouse claimed for our gang fifty yards behind Building Four.

None of us go alone. There's something about being alone outside in the night that's unsettling. Not in the woods, but around the school campus.

I realized that the first night here. I woke up in the dark feeling the need to relieve myself. No one else was stirring, but I remembered the outhouse Possum had pointed out to me. I figured I could find it by myself.

Better than walking into that stinky washroom in the dark and stepping on who knows what.

I crept down the narrow aisle between bunks to the open window. I descended the Virginia creeper—easy as going down a ladder. Then I stood looking off to the east.

There was a bright half moon in the sky. The night was warm. When I looked west, in the direction of the low stone building that was the lockup before it was locked shut for good, a chill went down my back. I thought about climbing back up the vine. But then I heard a soft scrabbling sound, like a big squirrel on a tree trunk. A second later, Little Coon dropped to the ground beside me.

"Don't want to come down here alone," he said in a soft voice, rubbing his hands together.

There was enough light from the half moon for me to see his face—how serious his expression was. He pointed with his lips to the west. The direction of the old jail building half a mile away, a deeper shadow in the center of the dark field.

"Don't never go near there at night, Jay Bird."

The hair stood up on the back of my neck. A chill went down my back.

"Haunts," Little Coon whispered. "Some died in there, you know."

I closed my eyes and shook my head. The last thing I wanted was to know more about that. Or to be back there in one of my visions. Somehow, that worked. I opened my eyes and I was still in the present.

"Okay," I said. "Let's keep going."

Then, without another word, the two of us made our way east to the outhouse.

I thud down the stair, one ripple in a stream of boys all dressed alike in doughboy duds. Army surplus and never used, we've been told. But Ira, one of the boys in our all-Creek gang, swears that the uniform his older brother was issued when he was here five years ago had a bullet hole in it. Right over the heart. So I suppose it is possible I am kitted out in a dead man's clothes. Which seems only fitting seeing as how I am sleeping in a dead boy's cot, right under those initials of C.C. carved into the wooden rafter over my head.

Fortunately, though, since arriving here I've not shared any past lives in my dreams.

I line up proper. Back stiff, eyes straight. I don't twitch a muscle, having learned my lesson at inspection the first day. I shifted one foot and had it stomped on hard by our company officer. Ray Chapman is his name. He's determined, despite the fact he's been saddled with me in mid-semester, to win ribbons during Sunday Dress Parade. He's full-blood Cheyenne-Arapaho.

A *real* Indian. That's what Possum called him.

I've learned a lot in the seven days I have been here.

Little of that has been in the classrooms. The academic teachers here are lifelong employees of Indian schools and all are white. They know what to expect of us—pretty much nothing. So they give in proportion to their expectations. The only academic teacher who seems to give a hang teaches English to the middle grades. She's a round widow lady with snowy hair and pale skin. Her name is Mrs. Tygue.

"ATTENTION!"

I've let my mind drift again. As a result I'm a second late snapping to attention. Since we're all in one straight line, my slowness stands out like a sore thumb.

Ray Chapman, *Sergeant* Chapman, has the eyes of a prairie falcon. He sees my mistake right away.

"BIRD!" he bellows. His voice when displeased has the same volume as an angry bull.

"YES, SIR!" I reply, yelling as loud as I can.

I learned to do that my first day of being lined up. But only after doing a hundred push-ups. Ten for every time I didn't shout out loud enough.

Sergeant Chapman plants himself in front of me. He gives me what Possum calls "the stare." I keep my eyes front, not moving a muscle. Fewer push-ups that way.

"You are a useless pile of dog dung," he says.

"YES, SIR!"

The hint of a smile flickers across his face. Chapman's not a bad sort out of uniform. He has a sense of humor. It shows itself now and then in pranks he plays on us. Yesterday he had us all standing at ease, eyes front, hands behind us. Then he walked around behind us with a pot of mush ladling sizable spoonfuls into everyone's open palms.

Chapman's also the best dancer in the Indian Dramatics Club formed here two years ago.

"Man," Little Coon said, "you ought to see how he moves them feet of his."

I won't be learning any of that dancing. Every member of the club is a western Indian. Comanche, Cheyenne, Kiowa, and so on. No students from the civilized tribes like the Cherokees and Choctaws and Creeks—who make up half the population at Challagi—belong. Being so civilized, us eastern tribes don't dress up fine with such feathers. The stomp dances we do are not dramatic enough to show off to the public.

For the public.

That means, aside from when special guests are invited here to see a "real" Indian show, the members of the Indian Dramatics

Club don't dance where the rest of the students can see them. Even their practices are private.

The Indian club's main job is to perform off campus. Civic groups, fairs, and the like. They do it to raise money and represent the school in a positive way to the general public. That way the surrounding towns don't just see Challagi as the place Indian boys and girls are always trying to escape from.

Nearly a hundred, I've learned, tried that in the first three months of this new year.

Deserters is what they are called.

It's a big problem. The school pays local law enforcement officers for returning runaways. Everybody here knows that. Some have even seen the superintendent counting out bills into the outstretched hands of men bringing back runaways they've caught. As much as three bucks a head, Possum told me.

That explains why Sheriff Boyle, back in the hobo jungle, was smiling so much when he mentioned Challagi. Catching deserters has been earning him a pretty penny.

FORWARD MARCH!

We step out as one at the command. For once my feet are in perfect step. Sergeant Ray nods and turns his critical eye on the light-skinned boy behind me.

GET IN STEP, ARNETT!!

Staying in step. That is what the government decided was needed to keep a bunch of wild Indians in line. Turn them into imitation soldiers rather than have U.S. soldiers fight them.

"Idea here," Possum said, after my second day of drill, "is

to kill the Indian and save the man." He chuckled. "Even if it means marching us to death."

A few days ago I didn't really understand that.

How could you kill someone and still have them be alive?

Since I've been here I've begun to see the meaning of it. Make you obedient. Dress you like a white soldier. Drown whatever's free inside you so they can boss you around. Even though I don't feel like I am really an Indian—despite what Pop told me—I don't feel good being treated this way. I understand why so many would rather run than keep marching to a white man's tune.

Pop ran away from here. So could I. But if I ran, would Pop be glad to see me? Probably not. Much as I wish I wasn't here, I don't want to disappoint him. Not only that, would I even be able to find him? No, my only option now is marching, not running.

ABOUT FACE!

I've been so deep in my thinking about everything that I have almost forgotten where I am—marching in formation with my unit. But a week of drilling has made my feet more attentive than my brain. I'm turning and staying in step with everyone else before having a chance to think about it.

Our unit's no longer anywhere near the dorm where we started. We're at the parade ground area, half a mile from where we started. My body's been marching while my mind was on vacation.

COMPANYYYYY HALT!

And here comes Sergeant Chapman walking right up to me. Am I about to get it for messing up our formations by marching like a sleeperwalker? It'll probably mean a hundred push-ups for me if not five hundred.

Eyes front. Spine straight. Shoulders back.

"Bird," Chapman says. "Bird." Then he smiles and pats my right shoulder. "Best job yet, cadet. Not a wrong step."

I'm so shocked that I hardly hear him say dismissed. I stand there for a moment. But no longer than that. The sound of the bugle—number two of the more than twenty calls that punctuate our daily schedule—comes a second later.

Sergeant Chapman has played a joke on us again. He's marched our unit so far from the dorm that we'll have to scoot like the dickens to avoid being marked tardy.

I start trotting with the rest of the boys in our company. Back toward the dorm, to change into clothes for classes or work.

"Hustle up!" Ray yells after us. He's watching us, hands on his hips. Then he takes off himself, sprinting past us all as if we were standing still.

"Come on, slowpokes," he yells, turning to run backward. "Get the lead out. Catch up!"

I've heard Chapman is the fastest runner in the school, captain of the track team. There's no way I could ever beat him in a race. However, he's not running forward and I haven't gone my fastest yet. And this chance to run, really run, makes a voice in my head say *Yes!*"

I kick myself into a higher gear. Head down, arms pumping, I sprint past Ray Chapman. He's so surprised he almost tangles his feet as he turns to run in earnest.

Of course he reaches our dorm ahead of me. But I'm not far behind him. Everyone else is at least fifty yards back.

Ray Chapman nods. We're both leaning forward, hands on our knees as we try to catch our breath.

"Bird," he finally says, a smile on his face "You can fly. Think about the track team. Okay?"

I've run so hard I can still barely breathe. How can I explain to him that the last thing I want to do is join anyone's team? My plan is to get out of here as soon as Pop gives me the okay. The sooner the better.

But I appreciate what he said. So I manage to gasp out, "Yes, sir, Sergeant."

"After drill it's just Ray," he says, straightening up. Then he walks away.

EXPECTING INDIANS

When I first arrived I was expecting Indians. Maybe not like those in dime novels or in James Fenimore Cooper's stories about the Mohicans. But real Indians, people way different from the kids I'd gone to school with.

I never envisioned what I did find here at Challagi. Full-bloods, Indian-looking boys and girls with black hair and brown skin, make up only about four of every ten students. The next big group are mixed bloods, kids with only one Indian parent who tend to be lighter skinned, lighter haired. They are real sensitive whenever a full-blood says they're not real Indians.

Then, there are the white kids. All of them have some Indian ancestry—or claim to. All of them are on the tribal rolls of one Indian nation or another. Most are from one of the historic communities that were reservations before allotment and the Oklahoma land rushes. A bunch of them look real white. Blond-haired and blue-eyed white. They're the ones who get called *stahitkey*, white boy, by some of us Creeks.

Us Creeks. I just said that, didn't I?

Some of those white-looking Indian kids grew up thinking of themselves as Indians, maybe even speaking some of the language. Me, I grew up just thinking of myself as a person. Being white means you have the luxury to do that. It means not worrying about who you are. You know your identity, even if you're a hobo.

It also means, outside of an Indian school, not being told you don't belong if you have light skin, blond hair, and blue eyes. Like what happens almost every day with Tommy Wilson. White-looking, he calls himself Creek. He grew up on historic Creek land. His father, like Pop, is full-blood and went to Challagi. Then he married a Norwegian lady.

Tommy sits next to me in Mrs. Tygue's class.

Tommy is a good kid. My first Monday at Challagi, he greeted me in the hallway.

"Welcome to Indian hell," he said. "So you're Muskogee, eh?"

I nodded.

"Tommy," he said, patting his chest. "Muskogee Creek like you."

Like me, I thought. *Right.*

I nodded again.

"Teacher here's old, but she's a good egg."

"Uh-huh," I said as we walked through the door.

"Got your English book?"

I shook my head.

He opened his to a page with the corner bent down. "This old poem," he said. "We had to read it. Today we talk about it."

I looked at the page and smiled. I already knew that poem.

"Thanks," I said as we took our seats.

"'Oh East is East and West is West, and never the twain shall meet,'" Mrs. Tygue read. She looked over the top of her thick glasses at the class. "Who can tell me what that means?"

No answer.

"Does it mean that those from other lands can never get together, never understand one another?"

She was met by silence. No one was raising a hand. Way different from my old white schools where those who knew an answer would be just about dislocating their arms waving to get the teacher's attention.

Mrs. Tygue's gaze settled on Tommy.

"Mr. Wilson," she said. "Stand up."

Tommy stood, an uncomfortable look on his face.

"Yes or no?"

Tommy looked over at me. I'm not sure why. I lifted one finger from my desk and then dropped it. He looked back at the teacher.

"Yes," he said, his voice barely audible.

Mrs. Tygue smiled. "Good. Now why?"

The uncomfortable silence that followed was even longer. Tommy wrapped his hands together and squeezed so hard that his knuckle popped.

I raised my hand.

Mrs. Tygue looked at me. "New student?" she said, pointing a short finger at my chest. "Can you tell us why? Stand."

I stood as Tommy sat, letting out a sigh as he sank back into his chair.

"The next lines," I said.

"Really?" Mrs. Tygue said, a skeptical smile on her face.

"Yes, ma'am."

"Are you certain?"

I nodded and then did something I could never do in my own voice, me being reticent to say more than a few words at a time. I recited Kipling's next lines of "The Ballad of East and West" from memory.

> *"Till Earth and Sky stand presently at God's great Judgment Seat;*
>
> *"But there is neither East nor West, Border, nor Breed, nor Birth.*
>
> *"When two strong men stand face to face, though they come*
>
> *from the ends of the earth."*

That earned me some funny looks from the other students, along with a very big smile and a "Well Done!" from Mrs. Tygue.

Right after that the bugle sounded to mark the end of the hour.

"Mu-to," Tommy said to me under his breath as we left the classroom side by side.

But he quickly peeled off as I turned to join up with Possum and Bear Meat outside the academic building.

"You like-um white boy?" Bear Meat growled, pretending he only spoke broken Indian English—like Mr. Parker, the old Cherokee man who's the boys' adviser in Building Two.

"Hunh?" Bear Meat said. "You like-um him, that white boy?"

220

He punched me in the shoulder. Playful, but still like getting kicked by a mule.

It's a big thing here, I knew now. Being labeled as a white student here at Challagi was almost as bad as being seen as an Indian in the white world. Maybe you were not in danger of being driven off your land—or even shot—but you still might be made to feel like an outsider a lot of the time. I'd come to realize just how lucky I was not to be seen that way. But it still didn't mean that I felt good about seeing people treated bad just for being born who they were.

"He's okay," I said, rubbing my shoulder to try to restore some feeling in it.

"Stahitkey," said Grasshopper as he and Little Coon joined us.

Grasshopper is the narrow-faced boy in Bear Meat's gang who is always chewing on something—grass, tree rosin, Wrigley's spearmint gum, paper—then spitting it out like that insect. As if to live up to his nickname, Grasshopper ejected from his mouth a piece of the eraser he'd just gnawed off his pencil. "White boys no belong here."

"At least it's better than being *stalustey*," Bear Meat chuckled. "Innit, Little Coon?"

Little Coon, whose name on the school's records is Louis Oliver, pretended not to have heard him. Of all the boys in what I suppose I can now call "our" gang, me being included now, Louis seems the most thoughtful and the most sensitive. He's also the one most likely, too, to do something diverting or funny whenever things get too serious.

"Oh my," Little Coon said, turning to direct our attention east.

"Take a look at what those old turkey buzzards are doing. Just a-circling over the old lockup like they thought it was something dead."

"Maybe," Possum said, rubbing the scar on his cheek with one finger—a gesture he seems to make without knowing he's doing it. "Old HD is over there and those buzzards, being close relatives of his, are swooping in for a family reunion."

We all laugh, but it's not all that funny. That head disciplinarian is no laughing matter. I've felt his gaze settle on me a time or two during the short period I have been here. I'd bet he wishes the new rules brought in by Superintendent Morrell weren't in effect.

Horse whipping and the like are forbidden now. I know that for a fact because just yesterday the HD grabbed Grasshopper—who was chewing gum—out of line at the morning roll call.

"YOU!" he roared, lifting Grasshopper up by his collar with his left hand as if he weighed no more than a puppy. The man's face was red as a beet. He raised up his big flat right hand.

The big ring the HD wears on his right hand glinted as it caught the light of the rising sun. That ring had slipped around on his finger so that it was inside his palm. Slap a man's face with a ring turned that way and it'll leave a gash. Out of the corner of my left eye I saw the look on Possum's face. And I knew right then who my friend's scar came from. Possum looked ready to step in. If he had, I would have been right beside him.

"Mr. Bayner?"

It was Superintendent Morrell. His calm voice made the HD stop, close his palm hiding the sharp-edged ring. He lowered

Grasshopper back to the ground and turned toward his boss.

"Yes, sir," he said. "Caught this one chewing gum."

Superintendent Morrell nodded. "Cannot have that," he said. "Rules are rules." He looked at Grasshopper who was standing head down between the two of them. "Spit it out into your hand."

Grasshopper did just that.

"Now stick it onto your nose and leave it there for the rest of the morning."

It was clear from the look on the HD's face that he was not happy about being stopped. But he went along with it.

While Grasshopper spent the rest of the morning standing at attention, the gum stuck on his nose and a sign reading **GUM CHEWING IS A FILTHY HABIT** hung around his neck. The only good thing about it, he said later, was it was more interesting than Mr. Pond's class that he got to miss.

Mr. Pond is the math teacher here at Challagi. He's a big, horse-faced man. In the classroom where he's supposed to be teaching, he hardly looks at any of us. Instead, at the start of each class, he writes a bunch of problems on the board.

"Do these," he says in his deep sarcastic voice. "Though I doubt that any of you dummies can."

Then he sits down, takes a swig of the cough medicine he keeps locked in the middle drawer of his desk, leans back in his chair, folds his hands over his chest, closes his eyes, and goes to sleep until just before the bell rings. That's when Mr. Pond wakes up, sort of gradual, stands, stretches, and points to his desk.

"You idiots, put your papers there. Now get out of here."

I hate seeing the others treated that way even more than I hate being treated like a moron myself. It's not right.

I think back to what it was like when I was on the road with Pop. There was none of that back then. Pop would not allow it. And more often than not it was true of the majority of men who were hoboes, true knights of the road. Thinking that makes me ache to be on the road again, living that free life, feeling the wind in my face as I leaned out of a boxcar while Pop was fixing up grub behind me. What a life that was! Even though Pop's aim was to have us a farm of our own again, I have to admit that I hardly ever thought about being back on our farm after our first month riding the rails together.

If it wasn't for my promise to Pop, I'd be having serious thoughts right now of heading for the hills. Or, to be more accurate, the rail yard. There's one in the nearest town where we got off with the horses, the one Pop and I walked from. Unlike other kids who've run away in the past, no one would be able to predict where I was headed. I'd be on the first fast freight, a hundred miles gone before they knew I was missing.

According to Possum, more Indian kids have run away from Challagi than have ever actually graduated. That ratio may be sort of skewed seeing as how there are a bunch of kids, like Pop, who ran away again and again.

"Back 'bout four year ago," Possum said, "they tried punishing kids who run away more'n once by expelling them. Think of that? Punishing someone by telling them they can't come back to the place they was trying to escape in the first place?"

Possum chuckled. "Like Old Rabbit said. Please don't throw me into that Briar patch, Mr. Bear!"

That expulsion policy ended when C.B. and a group of school staff—all former students themselves—asked for a meeting with the old superintendent.

"Giving a boy what he wants isn't what we'd call punishment," they pointed out.

"Why, I never thought of it that way!" was his response. The expulsion policy for runaways was abolished the next day.

To be fair, there are some here, more than you'd think, who actually chose to come to an Indian school. Bad as a lot of the so-called education is here, Challagi—like Pop said—is first rate when it comes to teaching farming. Some Indian students who've gone here, I'm told, are managing to do a lot better at farming and stock rearing using the modern methods they learned here.

There are other reasons why some Indian families—especially those who were Challagi students themselves—have sent their children here. They've done it to give them a sense of belonging.

Skinny's one of them. He's never tried to run away.

"Where would I run to?" he said. "Back where my family lived, we were the only Indians for miles around. The one school I went to, I was the only one with a brown face. Had to put up with other kids war-whooping when they saw me. Calling me Sitting Bull. Asking where my tipi was? Round here nobody treats me like I'm a wild Indian or a freak. Plus I got football here. Little town where my family lives don't have enough kids to form a team."

Being accepted as an Indian. That's what a lot of the kids

here feel good about. And that's what some wish they could be. Those mentioned earlier. *Stahitkeys* and *stalusteys*. White kids and black kids. Especially the *stalusteys*. Too dark to pass for white, they might do better in this world by passing as Indian.

"Phonies. Trying to get free room and board and an education all paid for by the government."

That's how Bear Meat sees the darkest-skinned students here.

Others, like Little Coon and Possum, are nowhere near so judgmental. Being my pop's son, I fall on their side of the issue. Far as I am concerned, it's what a man does and not how he looks that counts. I doubt that most of them really are fakers. They just come from families where there's both Indian and some other blood. Just like me. As far as the real dark ones are concerned—like some of those Cherokees from North Carolina—runaway slaves got adopted and married in over the years.

Actually, though those words *stahitkey* and *stalustey* get spoken now and then, it seems like no one ever goes out of the way to be mean to those labeled that way. They just don't always get invited into groups like our Creek gang. And in school activities like athletics or drilling, everyone gets treated alike. If some boy who's real black looking is a good football player, like Will Houma from Louisiana who's the starting right tackle, you can bet he is going to be welcomed on the school team.

Still, as I enter the mess hall with my friends, I can't help but notice that two tables—one in the boys' section of the huge mess hall and one in the girls' side—are occupied entirely by those dark-skinned kids labeled as *stalustey*.

226

CHAPTER TWENTY-TWO

ANOTHER DAY AT WORK

Another bugle call. The end of the noon meal and the start of the industrial part of my day. My academic sessions run from just after breakfast till lunch. Seven thirty a.m. till noon.

Every student spends half the day in academic and half the day in industrial. In my case, the industrial part's in the afternoon from one p.m. to five p.m. That suits me fine. Those who have industrial in the morning are often so worn out from the hard labor that they fall asleep in their afternoon classes. Not that there's that much to stay awake for.

In eighth-grade geography class, where the red-mustached, bald-headed teacher is Mr. Mallett, we learned the startling news today that the earth is round and called a planet. Also, that North America is a continent. Then Mr. Mallett put his feet up on his desk and went back to reading one of the magazines he buries himself in during every class.

Like the other awful teachers here, he's been working for the Indian education service for years. Teaching for him just means coming in to class each day, taking the roll, saying a word or two, and then spending the rest of his time sucking his mustache and reading cheap magazines. He doesn't even give tests. All we are expected to do is not interrupt his concentration on the pictures in the *Police Gazette* until the bugle sounds.

We don't do much studying. There's not enough geography books for every student—only five or six battered texts older than Mr. Mallett himself. So most of the students stuck in here every day either stare out the window or lower their heads down on their desks and doze off. Today when I looked around the room the only person awake aside from me was Possum, reading *The Call of the Wild*. He's a slow reader, mouthing every word and going back to read every page twice. But he's told me half a dozen times he loves the book. Especially the freedom in it.

Me, I've used the time to scribble in this journal I've started keeping—sort of like the one Pop kept. Writing in it makes me feel closer to him. Also it helps me to think about what I might say in another letter to Pop.

> *Another boring day, I start writing. How did you stand it when you were here, Pop?*

I've written a full page of thoughts like that by the time the academic building's annoying buzzer sounds. It goes off half a minute before the bugle. Despite the fact that I've had a month to get used to it, it still irritates the heck out of me when it goes off. It's pitched so loud it makes my teeth feel like they're being attacked by a dentist's drill.

Possum walks next to me as we head to our industrial class. Our Challagi schoolbags with our books and school supplies are over our shoulders. The bags are more like burlap sacks. The pack I arrived with is a lot better. But that pack was taken from me. Like such personal items as family photos, good clothing, keepsakes, and jewelry other Indian students arrived with at the start of the year, my pack is in "safe storage" in the basement of Building Four.

"Safe storage," Little Coon explained to me, "means anything valuable's about likely to still be there when you're allowed to look at your things as a baby chick dropped into a hawk's nest."

That pack of mine is empty. The only keepsake I really care about is that France Victory Medal I put in Possum's hidey-hole. And I've never owned a photo of Pop. I don't need one. All I need to do is just close my eyes to see his kind face in front of me.

But so far I've not been able to "see" what he's doing or about to do. That gift of mine of precognition—sort of viewing the future—only kicks in rarely.

"You look like you are *cah-gee-tay-tin* about something," he says.

Cogitating is his word of the day. In exchange for his continuing to show me the ropes here, being the Virgil showing me the way through the underworld—like Aeneus—I have been finding him a new word each day from my dictionary.

I just nod.

"So what are you cogitating about, Jay Bird?"

"Nothing much," I say.

In fact, what I am still thinking about is what I might say in my next letter to my father. I've written two of them to him so far. But I haven't sent them. That's because I haven't heard from

229

him yet, so I have no way to know where to mail them. I have them both—written on pages I tore out of my journal—folded up safe inside my copy of *Bullfinch's Mythology*—right next to the story of Theseus and the Minotaur. I've reread that story three times since I've been here. It makes me wish I could find a magic thread that I could follow to get out of the labyrinth of this Indian school. But then again, it was not Theseus's father who took him into that maze and told him to stay there. I almost mentioned that in my first letter to my father. But I didn't.

Nor did I mention the dreams I keep having of being in that dark place. A place without light. Where I can't open my eyes or hear . . . or breathe.

Except in that dream I also know I'm not me. I'm someone else.

I pushed that dream away, like brushing a spiderweb from my face, as I wrote.

> Pop,
>   How are you? I am fine. But I miss you so much. I am doing okay. I have a couple of friends. One of them is Possum. Remember him? He's the one who showed me around.
>   I guess you know what life is like here, so I don't have to say much about my days. Nights are hard. I have a hard time getting to sleep what with all the noises from the other boys around me. It seems like there is always at least

one boy who is crying or wakes up calling for his mom. That is how I learned the word in Creek for mom, after hearing it so many times. Ic-ki. I have been learning other Creek words, too. I guess that is funny, isn't it? Here at Challagi you get punished for saying even one word in Indian. But whenever the staff is not around, the guys in my gang are always talking Indian. So I came here speaking English and now I am learning Indian.

I am keeping out of trouble. So far I have only earned a few demerits. And I make sure to stay away from you know who. He was bad when you were here, and he's still bad. All the boys talk about him as if he was the boogeyman.

I have learned some useful things here, especially about farming. English is not bad and I have also done well in penmanship. I bet you can see that from my handwriting in this letter, can't you?

But the agricultural science classes have been very good. I have learned a lot about poultry. When we have our farm I think I can be very useful because of what I have been learning. Also on the weekends I have learned some things from the other boys in our gang. One of them, Little Coon, knows all about animals. We hunt together.

I have written a lot in this letter about me.

But what I want to know is about you. You must have been in Washington for quite a while now. I saw something in a Tulsa newspaper here at the school about the men like you coming to Washington. It said that they were Reds and they wanted to bring down the government. I know that must be wrong. I bet they are just men like you who want a fair deal.

I will send this letter to you as soon as you have written me so I know your address.

I love you, Pop. I will do my best to make you proud of me.

I am your faithful son,
Cal

Possum and I take as roundabout a path as we can to get to the harness shop, but not far enough out of the way to make us late. Plus, from the glint of light I see from the top of the water tower, I know we are being watched for any sort of infraction that will add marks to our red cards.

We don't want to get any of those demerits that used to earn a boy a whipping back in Pop's time. Now the only official punishments are to be assigned extra work or lose privileges—like being able to go into town on a weekend once a month or take part in get-togethers.

But both of us want to breathe the fresh air, listen to the birds that are flocking in ever-increasing numbers back into the trees and fields. So we take the route that leads us closest to the near meadow. Little Coon and I heard a meadowlark singing there just yesterday morning, and we saw the yellow of its breast before it disappeared into the tall grass beyond the cattle barn.

"Hear that," Little Coon said. "It was talking Indian. *Imi-tik-tanki, imi-tik-tanki.* Free time, free time."

No meadowlark is singing for us today, though. No geese fly over, honking at us to remind us how free they are in their open sky. As we approach the harness shop I find myself opening and closing my fists, trying to loosen them up. I'm already building callouses on my palms from the leather work. I sometimes wake up nights with my hands curled up like claws from the work of grabbing and manipulating the stiff horse harnesses we're making.

"Maybe," Possum says, looking down at my feet, "we'll get shoe repair duty today."

That would be nice. Shoe repair is easier work than the harness making.

Then Possum chuckles. "And maybe pigs are going to fly."

I chuckle, too, but I am now looking at my feet too. His words about shoes have reminded me just how uncomfortable mine are getting. I haven't been able to buy a pair of sneakers like his. We earn a few pennies a day from our industrial work. But I have nowhere near enough to buy shoes. I'm stuck with the bullhides I was issued my first day here. They've heavy, but not sturdy. They were so badly made out of already cheap material that they are starting to fall apart after weeks of my feet being tortured by them. I do have the polished black shoes I wear for

233

marching—as do all the other cadets. But that is all those shoes are for. Either sneakers or work boots have to be worn for the rest of the day.

Possum is still studying my busted bullhides.

"Least we can do today is try to get a couple of nails pounded into them clodhoppers of yours."

I nod.

"Why not get some sneaks like mine?" he asks as we near the harness shop.

I reach into my pants and pull out my empty pockets.

Possum shakes his head. "Didn't your Pop leave you no money on your account with the school bursar?"

It's a question that surprises me.

"Accounts? People do that?"

"That's how I got mine," Possum says. "Bought them in town with money my gramma put on my account."

"You think I have an account?" I ask.

Possum grins as we enter the harness shop at the exact moment that the bugle sounds.

"Do I look like the bursar?" He puffs out his cheeks, pulls in his shoulders, and messes up his hair so that he almost does look like Mr. Cash, the chubby white man who handles the school's funds.

I have to laugh.

"Look," Possum says, "didn't no one ever explain to you about accounts?"

I shake my head.

234

"One thing about Superintendent Morrell," Possum says, "that man is as honest as a June day is long. Believes a man should get paid for his labor. That'll teach us Indians how to be more like white men."

Like some white men, I think, remembering Just Jack.

"So," Possum continues, "every day we might earn a few cents from the industrial work we do. That gets put in our accounts. Summertime you get paid even more. Thirty-five cents a day for cutting grass. If you get assigned a garden plot, you keep some of the money for what vegetables you grow. Older boys might even be allotted a field to grow hay and grain. That earns you three dollars a day."

I think about the thirty days I've been here, looking at the callouses and cuts on my hands from the jobs I've been learning in the various shops and barns. It's a good thing I heal fast. And even better that my reflexes have been quick enough for me to keep from getting more than small injuries.

"Tell you what," Possum says, "soon as we have the time, I'll walk you to his office. Help you find out."

"BIRD, over here!" The heavy, nasal voice of Mr. Handler, the head harness and shoe repair instructor breaks up our conversation. He's a graduate of Challagi. Like most of those who teach trades, he's been employed here since his graduation twenty years ago. He's holding up a heavy handful of harness leather in one thick-fingered hand, cutting tools in the other.

"Sir!"

I hustle over to him before he decides I've earned a demerit

235

for typical Indian laziness—as he puts it, despite the fact he is an Indian himself. A dark-skinned North Carolina Cherokee.

Instead of handing me the stuff he's holding right away, though, he looks down at my feet—at the flapping sole of my right shoe to be exact. And a look that almost seems concerned actually comes over his face, which usually shows no emotion at all.

"Son," he says, "them the only work boots you got?"

"Yes, sir," I reply.

He throws the harness material and tools down on a bench.

"Come with me."

I follow him to the shoe-making part of the large, low building, back past the local farmer and his team of matched black horses that are being fitted with just-made harnesses.

"Sit," Mr. Handler commands. "Pull 'em both off."

I do as he says. I stand and watch as he takes first one and then the other in his broad hands, holds them up, and studies them. He shakes his head.

"I sure as blazes did not make this pair," he says. "One of my lazy Indian boys done this slipshod job. Not worth the powder to blow 'em to hell."

I'm not sure whether he means the shoes or the student who put them together. Probably both.

"Uppers are not half bad, but these soles . . ."

He rips the bottoms off both shoes and sends the soles flying like bats across the room, not looking where they land. What he does next happens with such a blur of movement that it is hard

236

for me to follow. Measuring, cutting, fitting, nailing into place. He's done in almost no time at all.

"Here," he says, tossing me my repaired bullhides. They hit me in the belly so hard that they almost knock me down, but I manage to grab them.

"Put 'em on."

I sit to slide on one boot after the other, pull the laces tight, and tie them. I stand up, stomp first one foot and then the other. My bullhides are still stiff and heavy, but as I walk back and forth in them, they feel sturdy for the first time.

"Thank you," I say.

"You can thank me by getting your butt back to making them harnesses."

"Yes, sir," I say.

Time to build more callouses.

Just as Possum described, Mr. Cash is a little white man with a round face. And a no-nonsense attitude.

"We're here to see about Cal Blackbird's account," Possum says.

"Your name," Mr. Cash said, as if Possum hadn't just identified me. "Name," he said again, pointing his pencil at me like it was a gun.

"Blackbird, Cal," I replied.

"Spell it," Mr. Cash says, licking his index finger and then using it to open a thick green ledger book.

I spell it as he runs the eraser end of his pencil down the page.

"Calvin?" he asks in a voice about as neutral as a blank sheet of paper.

"Yes, sir."

"Thirteen and twenty-eight," he says, tapping a line of writing so small I cannot read it.

"Sir?"

"Dollar and cents. Ten left on account. Three and twenty-eight earned."

He opens a drawer.

"Five," he says.

"Sir?"

"All I can disburse per month. Five." He holds out five one-dollar bills.

I look over at Possum. He holds up three fingers. His Converse All-Stars cost three bucks. Then he shrugs and holds up another finger, just in case.

"Four's enough," I say.

As we walk back toward our dorm I'm feeling happy. It's not just because I'll finally be able to have a pair of comfortable shoes—new ones, at that. It's because Pop left money for me. For a moment it felt as if he were here with me. Just a brief moment, but that and the prospect of my own Keds has put some sunshine into my heart.

"Best thing about this," Possum says, "is that today's Friday and tomorrow we have got us a town day. I know just the place for you to pick up a fine pair of sneakers just like mine. O'Boyle's Dry Goods." He grins over at me. "They sell penny candy, too."

"Good thing I got this extra dollar." I grin back at him.

Saturday morning.

Possum and me and a dozen other boys are riding the back of the school wagon sent in to town to pick up harness shop supplies. It's being driven by Mr. Handler, who saw us walking and ordered us to hop on board in that gruff voice of his, which I now realize covers up a soft heart. Hard as the work in his shop is—and as useless as it may be in this new world where cars are surely going to take the place of horses—he really wants to teach us the right way to do things. Unlike most of the academic teachers who are lifetime employees just looking to serve out their term before retiring.

I am quieter than usual. Not that anyone notices since quieter than usual just means only saying a word or two every hour as opposed to every half hour. I ought to be happy—getting away from the school routine and heading out to do something special. But being away from Challagi, seeing the open road ahead of the wagon, reminds me of all the roads Pop and I walked together over the last year. I'm doing what he wanted me to do. But I am still worried about him out there without me to look out for him. I hope I hear from him soon.

Possum nudges me in the ribs.

"Thinking about them new shoes?" he asks.

I guess I should be. So I nod and then go back to watching the road ahead as the horses clop along.

O'Boyle's is not our first stop in town. That first stop, which was along our way, is the train depot where we help unload some boxes being shipped East.

"Thinkin' of hitchin' a freight, Jay Bird?" Possum asks.

I just smile as I studied the train schedule, reading it from top to bottom, bottom to top, then back down again until I figure I have it fixed in my mind.

"Done?" Possum says.

"Done," I reply.

"Shoes now?"

"Shoes."

Five minutes later we're in O'Boyle's. No other customers are there as I walk up to the counter where a huge red-haired man is smiling down at us both.

"Shoes, I'd wager," he says, looking at my feet.

I nod and I'm handed a pair of black Keds.

I sit down, slip them on, lace them up. They fit my feet like a second skin.

"So whaddaya think?" Possum says.

I stand and walk back and forth down the crowded aisle of O'Boyle's, being careful not to knock over any of the various sized boxes piled precariously on all sides and filled with all sorts of stuff.

WHATEVER YOU NEED, WE HAVE GOT IT.

That's what the sign outside read. From the way every inch of the store is cluttered with goods, it just might be true were it not for the fact that the one thing Mr. O'Boyle does not sell is books—aside from copies of the King James Bible of which he has half a dozen offered at a quarter each.

I take another step, then hop up in the air and land without making a sound. It's as if my feet have springs under them with those thick rubber soles.

"Yes, indeedy do," the ruddy cheeked proprietor says. He rubs his huge palms together so hard you'd think he was trying to start a fire. "Plimsolls was what they called them when they first attached rubber to the sole of a shoe. Then in '92 along came the U.S. Rubber Company with their canvas tops. It was they who named them Keds."

I nod. Possum had warned me that anything bought at O'Boyle's would come with an explanatory lecture from the store's owner who was a history buff. And would have been a better teacher than most of those heading up our classes.

"Sneakers, folks started calling them. That was on account of how easy it was to sneak up on a man, them shoes being so silent and all. But what you have on there, young man, for the price of but two dollars and ninety-eight cents, are Chuck Taylor All-Stars, named for the famed Indiana hoops star, hisself."

He cocks his head to look at me and rubs his hands together even harder.

"You like-um them shoes, Chief? You want buy-um?"

I sigh inwardly at his attempt to talk the way some Indians do whose English isn't good. But there's no use in trying to correct him.

I just nod my head and hand him three dollars.

CHAPTER  TWENTY-THREE

TO HELP INDIANS

I've been at Challagi Indian Industrial School two whole months now.

The "noble mission of this fine institution" is to help the Indian.

I've now heard the superintendent say that more times than I can count. It is meant to teach the Indian a new modern way. To finally make him into a useful citizen after, as Superintendent Morrell puts it, "untold generations of meaningless savage life." To give him a true, higher purpose.

After the time I've spent here, though, it seems to me like the true purpose of this place is to wear the Indian out. I have done enough marching to have walked to California and back. The daily routine here starts at five a.m. with the first bugle.

TA-TA TA-TA-TA TA-TA TA-TA-TA

TA-TA TA-TA-TA-TA-TA-TA

Reveille, assembly, close-order drill, even before morning mess. That's true for the girls as well as the boys. They also have to march—but in their own companies. Then the day's work begins. Students handle all the maintenance work at the school. We grow all the food, work in the fields, clean the stables, feed the farm animals, fix everything that needs fixing.

We boys are all kept busy growing and building things that the school can sell. If we are lucky and are chosen to do certain jobs, just as Possum told me—like cutting the grass on the lawns—we can actually earn as much as thirty-five cents a day. The girls do all the cooking and kitchen work, as well as the sewing, making and mending things. Some of the boys who have sisters or cousins in the girls' houses have told me about what those girls have to do every day. They may not be plowing fields and picking rocks, but they do the cleaning and dusting and scrubbing of the floors as well. So they do not have it easy.

My first two weeks here, even though I thought my hands were used to hard work, I ended up with big blisters on my palms. I had cloth bandages wrapped around both hands. But it didn't prevent me from having to keep on working. Bleeding hands or not, if you don't do exactly as you are told you get demerits. If you stray off a walkway and step on the green grass you get demerits. If you are late to class you get demerits. If you make too many missteps in close-order drill or your uniform is not neat, you get demerits. It's not just the staff who can give you demerits. It is also the older students who've been chosen to be monitors. So someone is always watching you during the day, including that man on top of the water tower.

Get enough marks on your red card and you get punished. Loss of privileges is one punishment, being told you can't take part in social activities or go to town once a month. There're worse punishments, too, even though they no longer use the whipping post which is still standing by the parade ground. It's a log half buried in the ground with iron rings on it five feet up where a boy's hands could be fastened.

Being sent to break rocks down where the creek runs closest to the school grounds is still common practice. Making big rocks into little rocks, just like you were on a chain gang. Scrubbing floors on your hands and knees is another punishment you get for too many demerits.

My behavior since I've been here has been so good that I hardly have any demerits at all—even though the one thing that was on my mind all the time for the first week here was the one that would have earned the harshest punishment. Running away.

Not only do you lose all your privileges, as soon as they drag you back they shut you up in a dark room for a day or more with just bread and water and a bucket for a latrine. Among my friends, that has happened to most of them at one time or another. I sure as blazes do not want that happening to me.

By the time the last bugle comes at nine p.m., after evening assembly, some boys are so tired they can barely drag themselves up the stairs to fall into bed without even bothering to wash up or take off their clothes. They're too tired to do the one thing that so many of us dream about doing—running away and never coming back again.

Thinking of running, I continue to be a disappointment to Sergeant Chapman, our drill captain. He has now asked me three times to come to track practice.

"Make some use of that God-given speed of yours, Bird," he

keeps saying. "We could use you in the hundred and the last leg of the relay."

He's explained to me—more than once—the benefits of being on a sports team. Not only would I get time off from the various duties around the school, I'd be able to get away on trips to compete against other schools.

"Where's your school spirit?" he's asked me.

I have just listened and said nothing each time he's tried to convince me. I don't want to get involved in this place any more than I am. It's enough that I have a bunch of friends in our Creek gang—I don't need more than that. I don't intend to stay here a day longer than I absolutely have to. As soon as Pop gets back from Washington with his bonus money I am going to be out of here for good.

School spirit is something I don't care about or ever intend to have.

Although I no longer think about it all the time, the only running that appeals to me would be running away from here to wherever I can find my pop. Which I will not do because of my promise to him to stick it out till he either sends for me or shows up to get me.

I have to admit, though, that there would be benefits to being one of the athletic boys. They have a special training table in the mess hall with more food than the other students. The ones who get treated best are the boys on the boxing team. That is because Superintendent Morrell has a special love for that sport. That is why he has a special boxing class twice a week during our physical

245

education time where we usually just do such things as sit-ups, jumping jacks, and exercises using Indian clubs and medicine balls.

Once a month the school has boxing matches, where our boys either fight each other or boxing squads from other Indian schools. The school boxing coach is Mr. Handler, the brown-skinned Cherokee man who graduated from Challagi in 1912.

According to C.B., our dorm adviser, when Old Man Handler was a student at the school, he was the light heavyweight boxing champion and never lost a match. He might even have become a pro fighter—except that being a poor Indian he would not have been given a chance to win any real fights.

"He got an offer from a promoter in Oklahoma City," C.B. told a group of us one night before bed. "Went down there to see what it was about. But the deal was that he would have to look good for a round or two and then take a dive to whatever white boy he got matched against. Story is that he said 'Like this?' stepped in and knocked the promoter out with an uppercut. Then he came back here and has been here ever since."

Since then the only boxing he's done has been as a coach—in between his main job of running the harness and shoe repair shop. He's as good a coach as he is a harness maker—which is saying something. Though he does sometimes go on a bit about how this sport came to be in England with its Marquis of Queensbury rules.

England. That's where Pop and his regiment of 3,800 men went first before being sent to France. I remember Pop describing how it looked as they got close to the English shore.

246

And I'm on that boat. I can see the white chalk cliffs of Dover ahead of us as our troop ships near the land. I can smell the salt spray, hear the harsh voices of seagulls as they circle around us. . . .

"BIRD!"

I open my eyes.

Mr. Handler is staring at me and holding out a pair of boxing gloves.

"Your turn," he says.

Against who? I'm thinking as I slip on the gloves. Then I see who's stepping into the circle that is serving as our boxing ring. It's Bear Meat, a big grin on his face.

Oh my!

"Go get him, Jay!" Possum yells. Bear Meat, the leader of our gang, outweighs me by a good fifty pounds. From the grin on his face this is going to be all in fun—for him, at least. But I do not think he is going to pull his punches.

The other forty boys gathered around us are echoing what Possum said in various ways. Except none of them are cheering me on.

"Go to it, Bear!"

"KO in the first, Chief Bear!"

Mr. Handler ignores them all.

"Remember today's lesson?" Mr. Handler whispers to me, right hand on my gloves, left on Bear Meat's. Then he raises both hands.

"Touch gloves."

Bear Meat thrusts his gloves against mine so hard that it makes me take a step back. If that had been a jab to my chin it would have knocked me into next Tuesday.

Mr. Handler clicks the stopwatch he uses to time the two-minute round we'll be boxing—unless I get knocked silly a whole lot earlier.

"FIGHT!"

Bear Meat steps in with a lazy, looping roundhouse right. I duck under it and dance back, gloves up in front of my face.

"Come on, Jay Bird," Bear Meat growls, still grinning. He steps forward with a left jab that knocks my right glove back into my nose. It stings, but doesn't keep me from hopping to one side and avoiding the right cross that jab set up. This time, I circle to my right.

"Finesse it, Jay Bird," Possum hollers, using the word I taught him today out of my Webster's. That he pronounced it "fin-essey" doesn't take away from the pleasure of knowing I've got at least one person rooting for me.

The sudden thudding of Bear Meat's left against my right shoulder diminishes any pleasure I'd been feeling. I stagger to the left where my ribs—*THUD*—are greeted by Bear Meat's right hook.

That hurt. But despite having half the wind knocked out of me, I do not go down.

Bear Meat knows he's got me, though. He's no longer trying that hard. He's just pushing me around. He grabs me in a clinch.

I try to remember what to do. I dip my right shoulder, pivot up from my hips, and throw the punch we learned today. A right uppercut.

It lands square on Bear Meat's jaw, but all it does is just about break my own knuckles. Bear Meat steps back half a step and throws another punch of his own. A hard left hook.

WHOMP!

It lands square on my chin and knocks me flat on my backside.

I'm only there for a moment. I'm up on one knee, trying to keep going when I hear Mr. Handler yell "TIME."

I'm pretty sure it is well short of two minutes, but I'm glad he's taken pity on me. I was not going to quit, but if Bear Meat hit me again with one of those pile-driver punches it would have scrambled my brains.

Possum and Little Coon are helping me up. Bear Meat is walking around with his hands raised. He's got the right to do that. No question who whupped who.

Then he comes over to touch my gloves. There's a grin on his face and he's saying something. Maybe okay.

Mr. Handler's pulling off my gloves. The ringing in my ears is letting up enough that I can make out his words.

"I'm not going to ask you to join my boxing team, son. We got enough punching bags. But I give you credit for hanging in there. You got sand, son."

CHAPTER TWENTY-FOUR

STOMP DANCE

Despite all the hard physical work we have to do and nonstop schedule every day, there are warm nights when we still have enough energy to sneak out to the one place at Challagi that's truly free.

The woods.

It's where we can hunt with no one watching. Some of it with Possum's bow and arrows. Cook the game we get. He's a real William Tell when it comes to knocking down a squirrel from a high branch. And sometimes with his single shot .22—which he's been letting me use.

We can catch catfish from Challagi Creek, where it meanders through the trees. Sometimes—but not too often—a chicken finds its way out of the school hen yard and into our pot. We can eat better food here than is ever served in the dining hall.

The woods are where you can get away, where you're no longer here.

Deacon is the one who said that first to me.

Of all the boys in our Creek gang, Deacon's the best rock thrower. He's like a major league pitcher. He can knock a can off a fence from a hundred feet away with that side-arm delivery of his. He is also the most thoughtful of us, saying things that make you think. That's why he got that nickname, a nickname that's not entirely a joke. Like all the nicknames here at Challagi, it makes some sense. More sense than the discipline and stupid rules.

Like the one about dancing.

No dancing.

Not just here at Challagi, but everywhere. The Indian service actually published a broadside forbidding all Indians to dance. Because dancing is a waste of time. It encourages heathen behaviors.

That broadside was printed here in the Challagi print shop by Indian students. It was one of the first things Deacon showed me when I was rotated to the print shop after my two weeks in shoe repair and harness making. Him showing it to me sure made me laugh.

Not that the no dancing rule is funny.

What's funny is that anyone would imagine dancing as being a bad thing. Also, as I mentioned earlier, one of the things they encourage here at this school is the Indian Club doing western Indian dancing for visitors and performing around the area to create goodwill and raise money for the school.

The funniest of all, which brings me back to Deacon, is that they can't stop us Challagi boys from dancing. We just have to get far enough away into the woods along the upper reach of Challagi Creek. That's where Deacon leads our stomp dances.

Deacon is not much to look at. Average height, average build. His arms are long, though, which is one reason why he is such a good stone thrower. His skin's about the same color brown as mine. His hair is jet black, his face round and a little flat—though not as flat as the face of Pancake, who looks like he got hit by a frying pan. Aside from me, Deacon's the quietest one in Bear Meat's gang. But even though Bear Meat is our leader—some even call him "Chief" in a half-joshing way—once we get into the woods around the fire, it's Deacon who takes the lead. He grabs up a rattle and shakes it.

"*Oh-pan-ka-ha-ko!*" he shouts.

Stomp dance!

As soon as he yells that he looks about two feet taller. And everyone lines up behind him.

One of the strange things about Challagi, which might be hard for an outsider to understand, is how much freedom we boys have once we get off the main campus. All we have to do is be back in our beds before the first bugle call. But when you consider the fact that there're thousands of acres around the school with little hills and valleys, woods and fields, there's no way the authorities at the school could ever hope to keep total control weekends and during the nights. Some of those who run the school just seem to turn a blind eye.

Even old Mr. Rackett, who is the assistant disciplinarian and always looks like he is sucking on a lemon, ignores what happens in the woods or after dark. He's the one you see perched up on the water tower, the sun glinting off the binoculars he uses to spy on us.

Matter of fact, some of the Indian staff members, especially those former students who now work here themselves, not only tolerate our going into the woods campus but sometimes even take part themselves.

Mind you, it's only the boys. Not the girls. Those matrons in the girls' dormitories watch over them like hawks all through the day and owls all through the night. No one is allowed to sneak out of—or sneak into—those houses at night. It makes me feel sorry for those girls.

But we boys have a kind of freedom in the woods that's almost as good as what I felt riding the rails with Pop. Almost.

Even though I've been here two months, I haven't heard from Pop yet. I still wake up some nights whispering his name. Listening for his breathing, trying to smell him, to reach out and try to touch his back. But not as often as during the first month I was here.

Someone pokes me. Of course, it's Possum.

"Jay Bird, move your feet!"

I've been standing stock-still, even though the stomp dance has started. Daydreaming at night.

I do as he says, breaking into the shuffling rhythmic steps of stomp dancing.

I no longer feel like an out-of-place white boy, the way I did before. I feel like I belong to our gang. Maybe I'm not totally Indian, but I'm not the same as I was before. I'm seeing things another way.

And stomp dancing.

"Heee-yah heee," Deacon calls out.

"Whey-ya-hey!" the twelve of us all chant back as we shuffle

around the bonfire we've built in the clearing a little ways back from the creek.

"Heee-yah hee!"
"Whey-ya-hey!"
"Heee-yah hee!"
"Whey-ya-hey!"
"Heee-yah hee!"
"Whey-ya-hey!"

It keeps on like that, us dancing, repeating that chant as Deacon shakes his rattle that he made from a Number 3 can with river stones put into it. If you're not doing it, it might seem like it would be boring. But it's not.

The first night the gang brought me here to their camp along Challagi Creek was a warm Saturday night, the second week I was here. We'd left dummies made of old blankets in our beds to fool anyone other than C.B., who might make a visit to look in on our dormitory. No one worried about C.B. causing trouble about our being out at night. C.B. had been a student himself. He'd climbed down the Virginia creeper more times than any of us. He turned a blind eye to what we did at night, especially on weekends.

But every now and then Superintendent Morrell himself would visit the houses after bedtime to check on his charges. He never did more than just pause at a door and peer inside. Actually coming in a crowded dormitory, sometimes sort of rank with the smell of unwashed boys passing gas after a meal heavy with beans, was something that did not appeal to him.

Walking the trail by the light of a full moon that first time I felt like I was walking not just into the woods, but back in time. The only one with a lantern was Bear Meat, the rest of us trailing behind. Me the last in line. The rest of our group looked like shadows more than people. But I was comfortable with that. After all, I had behind me all those nights Pop and I spent camping back away from roads where no one could find or bother us.

Before long we came to the long creek that runs through Challagi's woods and the prairie. And now there were more lights to be seen than the moon and the distant stars in the sky above us. Along at least a mile of the creek I saw the glow of small fires, just about every hundred yards or so. I stopped to look at those campfires, squinting my eyes as I counted them. One, two, three, four.

Little Coon walked back to me, chuckling. "Ayup," he said. "That's how it is on a nice Saturday night like this'n. We got us a whole bunch of stomp dances tonight. More'n half the beds'll be stuffed with blankets back at the houses."

Possum came to join us. "Older Creek boys got their stomp grounds there," he said, nodding his head toward the closest fire. "Next there's two or three Cherokee gangs, a couple of Choctaw crews. The catfish in the creek won't be getting much sleep tonight."

When we got to our place along the creek, the moon was bright enough for me to make out the shadowy shape of a small cabin set back near the woods edge. That had to be the clubhouse Possum told me about. It had been built with boards liberated from the cast-off pile back of the carpentry shop. The roof was salvaged from an old building being torn down that would have just been burned. The moonlight glinted off the tin roof.

We went to the very middle of the clearing where I could make out a rough fire circle surrounded by stones.

"Fire keeper," Bear Meat said.

Little Coon stepped forward. "Present and accounted for," he said, his voice so mock serious that it was clear he was sort of making fun of our morning military drills. Then he tugged at my sleeve.

"Know how to make us a fire, Jay?" he said.

I didn't bother to say *ehi.* I just reached out and took the hatchet and the box of lucifers he was holding out to me.

There were dry pieces of plank cut into short lengths piled by the side of the fire pit, along with bigger logs. I took my time, splitting the planks down into pieces almost matchstick thin. Other pieces I shaved with the blade so that there were curlicues of wood all along their length. I arranged them into a conical shape, piling bigger pieces around them so the heat of the fire would rise up into the center of the little structure I'd made.

Then I knelt down low, struck the wooden match on a stone, sheltered that flaring match between my palms and gently thrust it in the center. The thin pieces caught right away, then the lengths with the shavings on them, then the bigger pieces. Before you could count to a hundred, the whole pile was blazing.

"All right," Bear Meat said, turning to Deacon.

They all knew I'd never stomp danced before. I'd told Possum that and he'd just given me that split-face grin of his.

"Shucks," he'd said, "that's true of half the boys who come here. And no wonder seeing as how not just their parents but

256

maybe even their grandparents went to Indian schools. You just watch and join in when you feel like it."

I'm not sure how long I watched that night or when it was I joined in. I just know that I found myself in that circle, dancing around that fire, and feeling fine.

We finish our first round of dancing. I'm breathing hard, but the night air is cool and clean. Just as it was on the first night I stomp danced. I feel almost contented as I put some more wood on our fire. That's the job that has fallen to me since that first night our gang let me be the fire maker.

As I pile on one piece of wood and then another, I find myself thinking about all the nights I tended a fire for Pop and me. Is he somewhere sitting next to a fire now?

The feeling of contentment leaves me. Once again I am wondering and worrying. That one question that came to mind was like opening a door. At first there's just a crack and then it swings wider. A cold breeze blows in from the other side. But all it brings me are more questions I can't answer.

What is my father doing now? Is he in Washington? Is he part of the growing army of Bonus Marchers I read about in the old newspapers I check every time I can get to the school's little library—which is a windowless room only a little larger than a closet. Sometimes those papers—which I now know are donated by Mrs. Tygue after she reads them—carry articles about the Bonus Army.

Whenever I read one of those articles all I can think about is Pop. Is he okay?

Is he ever going to come back for me?

That last question opens up a whole other door. Now I am not just worrying about him but about me.

How long am I going to be here?

Deacon has handed his rattle to Little Coon. Little Coon gives that rattle a shake. We're about to start another round of stomp dancing.

"Hold on," Bear Meat says, holding up his hand. He peers into the darkness around the big sycamores at the woods edge. "Who goes there? Step out and show yourself."

A shadow detaches itself from the other shadows and moves slowly forward.

"It's that white boy who keeps tagging along behind us," Dirt Seller says.

It's Tommy Wilson. The moonlight shines on his pale, uncertain face.

"Hunh," Bear Meat growls. "What you doing here, *stahitkey*?"

"Just . . ." Tommy says, "just watching."

"You don't belong here, *stahitkey*," Bear Meat says. "Get gone!"

Tommy lowers his head and mumbles something.

"Hold on." Little Coon asks, "What you say?"

Tommy lifts his head and repeats the word. *"Isti-cah-ti,"* he says, clearer this time. It's a word I know because Possum taught it to me. *Isti-cah-ti.* Indian.

"What?" Bear Meat says. "You saying you are Indian, white boy?"

"Muskogee," Tommy says, his voice even stronger. "That is what my dad says we are. Me, too. Even if my mama is white." He squares his shoulders. "I got Indian blood. Cal knows I'm Indian."

"My, my," Little Coon chuckles. "Don't that beat all? But what you doing here, Muskogee Boy? Why you follow us tonight?"

"Stomp dancing," Tommy says. "I like it. We did not have any Indians around where we live, but my dad taught it to me. I know what song you just did. He called it 'The Old Rooster.'"

Little Coon has sidled up to Tommy. "So," he says, "you know any other songs, Muskogee Boy?"

"One or two."

Little Coon looks over at Deacon, our dance leader. Deacon nods and so does Bear Meat. "Okay," Little Coon says. He hands the rattle to Tommy. "Let's hear one."

Tommy shakes the rattle, a little hesitantly at first as he looks at Little Coon who has stepped back and is rubbing his palms together. Then Tommy takes a breath and calls out the start of the song. His voice is sure and his feet start to move. Deacon gives Tommy's shoulder a gentle shove and Tommy shuffles forward, still singing as Deacon falls in behind him. Soon all of us are dancing, including me—an Indian boy who thought he was white, following a white boy who knows he's Indian.

All of us are joined together and free in a song older than our breath and stronger than all the Challagi rules.

CHAPTER TWENTY-FIVE

FIRST LETTER

This week I'm going to be working in the stables.

So far, during the nine weeks I have been at Challagi, I have done just about every possible job a boy can do. I've spent two weeks in the shoe and harness shop, two weeks in power plant maintenance and plumbing, a week in printing, a week in painting, two weeks in masonry, and a week in electric wiring.

That is what they do for new students—move them around so they can get a taste of the different trades they offer here. Some of what they teach really is useful—if you want to spend your life as a laborer. They do not train anyone to be doctors or lawyers, politicians, businessmen, or bankers here at Challagi.

The only trade shop I haven't been assigned is to baking. That's a job most boys want since you get to eat fresh-made things every day, right from the oven (when no one is looking). According to Bear Meat, who's one of the twelve student bakers who work there regular, they put out an incredible amount of food every week. Two thousand loaves of bread alone. Not to mention all the buns, corn bread, pies, and cookies.

The job I am going to have now, though, is what I think is the best one of all. Taking care of animals—especially horses.

It's hard for me to believe that it's been over two months since I got here.

It feels like two years—or forever—whenever I think about Pop, how much I miss him and the life we were leading.

But it feels like only two days have passed as I walk into the stable. There in the first stalls to the right are the pinto and the bay. They're the two cavalry horses Pop and I loaded onto the railcar and rode with all the way to the station. As I approach, the pinto leans his head out, shakes it up and down, and whinnies at me.

"My, my. Looks like old Satan there knows you," a voice says.

I turn toward the one who just spoke. It's a white-haired man who looks full-blood Creek. In the time I've been here it has gotten so that I can generally tell what tribe someone's from, if he's full-blood and not mixed. There's this sort of lankiness that most Creeks have, a look to their faces. Creeks do look different from Choctaws or Cherokees. And a lot different from western tribes, like Cheyennes.

The old man shuffles up to me, a gentle smile on his face. As he gets closer I can see he's not as old as I thought. His face is much younger than you'd expect with hair that white. And the way he is shuffling is not from age. I've seen it before in some of the vets Pop and I have met over the last year. It's from war wounds.

"John Adams."

"Sir?" I say.

"No, I am not the second president of the United States.

261

That's my name—or at least the one I was given, young'un. You the new boy, right? Blackbird?"

"Yes, sir."

Mr. John Adams chuckles. "Figured you would end up here sooner or later. Been hearing about you. Knew your pa. Best boy with horses we had back then. He still know that horse song I taught him?"

"Yes, sir."

"You ever say anything else but yes, sir?"

"Yes, sir." Then I add, "Sometimes."

Mr. Adams slaps his leg and laughs out loud, a laugh that is cut off by a grimace on his face. "All these years and I have still not learned not to slap this bad leg of mine when something tickles me," he says as he rubs his thigh. "Shrapnel. Some of it too deep to cut out without cutting a nerve, they told me. So even though I used to be full-blood Creek now I have to add that I have got a bit of German in me—German steel."

"My pop, too," I say, touching my left knee. "In here."

Mr. Adams nods. "So now he's gone off to Washington and bless his soul. Old Hoover has got a heart of stone, but maybe he and our other boys will make him change his mind. You hear Lowell Thomas on the radio that night?"

I nod. They allow us to listen to the radio in the common room of the dorm sometimes during our study hour between eight and nine. Lowell Thomas is the one whose deep voice is almost like the voice of God coming out of the speaker. Everyone listens as he tells America what it needs to know. On his network radio broadcast he'd spoken about the growing number of vets in Washington. "The March of the Bonus Army on Washington becomes more promising of excitement every day."

I've been following the news of the Bonus Army in the papers and whenever I can catch a little on the radio turned on all the time in the hall outside Superintendent Morrell's office. So I know that thousands and thousands of men have made it there. Black veterans and white ones alike, all with one purpose. The whole country is paying attention.

The vets have created a tent city in Washington. Some are camped out on the Capitol grounds. More are pouring in every day. Lots of folks have been helping them along the way. Railroad conductors have put on extra cars so that marchers could ride in them. But not everyone has been friendly to those veterans. Some are calling them Reds, saying they should be shot. Some marchers have been beaten and jailed.

"If I was a man with no job, I would be right there with 'em, young'un. Now let's go say hello to your friend here."

"Satan?" I ask.

"Well, that is what I calls him. Seeing as how he has a devil of a temper on him. Him and the bay. The other six are easy as pie to handle, but not those two. Don't help none that the men brought him and the bay here did not favor us with their names."

"Dakota."

"Say again?"

"Dakota is his name. The bay is Blackjack."

I walk over to the big horse's stall.

"Careful now," Mr. Adams cautions. "He bites."

But he makes no move to interfere, which doesn't surprise me. In the time I've been here at Challagi I've learned that the old Indian way is to let a young person try things rather than attempting to keep them away from danger. You learn by doing—and sometimes by getting hurt doing things the wrong way. That's why the industrial classes taught by the Indian instructors are always more popular than those taught by white men. And also why those who are in those classes taught by men like Mr. Adams make more visits to the infirmary. Like I did after putting a metal punch halfway through my palm my third day in the harness shop.

"Yup," Mr. Handler said, when I showed him my bloody palm. "Guess you can see why you have to keep your hand back whilst punching them holes. Now go get patched up."

I'm not really worried about Dakota biting me. But I'm also not one to tempt fate. That's why I'm reaching into my pocket as I get close to pull out what I've brought with me.

"Here, boy," I say, holding the apple out on my open palm.

Dakota reaches down, lips curled back. He takes the red fruit delicately and crunches it between his teeth as I stroke his neck.

"Son," Mr. Adams says, "you surely are just like your father."

"Jay Bird!"

I turn to look toward the stable door at the person who's just come looking for me.

"Mail," Possum says. "You got a letter!"

All of my friends know that I've been waiting to hear from

Pop. That's why Possum has hightailed it here to let me know that his cousin—who works in the school mail room and was told to keep an eye out for me—has alerted him that a letter's finally here.

I look back at Mr. Adams.

"Go ahead," he says. He points with his lips at the flat wooden tablet hanging on a hook by the door. "Just take that pass so as you don't get in trouble."

I'm holding the letter in my hand so tightly that the envelope is creased by the pressure of my fingers. There's no return address on the outside, but Pop's handwriting is easy to recognize. Plus, the cancellation mark over the stamp says District of Columbia.

Washington.

I haven't opened it yet. Eager as I am to do so, I don't want to do it where someone else might see me. I want to keep it between Pop and me. I'm not sure what the letter will say, but just getting it is good news. It means Pop is alive. Not having heard from him for so long has been hard on me. Not knowing if he made it to Washington. Or even if he was still breathing.

I keep the pass visible as I walk back to the stable. No one stops or questions me. When I re-enter the stable, Mr. Adams is grooming one of the big plow horses. He looks at me, sees the envelope in my hand, nods and points with his lips toward the little office room to his left.

"Go on," he says.

I go inside, shut the door behind me, and sit down on a stool. My heart is pounding. I slip my little finger under the flap to open the envelope. I take out the letter and hold it up to my face. Pop's familiar scent is on the folded paper. As is the paper itself. Unless I miss my guess, this letter was written on pages Pop tore out of his notebook. I bite my lip and then unfold it. For a moment I can't read the words. It all looks blurry to me. I wipe my eyes with the tail of my shirt. This time as I hold the letter up it comes into focus.

1ST JUNE

My Dear Son,

This is your father writing to you, Cal.

I hope you are doing well at Challagi. I am sure you are doing your best and have found friends. I am proud of you, son. I know it is not easy for you.

I am sorry it has taken so long for me to write to you. First I had to find paper and pen and then there was the business of getting an envelope and a stamp.

I am sorry if you have been worried. I have made it to Washington. I wish I could tell you my address so that you could write back to me, but I do not have an address. Even if I did, it is hard to say how long I will be here. We all hope to wait it out here, but there are rumors that the president might give orders for them to come to clear us out. I am staying in a camp city we have set up near the Potomac. There are hundreds of others like me here, thousands in the city. All of us are here for the same reason, to convince Congress and old Hoover to give us our due, as you know. It is exciting to be among so many others like myself, all of us back in the army again in a way.

We are a real army now. We have chosen a commander in chief, Walter W. Waters. He was one of the ones who first proposed us all coming to Washington back in March. He has been helping keep us organized, getting food, setting up places to stay and all that. He's also been negotiating for us with the police chief here, a Mr. Pelham Glassford who is a vet himself, a good egg, and sympathetic to our cause.

Because I know so much about the trains, I decided to help other men get here to Washington. So I have gone back and forth from Washington four times now, collecting other vets and showing them what lines to ride to get here. In one city we took over the railroad roundhouse until they agreed to put together a special train to carry four hundred of us part of the way here. Some other men here walked all the way from their homes. One came from Florida on foot all the way.

There is so much to tell, too much for me to put in a letter. Just know that I am okay and thinking of you. And I am hopeful that our business here will be successful soon. Meanwhile, son, hang in there. With luck I may be able to come and get you at the end of the school term.

I will try to write again soon.

I remain,
Your Pop

I read the letter a second time. Then I read it again. I know it's short, but it says so much in those few words. As much as I miss him, I am proud of him. And I will try to do my best to make him proud of me.

CHAPTER TWENTY-SIX

A BAD DREAM

July.

And I'm still here at Challagi. When the school term ended, many of the students went home for the summer. Half of our gang, in fact. Bear Meat, Skinny, Dirt Seller, and Grasshopper all went to help out their families on the little plots of land they have left—allotments meted out when the Oklahoma reservations were broken up by the Curtis Act of 1898.

I'd never heard about the Curtis Act before. And I sure as blazes did not hear a word about it in any of the classes taught at Challagi. I learned the story from other Creek students—mostly Deacon, who knows the most about tribal history and genealogy and the acts of Congress that affected Okie Indians.

The Curtis Act abolished the tribal governments and tribal courts in what was formerly supposed to be Indian Territory forever. It divided, like cutting up a cow, what used to be communal lands between individual tribal members. No Indian was allowed more than 160 acres, which left 90 million acres—the greater part of Indian land—to be given to white settlers.

"As if that wasn't bad enough," Deacon said while sitting round the fire after a stomp dance, "every Indian had to pay taxes on their land for the first time. So a lot had their land taken for non-payment of taxes. We also now had the right to sell our land if we wanted. And white men were ready to buy it."

"Specially after the oil," Little Coon added.

Deacon nodded. "Black gold, white men call it. We call it the black curse. A lot of that oil was on Indian lands. A few of us did get rich. But not so many as you'd think. Much of the Indian oil land was stolen by white men who got Indians drunk and had them sign their names on bills of sale and then did not pay them a cent. Some white men married Indian girls just to get their land."

"But . . ." I said. Then I paused.

Deacon looked at me and nodded again. "I know what you're thinking to ask, Jay Bird. Didn't people object once they sobered up? First of all, most courts will not take the word of an Indian over a white man. Second, if an Indian woman marries a white man, then ends up dead right after that leaving everything to her husband, there's not a soul left to object or ask if that death was suspicious."

I took a deep breath and shook my head. It all sounded like a bad dream. It made me understand even more why Pop wanted to escape from being an Indian. Why he didn't want to raise me knowing about all this. I cannot say he was right, but I see now he was trying to spare me the pain.

Bear Meat growled. "Some of us still got land. No one going to take it from us."

The firelight flickering over his determined face also made it possible for me to see the smile that came to Possum's lips.

"Bear Meat," Possum grinned, "is the littlest one in his family.

They're all bad men—even the women. Don't no one mess with the Chitto family."

Since two-thirds of the whole student body left it's been quieter here at Challagi, though Possum, Little Coon, and Deacon are still here. While some of the school staff remained quite a few others are gone, taking their once-a-year vacations. Now no one's perched atop the water tower with field glasses to observe our every movement.

Rather than the usual schedule of drilling and classes, those of us left here now have different roles to play—mostly as laborers and farmhands. Whether school is in session or not, animals have to be fed, grass has to be cut, and crops need to be tended. Plus there's all the upkeep on the many school buildings.

Why am I still here? Well, for one there is no home for me to return to. Not even twenty or thirty acres like the family farms that Grasshopper and Skinny and Bear Meat went back to for the summer.

For another, a second letter came in June from Pop. It was not delivered to me in the mail room, but by Superintendent Morrell himself who called me to come to his office at noon.

"Mr. Blackbird," the superintendent told me, gesturing to me with a wave of his massive left hand, "I have heard from your father."

He held out the brown piece of paper on which I saw my father's familiar writing. It was not letter paper, but something heavier. A piece cut from a brown paper bag. The date on the top was a week after the letter I'd received.

To Superintendent Morrell
From William Blackbird
Sir,

I apologize for sending this on such rough paper. Here in our camp writing materials are hard to come by, as is the time to send such missives as this.

I am writing to request that you allow my son, Cal, to remain there at Challagi Indian School during the summer months. He is a good worker, as I hope he has proven. I am sure he can be of use among the summer student helpers and might even warrant a garden plot of his own.

I am unable to return and collect him as soon as I had hoped. My own role as an officer and quartermaster in our Bonus Expeditionary Force requires my continued presence. Our army of veterans of the Great War continues to grow and we believe that our pleas for the payment of our bonus money will eventually be answered, though it may take till the ends of the summer. The papers have written well of us. We believe, with an election coming, that the president will see the wisdom of giving us our due.

Please inform Cal on my behalf and tell him that I am proud of him.

I held the paper in both hands and read it a second time, hearing my father's voice. Then I handed it back to the superintendent.

"Does this sit well with you, Mr. Blackbird?" Morrell asked.

As if I had any choice in the matter?

So I did the only thing I could do. I nodded.

That was three weeks ago. Since then I've been settling into my new role as a full-time farmhand. In addition to such things as grass cutting and whitewashing walls, I've been spending time in the stables. Mr. Adams has been teaching me how to work with the big Percheron horses. He also has detailed me to be the one most responsible for the feeding and currying of those retired cavalry mounts. I am clearly their favorite. Dakota, in particular. The big horse starts whinnying whenever I am within half a mile of the stables.

I have also been allotted a plot of my own to farm. Whatever I grow there can be sold with funds from the sale going into my account. There are no academic classes, but I have been able to study on my own using books borrowed from the library. A big box of novels and textbooks discarded from a high school in Oklahoma City was donated in June to our so-called library, housed in that small room in the academic building.

I was the first to get my hands on them. We do not have a proper librarian, but Mrs. Tygue suggested to the superintendent that I should be the one to go through the books and see they got shelved right.

My favorites among them are no less than ten novels by Sir Walter Scott and four by Robert Louis Stevenson. Possum, on my recommendation, is now working his way through *Kidnapped*.

The one I'm reading right now, before sleeping, is *Treasure Island*. I read it two years ago. But it has even more meaning for me now. I guess what I like best about it is that while I'm reading it, I am not here at Challagi. I'm off on that wild quest with Jim Hawkins and Long John Silver. For a time, deep in those pages, I'm not even worrying about Pop or missing him. For a time there's nothing but pirates and buried treasure on my mind. I close my eyes and drift off into a dream where Jim—who looks a lot like Possum—and I are walking along an ocean beach.

"NOO! LOOK OUT! NOOOO!"

That shouting, near-hysterical voice was so loud that it woke me up.

I look around. I'm in my bed in the half-empty dorm room. The still-open copy of Stevenson's adventure tale is clutched in my right hand. Jim Hawkins isn't there, but I'm not alone.

Possum and Little Coon are both staring down at me with worried faces. That tells me the one shouting was none other than yours truly. It pulled them out of their cots to the side of their crazy friend.

"Jay Bird," Possum says, "it was only a dream."

I shake my head, half to try to come fully awake and half to deny what my friend just said. I close the book, swing my feet out of bed. I rub my eyes, which are wet with tears.

"No," I say. "More than that."

I look at my two friends. The full moon shining in through the window casts enough light for me to see the worried looks on their faces. And despite what Possum just said, he knows that a dream can be a lot more than a dream. He's the one whose aunt had medicine dreams that were just as precognitive as the visions of Cassandra in the *Iliad*.

I know if I tell them what I just saw in my dream that they'll take it serious. I know, partially from what I've learned about being Creek and partially because a part of me has always known, that my dreams are connecting me to other people. People who've passed on—like Miz Euler's husband who got gassed in France—and people still living. My dreams are of things that happened, even before I was alive on this earth.

This dream was about the living. It wasn't just about something that was going to happen. It was more than that. It was about Pop, and in that vision I sort of was Pop, seeing through his eyes. It was night and there was noise and confusion all around me and the other men who were marching forward. There were lights, bright spotlights being beamed on us. We were on a bridge, facing armed men. We were not armed ourselves, but we were not going to let them get past us. We kept marching toward them.

"GET BACK! STOP OR WE WILL FIRE." That was what the man on the bullhorn was saying.

They won't shoot us, the man next to me shouted. *They won't never shoot us vets.*

And that was when the soldiers started firing. I felt the bullets entering my chest and I was falling, dying. . . .

And woke up shouting NOOOO!

275

Possum and Little Coon are still by my cot, looking at me. I'm amazed it's only them. I was hollering as loud as a bluetick hound on the trail of a raccoon. But as I raise my head and look around the room all I can see in the cots that hold other students here for the summer are sleeping bodies.

Possum smiles. "Yep, Jay Bird, they are all still ree-cum-bunt," using the word I taught him yesterday out of my Webster's. "That yell of yours was meant just for us, I suppose. Nobody else was supposed to hear it. So they didn't."

If he had said that two months ago I would have thought he was nuts. But not now. I just nod my head.

Then I realize someone is missing. Why isn't Deacon, whose bed is just past Little Coon's, also here by my cot?

I stand up and peer in that direction. It looks as if there's a body in Deacon's bed. But, then again, it looks as if the cots of my two other friends are also not empty. I walk over to Deacon's bed, pull back the covers. He's not in it. What it holds is a bedroll like the ones in Little Coon's and Possum's cots. Like the one they are fixing in mine.

"Put on your sneakers, Jay Bird," Little Coon says. "Deacon woke up a good two hours before you started yelling."

"Yep." Possum nods. "Seems he had one of them pree-mo-ni-shuns, too."

Little Coon nods. "Said the time had come for us to do something you needed done. Told us to wait till you woke up and then take you to our camp. That's where he is. Getting things ready."

CHAPTER TWENTY-SEVEN

TIME TO GO

Even though the moon is bright, I see the light of the fire burning next to the creek long before we reach the clearing where our gang's cabin is located. It's a much bigger fire than usual, far larger than to cook anything and certainly not needed for warmth on a balmy summer night such as this.

But the fire is not the only thing out of the ordinary. Right close to the creek, not far from the fire, is a flat shelf where the bank juts into the stream. It's a week since I've been here, but someone else in our gang clearly has been here to construct what's been built on that shelf. At first I took it for a big mound of brush, but as we come closer I can see it is way different from that. It's a rounded hut, sort of like a giant mushroom.

"Nice, innit," Little Coon says. "Three of us spent the last four days a-makin' it."

It's all covered up with blankets—blankets that I recognize from the stable.

"Horse blankets?"

"Yup," Possum says. "Long as we bring 'em back all clean and folded, Mr. Adams don't mind our borrowing them. Not that he gave us out-and-out permission, but he turned a blind eye, knowing how we'd be using them. Covering for the lodge."

The blankets are folded back on the fire side of what Possum just called a lodge. I peer inside and see that the structure the blankets were laid over is made of peeled poles lashed together with stringy roots and brown twine. It's not big enough to be a hut for living in. A single deer antler, looking like a hand with curled fingers, rests just inside. There's a hole in the ground about the size and depth of a good-sized cooking pot right in the center of the lodge.

"That's for the stones," Little Coon says, seeing where I'm looking. He gently grasps my shoulder. "Don't go inside yet."

I look at him in confusion. Then at Possum. A third figure stands up from the other side of the fire. Deacon. He was sitting so motionless that I hadn't seen him.

"Never seen a lodge before?" Deacon asks, his voice soft.

I shake my head.

"Sit down here."

I sit down close enough to the fire to feel its heat washing over me. It's a good feeling, peaceful. The fire smells different from any fire I've smelled before. I look closer at it and see that there are objects glowing red in the heart of the flames. It takes me a moment to recognize what they are. Stones. Each of them more or less round and half the size of a man's head. They're so hot that they seem to be throbbing—like hearts starting to beat.

"Stones are alive," Deacon says. "Fire just wakes them up more."

Little Coon and Possum sit down next to me. They've stripped off their shirts and sneakers. I do the same, feel the heat caressing my chest and my feet.

"Deacon was given this—taught to do it—by his granddad," Possum says. "So, because he is carrying it, he can do this. Make a lodge, run a sweat."

What is a sweat? I wonder. But I do not have to ask. Deacon begins to answer me before I've even finished that thought.

"Grandad Harjo," Deacon says. "He told it to me this way. There was a holy person a long time ago. Way before white men came. He showed himself to a boy who needed help. He taught him this way to cleanse his words, cleanse his body. Then that boy went on to help others in the same way. Now, Jay Bird, this lodge is here to help you."

Deacon keeps talking, his words punctuated by the snapping and crackling of the fire and the sound of hissing and cracking from the stones. Grandfathers, Deacon calls them. What he explains to me seems to be coming as much from those stones and that fire as from his voice.

I nod my head now and again as he talks.

Then he looks up at me.

"Are you ready?" he finally says.

"Yes."

He and I take off all our clothes and crawl into that lodge one after the other. I sit at the very back, facing the door that opens, I was told, toward the east. It's the direction of the dawn, the new day, the beginning of life. Possum, who is the fire keeper, moves burning pieces of wood aside with the pitchfork. He levers out a glowing stone, then carefully scoops it up. He reaches it into the lodge where Deacon uses that deer antler I saw earlier to guide that rock, pulsing with heat, off the pitchfork's tongs and into the hole in the center.

One stone, two stones, another and another. Even with the door open to the night air I feel the heat building inside the lodge. Eventually the hole is filled and Deacon holds up a hand to signal enough.

Little Coon, who's the door keeper, passes a bucket of water in to Deacon. Then Little Coon pulls the blankets down to close the door. Deacon and I are alone with the stones, their glow like that of miniature suns.

I can't say how long we're inside the lodge. It's as if time doesn't exist. Deacon prays and sings and I do my best to sing along with him. The heat is like nothing I've ever felt before, especially whenever he splashes water on the stones and steam rises to wrap itself around our bodies. Every inch of my skin feels as if it's on fire, yet it also feels cleansed at the same time.

Finally, after one more song—the fourth one, I think— Deacon lets out a long cry. It's just like that of a wild turkey, but so loud it almost shatters my eardrums.

Immediately the blankets are thrown up and aside as Little Coon opens the door.

"Go on out," Deacon says. "Don't dry yourself off. Go right into the stream and let its waters wash you clean."

Dripping with perspiration, I do as he says. I wade in up to my waist, then sit down so that my head is underwater. When I stand up again, the air feels cool on my body and all of my senses seem more alive than I can ever remember them feeling.

There's a huge splash next to me as Deacon jumps into the water himself. Then he pops up, sudden as a diving duck coming back to the surface. His upper body seems painted silver by the bright light of the full moon streaming down on us.

Little Coon and Possum are reaching their hands down to help pull us up onto the bank. As they do so, Deacon looks over at me and I see a glint of mischief in his eye. He makes a little sign. I nod.

"Now!" he says as he grabs Little Coon's hand and yanks him into the creek at the exact moment as I do the same with Possum.

As the four of us sit by the fire after the sweat, I know they are all feeling what I'm feeling. We're truly brothers. Whatever happens from here on in we'll always be as close as kin.

Deacon looks over at me.

"Tell us about it," he says.

I don't have to ask him what he means. I've never told anyone about my visions before. But being in the presence of friends who understand, who don't think such things are crazy, who even have names for the kind of seeing I've been experiencing makes all the difference. I look over at Possum and Little Coon.

They both nod. Go ahead.

So I tell what I saw, speaking more and longer than I ever have before. All three of them listen intently, not interrupting.

When I'm done I actually feel a little better, as if some of the weight's been lifted. But it's also made that vision stronger. And it's raised even the question in my mind that I have to ask.

"Does my seeing that mean it's going to happen?" I ask Deacon.

He stays silent for a good long time, gathering his words.

"My grandad," he finally replies, "told me that seeing that way can be more of a warning than a prophecy. Letting you know what might happen, not what has to happen."

Not what has to happen. Those words make hope start to flutter in my chest like a bird. It means what I saw might be changed. Pop could be saved. But there's only one person who can do that.

The summer days here are long, so it's after ten the next night when Possum and I climb down the vine. I have my pack with me. It holds the few things for my journey. It being summer I've only shoved in a light blanket and a change of socks and underwear. Money from my school account is in my right sneaker. My French Victory Medal, which Possum and I got out of his hidey-hole last night on our way back from the sweat, is in my left pocket, my jackknife in my right.

The near-full moon is almost as bright tonight as it was last night. That is both good and bad. Good because we will not need any other light to find our way. Bad because we might be more easily seen. So we keep to the shadows, avoiding the open pathways, staying close to the edges of buildings, moving as quiet as ghosts.

"Okay?" Possum whispers, hefting the pick as I hold the shovel like a rifle at parade rest. "You sure now?"

"Never surer," I whisper back to him.

"Me, too," someone whispers from behind me.

I would have jumped out of my skin if I hadn't recognized that voice as Little Coon's. I turn my head to look at him, the moonlight glittering off his teeth from a grin near as wide as Possum's.

"You need a lookout," he says, his voice low and soft.

I nod. What else can I do? Even though I wanted to avoid getting more of my friends in Dutch, he's right.

I'm sure about what I have to do, but there's still a knot the size of a boulder in my stomach as I lead the way to the stables.

"I'll set up here," Little Coon says when it comes in view, a dark shadow set back from any other building. Possum and I keep going, even though it seems as if I am walking through heavy mud the closer we get to the deserted guardhouse where unruly students used to be locked up. We stop, pause a while in the shadow of a big sycamore. My heart is pounding so hard in my chest that I'm afraid it might be heard like a drumbeat.

Possum plucks my shirtsleeve. "Let's go," he says.

We continue on, silent as shadows, until we reach the stable. Possum puts a hand on my shoulder.

"Here you are," he says in a soft voice.

I want to say something, thank him for being such a true friend—my first real friend. But there's a lump in my throat the size of a rock.

Possum chuckles. "Ain't no word in Creek for good-bye," he says. "Uncle Big Rabbit told me that's cuz we are always going to be meeting up again one way or another down the road." He gives my shoulder a gentle push. "Now go, Jay. You got yourself another road to travel for a while."

As I enter the building a soft whicker from the far stall greets me. Dakota has caught my scent. He nods his head up and down as I approach him

"Good boy," I say, opening the stall door. I pat his neck and he nuzzles his head against my chest so hard it almost knocks me down. "Ready to run?"

I don't put a saddle on him. That would take too long. But I've always been comfortable bareback on a horse. The bridle is all I need. I lift it off the hook, slip it into his mouth, walk him out of his stall, step up on the railing, and slide onto him. I adjust my pack over my back. Everything I need is in there. It's taken me no more than a minute to do all this. But there's no time to spare.

"Giddyup," I say, shaking the reins.

Dakota doesn't rear up, kicking his front hooves like the horses do in the cowboy movies. He was a cavalry mount, trained to charge into battle—not waste time with fancy moves. Instead, he bolts forward. We burst out through the open barn door onto the farm road. I'm gripping tight with my knees, one hand holding the reins and the other grasping his mane.

"GO!" I shout, kicking my heels into his sides.

As we pound along, we're not headed toward the main

entrance of the school. We're angling across the northern field, a wide expanse of prairie ahead of us. But that's all right. During the months I've been here I've gotten to know the lay of the land. The direction we're heading is the way I want to go, and a shorter way by at least a mile. The moonlight shining on the field, the scent of the prairie grasses being kicked up by Dakota's hooves, the warm night wind in my face, and the feel of the horse's strong, muscular body beneath me is almost like a dream.

PART 3

A DIFFERENT ROAD

CHAPTER TWENTY-EIGHT

ONE HAND ON THE RAIL

It's ten miles by road to the rail yard at the edge of town. But only seven cutting across the prairie as we've done. We haven't been at full gallop all the way, but still moving along at a good clip, Dakota's breathing easy and relaxed beneath me.

I slow him to a walk as we approach the depot. His long, tireless strides brought us here even quicker than I'd expected, quick enough to outdistance any pursuit, assuming anyone saw me going. Which is not likely. It's so early, just before dawn, that no one other than us is stirring. The streets are empty. I look up at the station clock.

If I have remembered the schedule right, there'll be a freight train here soon. It's not a passenger stop, but it has a mail car. So it will be slowing down to a near halt to drop off one mailbag and grab the other waiting on the platform.

I tie Dakota's reins to the hitching post near the watering trough in front of the livery stable. It's where Pop and I brought him and the other horses back in early April. So much has happened since then. Thinking about it all just about makes my head spin. But there's no time for cogitating now. I've a train to catch.

I run my hands along the big horse's sides, pat him a couple of times. He's not lathered up from his run. Seven miles is nothing for a cavalry mount. He should be okay without being rubbed down. He lowers his head down so I can stroke his forehead.

"Good boy," I say.

I push myself away from him and shift the pack on my shoulder.

Dakota is dipping his head to drink from the trough.

You'll be okay. They'll bring you back to the school. Don't know if I'll see you again. But I'll be remembering you.

I haven't yet heard a train whistle, but from the position of the hands on the station clock the freight I'm counting on should be here soon. I bend to place my left hand on the nearest iron rail, feel the vibration of the metal.

Yes!

I walk down along the tracks, staying low to keep from being seen. I almost trip over a pile of tools, left by some careless workmen—a five-foot-long claw bar, a track chisel, and a wrench. A hundred yards on, I stop, position myself in the brush at just the right place to make the run alongside the train and swing myself up onto a freight car before it picks up too much speed.

The screech of the train whistle cuts through the still dawn air. So loud it would make most men jump, but not an experienced knight of the road like me. I can't quite see the train yet, but its smoke is visible, rising high in the blue morning sky. The clacking of its wheels is getting louder and louder, so loud as it comes into sight that almost nothing else can be heard.

The freight's almost reached me. I turn and start to run. The engine passes me, its driver looking straight ahead. I let the coal car pass, then another freight car.

My feet are pounding on the loose stones along the track. Now! I reach my left arm—the one closest to the train—to grab the ladder side rail. My right hand takes firm hold of the rail parallel to it and I lift my feet.

I climb up three rungs, fast as a squirrel scooting up an oak tree.

I'm on my way.

WOUNDS

I don't look back as the train picks up speed. I make my way across the top of the car, then swing down through the open door of the boxcar. As my feet hit a slippery spot on the floor, I slip backward. A nail sticking out of the wall catches my shirt and rips it. But it doesn't stop my stumble. Arms flailing, I'm about to fall out through the open door.

"Watch it, young fella!" A strong hand with long, slender fingers has just wrapped around my wrist and pulled me back.

I look up into the face of the tall person who's just saved me. It's a dirty face, but a pleasant one. It's framed by long gray hair topped with a bowler hat.

"Thank you, sir," I say, surprised at how weak and cracked my own voice sounds.

"Ma'am."

"Huh?"

"Ma'am, young fella." The middle-aged woman I took for a man doesn't let go of my wrist. She flicks the cigar she was smoking out the door, then reaches her right arm forward to grasp my shoulder. "Come on over here."

She guides me to a corner where a bedroll and a few other things, including a large bag have been set up behind a row of packing crates. I smell food cooking and in the first light of dawn coming in through the door I notice a little camp stove set up with a pot of stew atop it.

"Take a seat," she says in a raspy voice, pointing at a crate. "Good thing I was just having me a smoke, otherwise you might have just tumbled head over teakettle out that door, sonny."

"Thank you, ma'am," I reply.

I sit on the small crate with a cloth over it the woman has set up as a stool. I've never met her before, but I'm not all that surprised to find myself in the presence of a woman hobo. There are more than a few women riding the rails in these hard times, though ours is largely a male society.

"Gale," she says.

"Huh?" I'm slow on the uptake because it's so early.

"That's my moniker, sonny. Gale, like the wind. And in whose presence do I now find myself?"

"Cal," I reply.

"Hmmm," she says, half to herself. Then she dishes out a plateful of mush and hands it to me. As I eat I take note of what's in that half open bag. There's bandages and a bottle of Witch Hazel in the top. I realize that I'm in the presence of an Angel of Mercy. A hobo doctor.

Pop told me about them. Knights of the road who make it their mission to care for other hoboes. Most are men, some of them former physicians. What they do is out of the kindness of their heart. After having lost everything material, they've still kept and shared their skills. Though I am not going to ask her,

I would bet this gray-haired woman knight named Gale has a story that is an interesting one.

"Your grub okay?" she asks.

"Yes," I say. "Thank you, ma'am."

"Fine," she rasps. "And you're a polite one, too, ain't you, Cal?"

I nod.

"And about as talkative as a clam, eh? So where you headed?"

"D.C.," I reply.

She reaches out to grasp the torn fabric of my shirt.

"Peel that off," she says as she turns to push aside the bandages to root deeper into that bag.

"Here, this'll fit you."

She hands me a shirt she's just extricated from its depths. It smells a little musty, but as I put it on, I find that it fits pretty good.

"Good," she says, eyeing me up and down. "So what's in D.C. for you, Cal? Going to visit old evil Hoover in his pretty White House?"

"My pop," I say. "He's with the Bonus Army."

Gale settles back onto the floor. "More power to him and them as is like him in the B.E.F.," she says. "But it is going to be getting right hot down there, you know? And I do not mean the tempachur. Been readin' the papers?"

"Some," I reply.

Gale nods. "Comin' to a head now," she says. "Old evil Hoover and that general of his—MacArthur is his name—they are seeing

Reds everywhere. When mostly it is just honest men who served asking for their due. Thousands of vets in and around the city. But not only that. There's women and children as well. Whole families. Most in the big camp cross the Potomac at Anacostia."

She snorts a laugh. "You ought to see how some is living there. Some in boxes and barrels. One fella is even sleeping in a coffin with a big sign on it reading **MY HOME IN WASHINGTON IS A BURIAL CASE**. Everyone as peaceful as can be, but all of 'em asking for that bonus to be paid."

Gale shakes her head. "Powers that be are not taking kindly to all those former doughboys setting up camp so close to the White House. There's close to two thousand in the old Armory building alone on Pennsylvania Avenue. Most of them are boys of the Sixth who served in France. Camp Glassford they call it, right within sight of the Capitol. Which makes Treasury Secretary Mellon and all his rich cronies right unhappy. They been planning to build a whole new Federal triangle there where the vets been billeted."

I'm listening with my mouth open. This gray-haired generous lady is like a walking fount of information. I've learned more from her in ten minutes about the Bonus Army than I've gotten from the last two months of reading papers and listening to the radio. And she's not done yet!

Gale looks out the door of the car at the morning prairie rushing backward, the sun turning the grass gold.

"For a while it looked good, you know. House passed the bonus bill. Even though old evil Hoover squawked like a wet hen about it. But the Senate sneaked out of town without even voting on it. And now that Congress is not in session, Hoover and his pet generals figure it is past time to get the BEF cleared out of the city. Next thing you know, it's martial law and blood being shed. You be careful, young Cal! You might just be walking into a war zone."

I shake my head. Despite the dream I had at Challagi where I saw Pop in mortal danger, it's hard for me to believe.

How could American soldiers be called upon to attack veterans?

"Were you there?" I ask.

Gale nods. "I'd be there still. Except I got word my daughter's sick. Which is why I am on this freight going to Kansas City. Fell asleep and missed my connection. So I am backtracking. Lucky for you, eh, Cal?"

I nod. Lucky for me for sure.

"Now, you just sit back and rest while old Gale fills you in on what to expect when you get to this land's biggest Hooverville."

I do just that, listening for an hour or more until Gale's voice and the rhythm of the train and the exhaustion I can't fight any longer conspire to make me drift off.

The last thing I hear before I fall into an exhausted sleep is Gale's voice.

"I'll be changing lines at the next stop. But you just stay in this car. And may the road be good to you."

When I wake up, the train has stopped. We're at the Kansas City rail yard. Gale and her belongings are gone. Nothing around me but empty boxes. I hear voices. Railroad bulls checking the cars. I slip inside one of the wooden boxes and wait.

The door is slid open a few feet and a ray of light shines in.

"Nobody here," a gravelly voice says from outside.

"Not like last month when we had them vets filling every car," another deeper voice answers. Then the door is rolled shut again.

The scrunch of the bulls' feet on the gravel of the roadbed fades away. The car jolts as the train starts moving again. I crawl out of the box and sit in front of the door. We're passing houses, farms, and fields, rolling alongside a river.

But I'm hardly aware of that. I'm seeing the scenes Gale described. All those men and their families in those camps. My father's there among them. Suddenly there's fire everywhere. People are screaming. "Tanks! Tanks are coming."

I'm hearing the rumble of heavy metal treads, the thudding of boots, the cracking of rifles. I'm seeing and smelling blood flowing in the streets.

I open my eyes. I'm back in the car, but that vision is still with me. And I know it's going to keep coming back every time I close my eyes until I can reach my father's side.

July 27th.

I've been traveling for two days. After Kansas City I spent the night near a hobo jungle at the edge of St. Louis. I looked in at the camp from the shadows without seeing anyone Pop and I knew. Being alone and just a kid, I figured I would be safer on my own. Not every hobo lives up to the ethical code. Without Pop to protect me I might get robbed of what little I have or worse. I slipped back into the woods and set up a cold camp.

And now this train on the Baltimore and Ohio line is taking me toward my final destination. I am hoping I'll get there in time.

Although I'm focused on what lies ahead of me—on finding Pop and making sure he is safe—I've had time alone for the first time since arriving at Challagi. Now that I've had time to think, I realize something. I've left behind the best friends I've ever had. In point of fact, aside from Pop, the only real friends I've ever had.

Before going to Challagi I thought I knew who I was. I thought I knew what road I was on. But now I know there's another road besides riding the rails and dreaming about having a farm again with Pop. Now there's the road of my being an Indian, a road I'm going to be traveling for the rest of my life whether I'm with Pop or not.

Until I got to Challagi, it was always just Pop and me. During the time I was in my old school there were kids I'd been friendly with. But none of them were like Possum or Little Coon or Deacon. No one I could really rely on other than my father. No one I could tell my dreams to. No one I'd trust with my life.

Thinking of them and the things we've done together brings a smile to my face. Does that mean I'm missing Challagi? That thought confuses me. I'm sure as shooting not missing most of the teachers, or the stupid rules, or the backbreaking work they had us do for pennies a day, or the dumb marching, or the way they treat us.

But I am missing our Creek gang. I belonged with them in a

298

way I never belonged before. I miss the freedom of the woods and fields, the joking, the stomp dancing. I miss having learned I'm not just Indian. I'm Creek. Even though I've only known about it for a short time it's like I've found a part of myself that was always there, but just hidden. I'm seeing myself—and Pop—in a different light. It's kind of like I've been growing up without ever having looked into a mirror and recognizing myself.

What will I do when I find Pop? And where will we go after that? What road will we be on?

I shake my head. Right now it's my turn to take care of him. All I should think about is finding him. Soon.

CHAPTER THIRTY

TANKS ON PENNSYLVANIA AVENUE

Washington. It took me two more days on the road to get here.

Part of me is in awe of the crowds of people. Every sort of person you could imagine seems to be here. People in suits and ties, women in nice dresses, others just in casual clothes or their shirtsleeves. There are mothers with baby carriages, young couples arm in arm, shoppers with their arms full of packages. It's a busy place.

Another part of me is in even greater awe of the mammoth buildings that make you feel small. Like the huge spike of the Washington Monument where I stood for a moment craning my neck to look up to its top. Or the Treasury Building with its huge columns next to me here where Pennsylvania Avenue turns the corner.

Right now I'm looking at the White House. There're police cars all around it and traffic has been cut off. Patrolmen in tall black boots are everywhere. There are chains on the gates to the marble building set back behind broad, neatly mowed lawns.

"Old Hoover's in there," a familiar voice says from behind me. "Locked himself up safe from all us Bonusers."

I turn to look up at the dark, handsome face of Corporal Esom Dart, the man Pop and I helped to escape the sheriff months ago at the hobo camp. I can't stop a big grin from coming to my face. What luck! It's not just that I'm glad to see that he's okay. It's also that I'll bet he knows where I can find Pop. He's a sight for sore eyes.

He's in full army uniform, the Croix de Guerre and half a dozen other medals pinned on his chest. There's also a wet bandanna around his neck. Water's dripping from it onto his jacket. A canteen hangs on his belt.

"Still got that medal I left you, pal?"

"Yes, sir," I say, patting my shirt pocket with my left hand as I hold out my right to take his.

"So," Corporal Dart says, shaking my hand, "what you doing here in this powder keg about to blow?"

"Pop," I say. "I gotta find him."

Esom Dart nods. "Come looking for your father? Not staying safe at that school where he left you?"

I shake my head.

Corporal Dart's serious face breaks into a smile and he laughs out loud. "Pal, you never do waste a word, do you?"

"Guess not," I reply, smiling back at him.

"Well," the corporal says, "I left your father not an hour ago. I was out on recon and need to report back. Let's go."

"What's happening?" I ask as we turn away from Hoover's fortress toward the Capitol Building.

"Too much to tell, pal."

We push our way along Pennsylvania Avenue. Thousands of civilians fill the sidewalks here. Police are stationed in the street, keeping folks from crossing to the other side occupied by veterans and their families. Seeing all those grim-looking cops puts a knot in my stomach.

"Police came an hour ago," Corporal Dart says. "Chief Glassford on his motorcycle, warning everyone troops were coming. Told us Bonusers to leave. But how can a man go back to his home when he don't have any home to go to?"

Some of the men on the other side are holding signs. **BONUS NOW. MY CHILDREN ARE STARVING**. One man's head is wrapped with a white cloth that's stained with blood. They're white, but return the salute Corporal Dart gives them.

"Camp Glassford men," Corporal Dart says. "They were there this morning when the police tried to evict them. Two got shot dead. Some left and went across the river. That's where most of us, like your Pop and me, have set up our billets. Over the Anacostia River drawbridge to Camp Butler. There's seven thousand vets and about six hundred women and children there. Black and white all together. Streets laid out, sanitation in place, regular patrols to keep order."

We're passing another group of men, both Negro and white, standing on the opposite sidewalk singing.

"All you here—all you there

Pay the bonus, pay the bonus everywhere.

For the Yanks are starving,

The Yanks are starving,

The Yanks are starving everywhere."

"Black vets and white vets together," Corporal Dart smiles.

"Here, leastwise for now, that color line's gone. We have got us a piano across the river in Camp Marks. A redneck boy from Georgia and a brown boy from Harlem taking turns playing it, singing 'It's Only a Shanty in Old Shanty Town.'"

We turn south. A jumble of buildings fills the block on Third Street. One big old structure stands several stories tall—its side wide open to the elements. All around are men and women, tents, rough lean-tos. American flags are everywhere, some hanging from abandoned buildings targeted for demolition, others being held up by men standing at attention.

"Camp Glassford," Corporal Dart says. "Named it for that chief of police. A vet himself. He's been treating us all with respect. Especially since us vets have vowed to keep it peaceful, no matter what. But Hoover wants us all gone. You mark my words, pal. If they do bring in the army to drive us out, old Hoover is going to get voted out in favor of that new man Roosevelt. And now he's about to let his big dog off its leash—General MacArthur, who views us all as commies."

I hear a muffled roar from back up the wide avenue.

It's people shouting. I can't make out the words at first. Then, as the sound gets closer—like a flood rolling down a riverbed—I do.

They're coming.

Now I hear the quick clop of hooves on pavement. A troop of mounted men coming into sight. Hundreds of them on horses as big and beautiful as Dakota. It's a stirring sight for sure. Some of the vets across the street start to applaud. Maybe this is a parade to honor them for their service.

Behind the cavalry comes the thud of marching feet. Infantrymen. Then, metal treads clanking, tearing up the pavement, half a dozen tanks rumble into view.

A mounted officer raises his sword. The crowd goes still as the saber flashes in the sunlight like a kindled torch. Behind the cavalry, foot soldiers are fixing bayonets. They're pulling gas masks down over their faces—no longer looking human now, but alien-headed monsters.

"Lord Jesus, help us," Corporal Dart says, his voice a harsh whisper. "Run!" He grabs my hand, pulling me back from the avenue as the cavalry officer shouts a command.

"HERD THE CROWD NORTH!"

A group of troopers ride straight at the peaceful onlookers, swinging glistening swords, hitting people with the flat of their blades.

"MOVE!" cavalrymen are shouting. "MOVE!"

The people are trying to escape, but the crowd's too thick for anyone to move fast. A trooper slaps a mother with a small child in the back with the flat of his saber to push her along, knocking her to one knee. As he swings the blade back, its sharp tip slices the ear of an elderly man and blood spurts out.

We've managed to get clear, south of the attacking cavalry, pressed against the side of a building. Bad as it is for the crowd, it's worse for the vets on the other side. The men with gas masks are lobbing grenades into the Camp Glassford encampment. Vets are coughing, stumbling, falling back among the ruined buildings. Clouds of smoke rise as MacArthur's soldiers torch tents and rough-built shelters. In front of one wooden shanty, an American flag on a pole waves—the rising heat stirring it into motion before it, too, blackens and bursts into flame.

The acid scent of tear gas reaches us, burning my nose, making my eyes water.

Corporal Dart pauses to pull up his moist kerchief. He yanks a second one from his pocket, pours water on it from his canteen, and ties it over my nose and mouth.

"Pal," he says, "we got to keep moving."

Men and women who've escaped from the encampment are running all around us, hoping to find safety across the river in Camp Marks.

The drawbridge over the Anacostia is down. We pound across, not stopping to look back till we reach the other side. Crowds of coughing, crying people stretch all the way back to the distant Capitol. Smoke is veiling the Capitol dome and spreading out over the central part of Washington, but there's no sign of cavalry, soldiers with bayonets, or tanks. They must have stopped at Camp Glassford.

"You all right, Esom?" a voice says from behind us. It's a tall, slender man with light brown skin. "War zone up there."

Corporal Esom Dart pulls down his bandanna and coughs to clear his throat as the man passes me a handkerchief to wipe my eyes.

"Alive," Corporal Dart says. Then he clears his throat. "So far. This is Will Black's boy, Cal."

"Sir," I say, taking the man's slender hand.

"So they finally did it?" he asks.

"Yup," Esom says. "Here next, I suppose."

I'm amazed at how clean and well-ordered everything is over here on this side of the bridge in what they're calling Camp Marks. There are all sorts of makeshift shelters—from tents and miniature bungalows made from scrap lumber to the boxes and barrels Gale told me about. Streets are neatly laid out and named.

For some, life's going on as if everything was normal. Children are playing. Women are doing washing and preparing meals. People are sunning themselves. There's that piano I was told about. A young brown-skinned man is sitting at it playing a catchy song while folks—white and black—gather around listening. They don't know what's happened.

But down on the bank of the Anacostia itself are men and women acting as doctors and nurses. They're binding wounds and washing the faces of Bonusers near-blinded by tear gas.

"Look," Corporal Dart says, pointing ahead of us. "There's your father."

His back is turned and he's fifty yards away, but I recognize him right off. He's standing with a group of men—a policeman with a lieutenant's bars on his uniform and several other D.C. police. They're all listening to a thin, square-jawed man wearing an officer-style uniform speak, his face angry.

"Camp Commander," Corporal Dart whispers to me. "Captain Eddie Atwell."

We're close enough now to hear what he's saying.

"We do not blame the municipal police department," he says.

"Your men have given us a square deal. But we blame the army and the president. We have drawn a line at the bridge."

The police lieutenant raises a hand. "Now, Eddie," he says, "MacArthur is not about to be turned aside. Once that son of a sea cook makes up his mind, doesn't matter how dumb it is, he is going straight ahead."

Atwell reaches out a hand to rest it gently on the policeman's arm.

"Ira," he says, "you are a vet like us. You know we're not Reds or criminals here. We've checked the papers of every man here at Camp Marks and they are vets, every one. We've been asking for our due. Peacefully. But if they come to the camp tonight, I will meet them at the gate."

"Eddie . . ."

"No, I will kill the first man to put his foot across the line."

Those words send a shiver down my back. Those troops coming are cavalrymen with swords and infantry with fixed bayonets. They have tanks. If they cross that bridge and shooting starts, this could turn into a massacre. Just like what I saw in my vision!

I don't think Pop has seen me yet. But I'm wrong. Without turning around, he drops his left hand from his waist to point at the ground. He's signaling me to wait.

"Tell you what, Eddie," the police lieutenant says, "let's just keep talking, walk around and see what the situation is. You know they're the army. And you've got seven thousand people here with hundreds of women and children among them."

307

Atwell looks behind him, taking in the camp, maybe imagining the chaos that might ensue.

"Okay," he says. "Let's do that."

Atwell, the policemen, and half a dozen of the vets gathered around him move off. Pop does not go with them.

He turns to me, the expression on his face half concern and half delight.

I want to tell him everything that's happened since I saw him last, how my dream sent me here, how he has to leave before something awful happens.

But all I can do is say "Pop!"

Then his arms, thinner than when I saw him last but no less strong, are wrapped around me.

"Cal," he says, "Cal!"

I'm sitting with Pop by the fire pit in front of his camp. His billet's nothing more than a tent with a camp chair and a cot and a few rugs spread out on the dirt floor. But it feels more like home to me because Pop is there.

I've been talking for the better part of an hour—even more than after our sweat back at Challagi. Pop's just listened, not interrupting even once. I've told him everything, even about my vision, and he's just listened, nodding now and then, understanding and believing me as he always does. Now that I have finally stopped squawking—like a jaybird—my throat is sore.

"Cal," Pop says, "that is quite a story." He touches his heart, then holds his hand out, palm up. "I am sorry for the pain you've felt. But I'm glad for you, too. It sounds like you found some real friends."

I grab and hug him so hard it squeezes his breath out.

"Cal," he says, chuckling, "leave me one unbroken rib."

I let go of him and we just sit there, smiling at each other for a spell.

"What now, Pop?"

"Hard to say," he says. "There's no telling when MacArthur's troops are going to come across. But one thing I know now for sure. No way are you going to let me try to make a stand at the bridge. Right?"

My being here is going to change things. Pop's not going to sacrifice himself with me by his side.

I nod my head, the smile on my face now a grin.

"Thought so," Pop says. "It's good just to sit here with you, son. I've missed you."

"Me too," I say.

I reach into my coat and pull out the letters I've written. Two dozen of them, all held on to for want of an address to reach him. I hand them to Pop. As he takes them, he wipes his cheek with the back of his left hand.

"Got something in my eye," he says.

Whatever it is, it's stubborn about being wiped away because as he opens, unfolds, and reads each of my letters, he keeps wiping his eyes with a kerchief he pulls out.

It takes him a while because he reads each letter more than

once—as if trying to memorize every word. Then he carefully refolds and puts each one back in its envelope when he's done.

"Son," he says, stowing the big sheath of letters into a coat pocket near his heart, "I am going to keep these for as long as I live."

Just like I am going to hold on to the one letter I got from him.

Eight hours have passed since the destruction of Camp Glassford. The fires across the river have died down. No more smoke is rising. We have still not been invaded. But it sure looks as if it's going to happen soon. Pop and I are both standing near the drawbridge across the Anacostia. My pack is on my back. To my satisfaction, Pop has stuffed his own pack with a few of his belongings. His tent, the camp chair, the cot, and the rugs have been left in place. Maybe we'll come back to them. But I suspect not.

Tanks have been brought up on the other side of the river. They're placed to block anyone from leaving or coming to help us. Behind the tanks are rows and rows of infantrymen. Hundreds of them. A big black army staff car, General Douglas MacArthur's, no doubt, is also parked over there.

But it's not just the army. There are hundreds of civilians as well. They're not there to support the coming assault. What happened hours ago has turned sentiments our way.

As Eddie Atwell carries a big white flag across the bridge, some of those civilians start cheering.

"HOORAY FOR OUR BONUS BOYS!"

Though the sun has set, it's bright as day. A big

searchlight—like the one in my vision—has been set up over there.

A tall man in a uniform steps out of the staff car.

Civilians in the crowd start hooting.

"DOWN WITH MACARTHUR!"

"MURDERER!"

"BOO! BOO!"

"DOWN WITH HOOVER!"

Half an hour passes. Atwell comes back across the drawbridge.

"We've got an hour's truce to evacuate!" he shouts.

It's as if an electric shock has been sent through the camp. The searchlight is being played on the front line of huts and tents of Camp Marks. People are starting to panic.

"Time to go," Pop says. His voice is calm, but it's also sad.

As we trot together away from the bridge, it's chaos all around.

"The soldiers are coming to kill us," someone is shouting.

Car engines are being started, mothers are calling for their sons and daughters. There's no back road out of here, but cars might make it going across lots. Families without vehicles are running, carrying their children. They are heading toward the hills behind the camp. That's where Pop and I are going, too.

Our night vision being better than most, we help some of those frightened people. First a pregnant woman carrying a baby. Then an old vet, chest covered with medals. He's gasping, lungs having been weakened by mustard gas.

By the time we've reached the highest hill, the army has

already crossed the bridge. What was once the home of thousands is a scene like hell itself. So many blazes have been set by the soldiers that the burning tents and shacks light up the sky. It is a night on fire.

"Who would of thought this could happen here in our own country?" Pop says.

I offer no answer. He's silent for a bit before he speaks again.

"Unless," he says, "they were hoboes or Indians."

"Like you and me, Pop," I say.

That surprises him some. But then he puts his arm around my shoulders.

"*Ehi.* You could say that," he replies.

Being experienced knights of the road, it was easier for Pop and me to figure what to do and where to go when everyone was driven out. We just waited on that hill till dawn. Four hours later, following trails and back roads Pop knew, we reached a rail yard in Maryland.

Pop came to D.C. with nothing, so he had nothing to lose. And because I had come looking for him, I had everything to win.

An hour after we were on a train, out of there. We had each other again.

We kept heading west. Five days later, when we hit Kansas City, I spied a couple of quarters in a deep crack in the wooden sidewalk by the rail station. Pop and I decided we should treat ourselves to a movie.

It was *Destry Rides Again*, starring Tom Mix. The film was pretty good, but what tickled us was that when Hoover's face appeared on screen in a newsreel every single person in the theater hissed and booed.

Pop and I didn't talk much at first about what we'd both been through. We just traveled and made do. We worked whenever we could to earn an honest dime and lived by the code. Life wasn't easy, but we were together.

There was an election coming up. Hoover was going to be running against a man who'd promised a new deal. We all knew old Hoover's goose was cooked. It wasn't just the Depression but what he did to the BEF and what he said afterward.

One day, as we sat around the fire in a jungle camp near Santa Fe, Pop looked over at me.

"What now, son?" he said. We'd heard that another Bonus march was being planned to take place after the country got a new president.

I stirred the fire with a stick. It was a question I'd been expecting. And I was half surprised at the answer I found myself giving.

"Going back," I replied.

Pop knew what I meant. He and the other vets had to try again and keep trying until they won their rightful bonuses and Pop got that farm. He was never going to quit trying, so I couldn't give up either. With Hoover gone—as most folks expected now—there might actually be a new deal. Pop taking up the fight again would also mean my going back to Challagi. The semester would be starting in a few weeks.

"You sure about that, son?" he asked.

"Sure," I replied.

Though it might take some explaining, I knew I'd be accepted back as a student after running away. Pop would come with me and clear things up with the superintendent. There was so much sentiment in the whole country in favor of the Bonus Army that my leaving to support Pop might even make me sort of a hero in Morrell's eyes. Not only that, having another full-blood Creek on the school rolls would get them that government subsidy.

As much as I loved being back with my father, I was also missing the boys in our Creek gang. Even Bear Meat. I'd never been with another group of people my own age who understood me and wanted the best for me—as I did for them.

For all that was wrong at that Indian school, I had brothers who'd welcome me back. I could learn more about agricultural science, spend time in the horse barn and see Dakota again. I'd dreamed about him not long after we left Washington and I'm sure that dream of his being safe and sound back at Challagi was true.

I might even join Ray Chapman's track team. I was a gentleman of the road and would always be the son of Will Blackbird. But I now understood that being Cal Blackbird meant I also had another road to follow, the road of being a Creek Indian.

I didn't say any of that out loud, but Pop sat there nodding as I was thinking it and I knew he understood.

He smiled.

"Are you ready, Cal?" he asked.

"You could say that," I replied.

Afterword

Two Roads takes place at a tumultuous time in American history. While it is, first and foremost, a story about a young man trying to understand what path he must travel, its backdrop is 1932—when this nation was deep in the Great Depression.

It was a period when, after the stock market crash of 1929, average family income dropped by 40 percent. There were over two million homeless, people of every social class and background, living in shantytowns called "Hoovervilles" and hopping freight trains as hoboes. Among those hoboes were no fewer than 250,000 teenagers—whose story was dramatically chronicled in a 1997 PBS documentary called *Riding the Rails*.

The life of the hobo, including hopping freight trains and living temporarily in shantytowns near the tracks called jungles, might be said to have begun a century and a half ago after the Civil War. That was when large numbers of out-of-work men, most of them veterans, used those trains as the fastest way to go—often West—in search of jobs.

It's important to recognize—as my late friend the folk singer and social activist Bruce (Utah) Phillips—always pointed out to me—that a hobo is neither a bum nor a tramp. Hoboes are essentially migrant workers, impoverished homeless people who will readily accept employment and pride themselves on being honest. Tramps, who only work when forced to, and bums, who refuse to work at all, are looked down upon by real hoboes.

The nomadic life of a hobo, a "Gentleman of the Road," experienced by my main character and his father, actually did include that "ethical code," which Cal likes to quote. It's been a popular, often romanticized subject in song and story. I grew up hearing such songs as "Hallelujah, I'm a Bum," "The Big Rock Candy Mountain," and the Kingston Trio's "Fast Freight." There are many books about the hobo life, from Jack London's *The Road* (1907) to *Citizen Hobo* by Todd DePastino (2003).

Nineteen thirty-two was also when an almost forgotten event took place, which precipitates the action in this story—Cal's father leaving

315

him to join the "Bonus Army." Forty-five thousand veterans of World War I—men like my main character's pop—set up camp that summer in the nation's capital. These men had been promised eight years earlier a bonus payment based on their service to the nation. Called the "Bonus Army" by the press, their weeks of peaceful protest saw white men and black men from all over America marching and living together in a common cause as they petitioned Congress. It may be seen, perhaps, as a forerunner of the Civil Rights movement and later marches on Washington. The whole story of this American epic is memorably told in *The Bonus Army* (2004) by Paul Dickson and Thomas B. Allen.

However, these veterans were labeled as Communists, impostors, and insurrectionists by President Herbert Hoover who sent his Army Chief of Staff, General Douglas MacArthur, to evict them by force, including mounted cavalry and tanks on July 28, 1932.

Widely condemned by the American public, that brutal treatment of peaceful American veterans was a factor in the election of Franklin Roosevelt—who promised a "New Deal" for the country—as president that fall. (It is estimated that Roosevelt's WPA program alone employed 8 million between 1932 and 1940.)

The other major element in Cal's story is the Challagi Indian Boarding School. Although the Challagi school is a fictitious one, it is patterned after an actual Indian school in Oklahoma, the Chilocco Indian Agricultural School. Anyone wishing to understand more about Indian boarding schools in the early twentieth century should read K. Tsianina Lomawaima's excellent book *They Called It Prairie Light, The Story of Chilocco Indian School.*

This is the fifth book I've written in which federal Indian boarding schools play a central role—including my biographical novel *Jim Thorpe, Original All-American*, and *Code Talker.* Although the Carlisle Indian School, established in 1879, was the first off-reservation Indian boarding school, mission schools subsidized by the federal government first began around 1810. My young adult novel *Walking Two Worlds* tells the story of the struggles of Ely Parker/Hasanoanda at such a school in the early nineteenth century.

The objective of such schools was not just to educate Native Americans. It was to solve what the government called "The Indian Problem." Rather than continuing to fight expensive Indian Wars—fought again and again because Native Americans stubbornly refused to give up their lands—schools could be used to assimilate and acculturate. As Richard Henry Pratt, founder of Carlisle put it, to: "Kill the Indian and save the man." In other words, cultural genocide.

These schools were largely paramilitary institutions in which Native students were stripped of their native languages and cultural identities, drilled, dressed in uniforms, and separated from their families for years at a time. There was often abuse and harsh punishment. In the four decades of its existence, more Indian students ran away from Carlisle than graduated. When *The Problem of Indian Administration* by Lewis Meriam came out in 1926 it laid bare the awful conditions found to a greater or lesser degree in all of the dozens of federal Indian boarding schools. Overcrowding, unsanitary conditions, unqualified staffing, near-slave labor were among its findings.

Not only that, even after the Meriam Report—which did produce positive changes—recommended that Indian students be educated at community schools near their homes, Indian boarding schools continued to grow. By the early 1970s, some sixty thousand or more Native Americans were attending boarding schools. It was only after the 1970s that such boarding institutions were largely abandoned to finally be replaced by community-based schools.

For Native kids—often taken by force—arriving in one of those faraway schools was a terrible change from the loving support of their family environment. Yet, as Jack Thorpe, son of the famous American Indian athlete Jim Thorpe, put it to me, "Even though Dad had been in Indian boarding school himself, that was where he sent me and my brothers."

Why, if life at Indian school was so draconian, would Jim Thorpe in real life and Will Blackbird in my novel deliberately send their sons to an Indian boarding school? Why, in fact, did so many graduates of Indian boarding school not only send their kids to such schools, but also praise their own experience.

The answer can be found not so much in what was intended by the creators of these schools as in what the Indian students themselves made of the institutions. As Lomawaima so succinctly put it in *They Called It Prairie Light*, "Indian people made Chilocco their own." Rather than being made "less Indian," the Indian schools actually served to confirm their Indian identity, not just as members of a particular tribal nation, but in a Pan-Indian sense. This identity was strengthened not in the classroom but in their interactions with other Native students. This was especially so by the 1930s when many Native students, like Cal, came to the boarding schools already speaking English and knowing little or nothing about their original tribal communities.

317

Some already knew what they wished to gain from an Indian boarding school—for example, agricultural skills that could be used on their farms or trades so they could make money in the larger economy now that traditional ways of subsistence were no longer viable. They made use of the boarding schools as places where they would not be assimilated or acculturated—as Pratt and others intended—but given the tools to adapt, survive, and even thrive.

More than anything else, surrounded by other Native students who often became lifelong friends or spouses, they could feel Indian, exist within a sort of new family that would take the place of their family of origin. Although Native languages were forbidden, they were spoken when no white teachers and staff could hear them.

Though I never attended an Indian boarding school, many of my generation did and the stories they told me bore out the powerful undercurrent of Native identity found in those institutions. Barney Bush, a Shawnee poet, chuckled about how they used to steal the bass drum from the band room, go up in the hills above the school, and play powwow songs. Phil George, a Nez Percé traditional dancer and tradition bearer—who also served in Vietnam—told me some of the best stories he learned were from other Native kids when they were locked together in the school basement for punishment.

Louis Little Coon Oliver (1904–1991), a Creek elder I met when he was in his seventies, told me similar tales about his time in Indian schools. I had the honor of being his editor and publisher when his first book of poetry came out in 1983. After leaving Bacone Indian University, Louis rode the rails and hitchhiked all over America before returning to live out his life in Tahlequah, Oklahoma. The character of Little Coon in this novel is meant as a tribute to Louis, who always found something to joke about—at the same time as he was teaching. He would make you laugh in a way that also made you stop and think.

It's my hope that this small novel—based not just on years of research but also on the countless stories of boarding school life I've heard over the last five decades from friends and elders who were kind enough to share them with me—will do the same. Entertain with a good story while also, though not in a preachy way, teaching something about parts of American and Native American history that should be better known.

DISCUSSION QUESTIONS

1. *Two Roads* takes place in 1932, the same year in which many other important movements and events took place in the United States. Can you describe one of these significant historic moments? How does this real-life event affect Cal and his father in the story?

2. What do you think is the meaning of this novel's title, *Two Roads*? Does it just refer to the physical journeys that Cal and his father are taking? Or could it mean something more?

3. We see other men in this story who, like Cal's Pop, are veterans of World War I. What were the effects of World War I on these characters? Do you think an American soldier today would have similar experiences?

4. Cal is proud of the fact that he is a "hobo" with an "Ethical Code." How does his belief in this ethical code affect his character growth throughout the novel?

5. When Cal learns about his Creek identity, how does this new-found knowledge affect his life? There were so many negative attitudes and harmful stereotypes forced upon Native

Americans in the U.S. in 1932. How does Cal feel about these attitudes and stereotypes at the beginning of the book, and how does he feel by the end?

6. The Challagi Indian School is a fictional school modeled after the real-life boarding schools that the United States government forced several generations of Native American children to attend in the late nineteenth century and during much of the twentieth century. What were the goals of these schools? How did Cal and his fellow students cope with the hardships they endured while at Challagi?

7. What does Cal learn at the Challagi School? Who does he seem to learn the most from? What do you think of his teachers? Why do you think he chooses to return to the school at the end of the novel?

8. What was the Bonus Army? Why did they march to Washington and set up their encampments there? Do you know of other marches on Washington for social justice and social change that have taken place since 1932?